The Stuart Agenda

by

Alan Calder

To Eric

with best wishes

Alan

Feb 2012.

Willow Moon Publishing, LLC
201 St. Charles Avenue, Suite 114 -152,
New Orleans, Louisiana 70170

www.willowmoonpublishing.com
Contact Information: info@willowmoonpublishing.com

The Stuart Agenda

COPYRIGHT © 2011 by Alan Calder
First Print Edition December 2011
ISBN: 9781468055900

Cover Art by Jennifer Sonnier
Photograph by Alan Calder

Published in the United States of America

Dedication

To Jennifer, Fiona and Laura for their constant support and all the people who helped along the way, especially Lindsay Townsend.

The Stuart Agenda – Historical Preface

The Stuart Dynasty ruled Scotland from the Middle Ages until the Union of the Crowns. After the Union, Stuart Kings rarely visited Scotland. They were deeply embroiled in problems of religion and national governance. The Stuarts were much wedded to the idea of the divine right of Kings, something that the Westminster Parliament regarded as a constant threat to its growing aspiration to be the power in the land.

1603

Union of the Crowns. James VI of Scotland follows Elizabeth I of England as first King of Britain.

1649

James' son, Charles I, is beheaded over his insistence on autocratic rule and dangerous flirting with Catholicism. Cromwell takes over.

1660

Charles II is invited back to claim his throne after the death of Cromwell.

1685

Charles dies without legitimate heirs. His younger brother, James II, takes the throne.

1688

James II is forced to flee to France after insisting on his divine right to rule and reinvigorating Catholicism against the mainstream religious sentiment. James' daughter, Mary, and William of Orange take the throne in "The Glorious Revolution."

1690

James II returns to reclaim his kingdom but is defeated in Ireland at the Battle of the Boyne by William of Orange, the King Billy of Northern Irish Protestant folklore.

1702

William of Orange dies after Mary, who succumbed to smallpox in 1694. They had no children. Mary's younger sister, Anne, takes the throne.

1714

Anne dies in 1714 without leaving any surviving children. The English king-makers then pass over the claim of James, the Catholic Old Pretender, son of James II, from his marriage to Mary of Modena. The Protestant, George of Hanover, is invited to take the throne. He had Stuart credentials through his grandmother, Elizabeth, who was a daughter of James I.

1715

The first Jacobite Rebellion in Scotland fizzles out in defeat at the battle of Sheriffmuir when the Stuart champion, the Earl of Marr, was defeated by the Government's Duke of Athol. A belated six-week visit by the Old Pretender himself was too little too late.

1745

The high point of the Stuart fight-back came when the Old Pretender's son, Charles Edward Stuart, the Bonnie Prince Charlie of Scottish folklore, landed from France to lead the second Jacobite Rebellion. After some impressive victories, he was finally defeated on Culloden Moor in April 1746 by the Duke of Cumberland, effectively ending serious Jacobite resistance to the new Georgian order.

The official history says that both Bonnie Prince Charlie and his brother, Henry, a Catholic Cardinal, died without leaving legitimate heirs. This greatly pleased the Hanoverians, who did not relish any more Jacobite attempts to supplant their now established dynasty. That effectively ended the direct Stuart bloodline. This situation left the diverted Catholic Stuart bloodline running from Charles I through his daughter, Henrietta, to the Kings of Sardinia, then Bavaria.

However, the Hanoverian spin doctors airbrushed out of history the late marriage of Bonnie Prince Charlie to Marguerite, Comtesse de Massillan, in 1785. That union produced a son, Edward James, whose descendants still covet the lost crowns of the Stuarts.

Chapter 1

Scotland, May 2035 - Gordonstoun School

"What a match! What a tackle! Pity the lanky guy had weak knees. I'm very proud of you." The message on Robert's z-phone was from his stepfather in Paris. He'd been receiving live feed from the evening inter-house rugby game via Robert's ear-stud camera, giving him his stepson's view of the game. The praise made Robert feel better, and helped to neutralise the guilt he felt about inflicting a serious leg injury on the lumbering Prince Henry with his try-stopping flying tackle. But didn't the haughty heir to the throne need to be taken down a peg or two? Robert drifted off to sleep, wondering whether a week or two on crutches would plant a few seeds of humility in the royal persona.

Deep in the night, Robert slipped out of a fitful sleep, disturbed by a sound that didn't fit the normal pattern in his room at Gordonstoun's Round Square House. It wasn't the moan of the wind round the high gables outside or the distant voices of other boys in the building. It was in the room. Instantly fully awake, on his guard, and feeling vulnerable as a foreigner, his adrenalin rushed to meet the unwelcome intrusion. A threatening silhouette came toward him out of the paleness of the window blind. He slid quickly from under the duvet and launched his six-foot length at the intruder with a flying rugby tackle, similar to the one that had felled Prince Henry earlier in the day. The force of the tackle sent the intruder backwards with Robert still locked round his thighs. They careered into Robert's desk, sending his touch-screen flying and scattering books in all directions before slithering to the floor. Robert was now on top of his struggling would-be assailant and delivered a short right hook into his face to ensure the attack was over. Robert then leapt up and touched the wall, activating the wallpaper LEDs.

"It's you, Simkins." Robert looked down at the contorted face of Prince Henry's friend and lead sycophant who sat up, clutching his bloody nose. Robert's tone hardened when he saw the baseball bat lying on the floor.

"I don't believe this. Did that creep Henry send you? Is he pissed off with me for that tackle?"

"No, he didn't send me. He's been to hospital because of you and your mad tackling. He's going to be on crutches for a month. We're

1

not putting up with it, especially from a Frog."

"Think of it as international experience then," replied Robert with mock gravity, swallowing the insult and resisting the temptation to ram Simkins' words back in his mouth.

"You should go back to France. This school isn't big enough for both of you now," said Simkins, getting up from the floor as the door to the room opened and Andrew MacDonald, Robert's neighbour, appeared.

"What's going on? I heard an almighty clatter."

"Simkins came to duff me up for hurting his master," said Robert, picking up the baseball bat.

"That's a bit strong, Simkins, you could kill with that thing."

Robert couldn't help blurting, "Henry's a clumsy carthorse. He shouldn't be allowed on the rugby pitch."

"It's Prince Henry to you, even if you are a Republican Frenchman. He'll soon be the Prince of Wales, don't forget. You just can't treat him like that," Simkins answered.

"Get your arse out of here, Simkins, I've had enough of this."

"This isn't over; we'll get you," said Simpkins as, he scurried from the room.

"That tackle sure is causing trouble. You've pissed off Henry's camp big-time. You should have let him score."

"What? You must be joking," replied Robert, who struggled to put his feelings about the Prince into words.

"Perhaps you just don't like deferring to a Prince."

"Andrew, you're a MacDonald of the Isles, aren't you?"

Robert closed the door, the back of which was adorned by a picture of the Scottish rugby team.

"Sort of, my father's cousin is *the* MacDonald, Lord of the Isles."

"Sit down for a minute, Andrew, listen to this. You know me as Robert Lafarge. My stepfather, André Lafarge, is a successful French businessman. My real Dad died. His name was Stuart. We're the true line descended from Bonnie Prince Charlie."

Robert felt a deep sense of relief to share his burdensome secret with someone who would be likely to understand what it meant.

"So that explains the thing between you and Henry. It's the battle of the rival houses, Stuart against Windsor."

"Anyway, our families were locked together in the Jacobite

struggles, Culloden and all that, and the rest is sad history."

"Robert, if you ever need my help in that cause, you know you can rely on me."

****

Robert couldn't get back to sleep. The incident with Simkins had stirred up a ferment of history and personalities that was beginning to bubble over. First of all, he questioned what he was doing at Gordonstoun. Without much warning, he'd been removed from the familiarity of the French education system and parachuted into the famous Scottish school, mainly at the behest of his Uncle Leo and Aunt Françoise. After the death of his father when he was five years old, his uncle and aunt had played a big part in his upbringing. He regretted that he had not paid sufficient attention to many of Uncle Leo's attempts to educate him on Stuart history. His mother seemed to go along with the move to Gordonstoun, on the grounds that it would be a better base for an international career. His stepfather limited himself to a chauvinist grumble about leaving France.

At Gordonstoun, he often suffered from homesickness and hated the Scottish cold and especially the food. Even drowned in milk and honey, he detested porridge. On the positive side, he was enjoying school rugby which in his mind had developed an importance beyond his formal studies, something of which his stepfather would probably approve.

But, most of all, the day's incident made him more keenly aware of his heredity, his descent from Bonnie Prince Charlie, whose Royal line had been replaced by the *Hanoverians*. Uncle Leo would not tolerate them being referred to as the de-Germanised Windsors.

As he tried to get to sleep he made a commitment to read more about his illustrious ancestor but sleep refused to take him, so he got up and began searching the Cybernet for references to Bonnie Prince Charlie. This quickly threw up a virtual tour of the ill-fated Jacobite campaign of 1745 to 1746. The site enabled him to walk in the footsteps of and see through the eyes of his ancestor. He put the headset on, chose his viewpoint and started the walk.

He was immediately transported to the deck of the French ship, *Du Teillay*, passing the vast cliffs of Barra Head on Berneray, the rugged southern sentinel of the Outer Hebrides. It was the 22nd of July 1745. The ship sailed on into the Sound of Barra, the French tricolour

3

billowing provocatively behind, anchoring off the Island of Eriskay. He got into a rowing boat with his seven companions in arms and made for the beach.

The warning cries of the gulls and the skirl of the pipes welcomed him as they scrambled ashore onto the white sand to be met by members of the MacDonald Clan.

Their faces soon turned from joy at the return of their spiritual leader to sadness that he didn't have a large French army behind him. The MacDonalds shook their heads and the party went back to the *Du Teillay* to head for the mainland at Borrodale. Messengers were sent out to call the clans to raise the Prince's standard at Glenfinnan on August 19th 1745. After a long, exhausting walk, the party rowed up Loch Sheil between the haunting dark mountains on either side to Glenfinnan village.

The clans began to arrive in the late afternoon and into the next day. The spectacle of the raising of the standard and the blood-curdling cries of the Highlanders saluting their leader made the hair stand up on the back of Robert's neck and tears well up in his eyes. Through the long night, Robert walked and rode with his ancestor south to his triumphant entrance to Edinburgh, on to his numerous victories all the way to Derby. There the Prince railed in disbelief as his generals insisted on retreat back to Scotland when they were only a hundred miles from a panicking London. The trail back then led inevitably to Culloden. At this point, Robert switched off the display, emotionally and physically exhausted. He wanted to walk the ground at Culloden for himself.

****

After an hour of sleep he trudged in late for breakfast, still reeling from the emotional impact of his nocturnal journey. He picked up two boiled eggs and a heap of toast from the self-service counter before sitting down beside Andrew MacDonald.

"No further disturbances in the night?"

"Only self-inflicted. I spent most of the night on the Cybernet."

"No wonder you look tired."

"Well, look what's just crawled in," said Robert, as Simkins appeared at the door, sporting a ripe black eye, followed slowly by Prince Henry on crutches. Robert felt the tension in the dining room rise as every head turned to see the Prince, many of them then turning on Robert, conversations falling to whispers, all waiting to see what would happen.

"I suppose I should go over and ask how he is."

"You could offer to carry his tray for him."

"No, that's Simkins' job. I'll let the sods sit down." Robert was not surprised that nobody approached the Prince to ask for his health or commiserate. Before long, the tension passed and people began to drift out for the morning classes. Robert got up and strode over to the Prince's table.

"I'm sorry about the injury. I'm glad it's not worse. I've seen legs broken that way."

"So, I'm lucky that you were going easy on me, am I?"

"No, I didn't mean that."

"I'm going to lodge a complaint. That was dangerous play."

"I told you we weren't going to put up with it," added Simkins.

"When did you tell me that Simkins? Does Henry know that you came to play baseball with me in the middle of the night? Should I lodge a complaint about that, with the police, perhaps?"

"That had nothing to do with me, I was at the hospital," protested Henry loudly.

"Let's forget the whole thing, shake hands on it," said Robert, offering his hand to Henry and trying to look him in the eye. Henry's long thin face stiffened, his eyes unable to meet Robert's, refusing to make peace, camped firmly on his injured pride. He slapped Robert's hand contemptuously aside as Simkins cackled a gloating laugh.

"Have it your own way, but don't try to go past me on a rugby pitch again. Stick to chess, I hear you're good at that. And join the A level charm class as well."

Henry's face flushed at being spoken to so directly. He struggled to his feet and scuttled crablike out of the dining room on his crutches, followed by the faithful Simkins, who glowered back threateningly at Robert from his safe retreating distance.

Robert sat down in Henry's seat and put his head in his hands. Images from the night filled his vision, he felt Bonnie Prince Charlie's footsteps stamping on his back; history was taunting him, driving him. He wrestled with his feelings of anger. Did he want to complain himself, leading possibly to Prince Henry's further humiliation? Or did he want to nurse his anger into his growing consciousness of being a

Stuart? Perhaps he would find what he was looking for at Culloden. He would go there with his Uncle Leo.

Chapter 2

16 Years earlier

France, 2019 - French Justice Ministry, Paris

Leo had been called unexpectedly to the office of Hervé Dubois, the French Minister of Justice. Hervé was an old family friend, especially of his brother, David, and a legal colleague before his political career.

A few minutes before 10 a.m., in bright sunshine, Leo entered the Hotel de Bourvallais in the Place de Vendome, home to the French Justice Ministry for over two hundred and fifty years, although originally the home of Louis XIV's Chancellor. He felt very comfortable in the opulence of the surroundings. He'd been there many times before as a member of official committees or enquiries and imagined that the state had found some new task for him. Leo signed in at Reception and was led up the staircase of Honour, past the magnificent Gobelin tapestries to the Green Room, one of the large first floor rooms overlooking the Place Vendome. He had expected to be led to the waiting area outside the Minister's private office, to suffer the obligatory ministerial lateness demanded by the dignity of his office, tinged with a degree of institutional Latin arrogance.

The change from normal procedure unsettled Leo a little and he used the mirror above the fireplace to straighten his already perfectly horizontal bowtie and flick imaginary surface contaminants from his immaculately cut dark-navy pinstripe suit. The perfume from the large vase of flowers calmed him as he began inspecting the room more carefully. He was looking at an early Aubusson tapestry, set in the otherwise bare room with green wallpaper and curtains, when the door opened and the Minister, Hervé Dubois, bustled in starting a running commentary on the décor of the room as soon as he entered, heading for the windows overlooking the Place. The Minister's lack of height was mitigated by a stand of hair which projected four centimetres vertically from his scalp, before slicking back in improbable black waves. Leo also suspected that he wore shoes with height assisting heels, minor vanities in the scheme of the possible for French politicians. Leo admired the feisty Minister who hailed from Midi *paysan* stock. Despite his street fighting credentials as an ex-mayor of Marseille and ex-Minister of the Interior, Hervé Dubois had a considerable intellect, the equal of any of the disdainful, arrogant *polytechnicien* class who dominated the top of French politics.

"Yes, Napoleon's shadow falls on us every morning from the top of the column, reminding us to uphold his *Code Civil*," said the Minister, in a banal reference to his constitutional duty. Napoleon again, thought Leo. It was impossible to move in Paris outside his shadow. The Minister appeared to be bustling more than normal; was he a little nervous?

"I'm wondering whether you have some more work in mind for me. Perhaps a committee to chair or an enquiry to lead," suggested Leo.

"No, it's nothing like that Leo, it concerns your brother, David," replied the Minister, losing eye contact with Leo.

"David?" Leo felt a knot of apprehension in his stomach at the mention of his brother's name.

"We've got some new information about his death. I thought you would like to know," answered the Minister gravely, lowering his voice and leading Leo conspiratorially along to the window which had just fallen into the shadow of the Vendome Column, acting as a giant sundial in the square outside.

"What information?" asked Leo.

"We were, of course, all very sad at the time of David's death. He was a friend of mine and a great journalist. It was a huge loss," continued the Minister, looking down into the square.

"Yes, we all appreciated your support at the time of his accident, Minister," said Leo, who also looked out of the window at the busy throng of pedestrians in the square, wishing that one of them would turn and wave up at him, wearing David's face. David's memorial service had been the saddest event in his life, a sadness prolonged by the fact that David's body had never been found.

"Well, that's just it, Leo, we don't think it was an accident."

"What are you talking about, Hervé?" asked Leo impatiently, dropping the polite form of Ministerial address. "David died in a boating accident; the gas bottle on his yacht blew up during a fire."

Certainty began to fray at the edges, feeding a doubt that he had buried deeply at the time of David's death.

"Leo, he was killed by a bomb, not the gas bottle," replied the Minister, taking Leo's arm in a gesture of comfort.

"How do you know this? What proof have you got?" The pain that he thought he had grieved away welled up again, buffeted by disbelief that such a fate could have befallen his hero. Leo had truly loved his brother, who was eight years older than him, an age gap that eliminated the rivalries of closer siblings. He had idolised the brother who introduced him to every sporting and manly pursuit and who had always looked out for him. He had felt David's loss much more than that of his father. His head was suddenly full of images of the idol of his youth: on holiday with him in Scotland, striding over her mountains, swimming her lochs and catching mighty salmon. Then there was Monique, or plain Monica before the French affectation. She was the woman who'd turned David's head.

"The affair was investigated by the security service, the DST. They thought the Brits did it but couldn't prove anything. The Brits had a motive. David was a very good investigative journalist and we know that he was working on a big story about the British Royal Family," said the Minister.

"Not those Hanoverian bastards again? But why are you telling me this now, all these years after it happened?" he asked, as a painful picture of his dead brother floating in the water, came into his head. The pain was somehow enhanced by the added tragedy of his nephew, Alexander, David's only son, being killed in a car crash.

"It's just been confirmed. We've interviewed a friendly MI6 spook who's retired to Provence. He owed us a favour and threw that information in along with other things that we really wanted."

"This is dreadful news, Hervé, but thank you for having the courtesy to inform me," replied Leo, turning away, as the impossible dream flashed through his head again. This time, after the Stuart Prince cut the Hanoverian dragon's head off, the claymore carried on unaided, slashing at the body until it found the heart, still beating. The next swing of the claymore cut the heart in two, sending a froth of Hanoverian blood in all directions, dousing the Stuart Prince, who licked his lips, savouring the sweet saltiness. The claymore then continued until the dragon was reduced to a mound of bloody pulped flesh. Leo felt sad and elated at the same time. His adrenaline pumped in sympathy, smelling the dragon's blood as a huge righteous anger reared up inside, making him tremble. Onto the cusp of his anger floated a dangerous consuming desire for revenge. Despite its empty fleeting sweetness, at that moment, he wanted it above all things.

"What are you thinking, Leo?"

"I want to avenge my brother's death. I feel like cutting a Hanoverian throat," he replied angrily, turning from the window and throwing his head back like a frightened horse.

"Leo, anger isn't the answer, step firmly on it. You want to get even, don't you?" he suggested, his small eyes narrowing to slits, a half smile displaying his small but perfect teeth.

"But how?"

"Our intelligence tells us that the Scottish Nationalist Party is about to split. A lot of them are fed up with the drift to a kind of UK federalist compromise and the lack of economic progress."

"And of course that's left the Hanoverians unchallenged in Scotland."

"The talk is that a breakaway Scottish Independence Party is about to be formed. It'll campaign for nothing less than total independence with a new constitution for Scotland."

"A new constitution. Would that give the Stuarts an opportunity to retake the Scottish throne? Would that be vengeance enough and a fitting tribute to David?"

"That's more like it, Leo. The timing is good. There are interests in Europe who are fed up with English Euro-scepticism. They want to see Scotland as an independent country within the EU, just like Ireland, and the English weakened. I'm sure they would help you achieve that."

"Those interests, who are they?" asked Leo, going cold as he crossed the line between dreams and reality, where dragons were much more dangerous and could be relied upon to bite back.

"They're in Brussels of course. Go and see Albert Delavarenne," replied the Minister comfortingly, giving Leo a business card.

"I presume that your support is unofficial, Hervé?" Leo looked down at the card which bore only a name and a mobile telephone number.

"Support for what?" replied the Minister, with a full smile this time, showing just too much ribbed gum-line above his teeth.

"OK, I'll go to see your Albert."

"And why don't you discuss it with our mutual friend Cardinal McKerran? He's a Scot, and the Vatican will surely have a position."

"Good idea, I'm dining with him tomorrow night."

Leo looked at the Minister in wonder. Hervé was right, the old peasant. Why did he have to slay the dragon? That was an impossible dream. Why not capture a part of the dragon's territory, the part that was most rightly his own family's through birth? It would not be a slaying, more like cutting half the tail off, a most annoying injury but hardly fatal.

****

Back out in the daylight, Leo walked in the shadow of the Vendome Column to its plinth, which depicted scenes from the battle of Austerlitz. The metal cladding of the Column was made with the bronze from 1200 captured Russian and Austrian cannon, the victory ordained by the military genius of Napoleon Bonaparte. Leo stood there silently for a few minutes, charging himself with the battle energy that still flowed from the pores of the gunmetal. As he left the square, a bank of small white clouds was visible on the southerly breeze, white horses ready to bear the cause northwards.

Walking back to his office, the revelations from the Minister filled Leo's cup of cynicism to overflowing. The recurring attempts by the last few Royal Hanoverian generations to present themselves as model families leading the nation had already been shot through by the end of deference and the harsh glare of press scrutiny. Their lives were a sham, covering often rampant dissolution. They were hardly fit for purpose, thought Leo, who quickened his step as a light misty rain fell from the now thickening cloud. He eagerly subscribed to the conspiracy theory that Diana, Princess of Wales, had been eliminated by the Hanoverians when she became a threat to their cause. It looked as though his brother had shared the same fate. At last he had a way forward, a cause to commit himself to.

****

The following evening, Leo emerged from the Chatelet Metro station, into the Rue de Rivoli. He had come from Gare de Lyon, the terminus for his train from Fontainbleau, fifty kilometres to the south, still in shock at the news he had been given by Hervé Dubois.

Leo was not unusually tall, about five feet ten, with a quick long stride which easily consumed distance. His wife often complained about his walking pace, even when she was not wearing high heels. On that surprisingly mild autumn evening, he was wearing a beige lightweight wool suit; he abhorred the untidy corrugation of the more fashionable linen. A light-blue shirt and a dark-blue trademark bowtie completed the picture. He had a tanned longish handsome face and carefully cut greying hair, worn on the long side, giving plenty of opportunity for hand-combing, which was an established part of his body language. He strode along the side of the square in front of Notre Dame Cathedral, shimmering in an ethereal Monet-esque glow ordained by the rapidly falling sun. He passed street sellers peddling cheap trinkets, his marching feet disturbing small heaps of leaves from the fall that was well underway. He drew admiring glances from impressionable female tourists who wondered if he was famous and identified him as an alpha male and at least, a left bank intellectual.

Passing the iconic cathedral reminded him again of his lineage, buried by English kingmakers in the seventeenth century, and rubbed salt in the deep wound, reopened by news of his brother's murder by the British. As he skirted around the quieter back of the cathedral, gaggles of tourists gave way to knots of lovers: some walking hand in hand, some locked together watching the river life pass by, some looking into each other's eyes, practising Rodin's kiss, all wallowing in the sensuality of Paris.

Leo then crossed the historic Archbishop's bridge that led him onto the left bank of the Seine near to where the Archbishop's palace had stood, before it succumbed to the destructive forces of *egalite* in the early nineteenth century. The left bank was thronged with tourists making their way to the many restaurants along the *Quai*, or deeper into the Latin Quarter.

Leo was optimistic about the coming encounter. He hoped that it would provide valuable support to the edifice that he was constructing, a bridge linking revenge and a road to the north, leading all the way to Scotland. The apartment was in a side street, a block away from the river. It was externally anonymous and internally sumptuous, one of the perks of the Catholic hierarchy. Leo thought with a smile, that he would get a better dinner than the punters in the Latin Quarter.

Cardinal McKerran was already there, his ample frame encased in appropriate high Catholic finery; vestments of red-trimmed black silk. The Cardinal chaired the Vatican Constitutional Committee, of which

Leo was a member. The meeting rotated around the capitals of Europe and Leo had invited the Cardinal to dine privately with him on the eve of the Paris meeting. The Cardinal had agreed, even insisting on providing an appropriate venue. The men had a good relationship, based on mutual respect for each other's intellect and professionalism. Leo wanted the Cardinal's view on his thinking so far. He considered him an ideal choice from an intellectual and historical perspective and a low risk one, if there was no meeting of minds.

Dinner began at the highly polished walnut table, which was capable of seating at least eight. The Cardinal occupied a carver chair at one end with Leo sitting on his left. A large lit candelabra delineated their corner of the table which otherwise seemed to be covered with glasses. They sat under the steely gazes of past prelates, whose portraits adorned the walls and who no doubt would have relished the conspiratorial atmosphere being created by Leo.

During the first course, Leo let the Cardinal elaborate on the objectives for the following day's meeting. For the second course, scallops were served, a culinary no-go area for the mollusc-sensitised Leo, giving him more of an opportunity to lead the conversation. He quickly turned it to Scotland and the Stuarts, safe ground since the Cardinal was also a Scot. The delicate faint smell of the scallops revived unpleasant memories.

"The Vatican always had a soft spot for the Stuarts. You took my ancestors in and cared for them after the Hanoverians persuaded the French to throw them out," Leo reminded the Cardinal.

"I suppose we did, and we buried the last of them together to tidy it all up. A tomb in St Peter's was surely a fitting end to that tragedy," replied the Cardinal sadly, reminding Leo of the magnificent monument to his ancestors at the very heart of Catholicism.

"Need it be the end, Cardinal? I think that Scottish Independence is coming. Could that offer a new beginning for the Stuarts?" asked Leo quietly, lest the gazing prelates and the walls hear his oblique approach to treason.

"You mean a fresh Stuart monarch replacing the Hanoverians in an independent Scotland?" replied the Cardinal, with a knowing smile.

"Yes, just that. It's what I've been dreaming about recently. I know it won't be easy and I'll need allies."

Leo so wanted to talk about David but something held him back.

His thirst for revenge, while natural and entirely correct as a motive, would appear un-Christian to the prelate and unlikely to engage his sympathy. As he looked up, the eye of the archbishop in one of the pictures on the wall caught his. The pink round face expressed relaxed agreement, a small comfort to Leo.

"Yes, we're watching the Scottish situation closely. But would the Scots want a republic or a monarchy? I think most would say a republic, if you asked them in the street today."

"I don't dispute that in the current climate. But is Scottish republicanism not a reaction to a failing Hanoverian monarchy?" added Leo, who was experiencing a curious tingling sensation, as he fully laid bare his new ambition for the first time.

"I suppose that raises the question of legitimacy. Who among the Stuarts is the rightful claimant to the Scottish throne?" asked the Cardinal, as he pulled his chair in to tackle the main course, *confit* of duck, the candlelight flashing off his enormous gold crucifix as he leaned forward.

"Well, of course, the eighteenth century Hanoverian spin doctors wrote the official version of history. They claimed that the main Stuart line terminated with the deaths of Prince Charles Edward and his brother Henry, without any legitimate heirs," began Leo, who was dissecting a piece of crispy duck skin, his favourite flavour, away from the flesh.

"No hope for Henry, like me, he was a Cardinal in the Catholic Church."

"But Prince Charles Edward did marry for a second time when he was sixty-five years old. The lady was Marguerite, Comtesse de Massillan. A year after the marriage, she bore Charles a son, Edward James Stuart, who carried on the Stuart bloodline and my branch of the family is descended from him."

"So the Hanoverians conveniently airbrushed that out of history. I'm sure the Vatican Library will have a copy of Prince Charles Edward's marriage contract. Leave that to me?"

"Will you support us?"

"I'm inclined to agree with you that there might be an opportunity, Leo. I know that we have some very old scores to settle with England and the Hanoverians but the Vatican won't be able to offer you any material support; we're no longer involved in national intrigues of this kind. However, I would personally be delighted to see a Stuart back on the Scottish throne and you have my personal support and blessing."

"Thank you, Cardinal," stammered Leo. The strength of the Cardinal's support had finally kicked open the doors already unlocked by the revelations concerning his brother's death. Through the open door charged the savage dogs of revenge, demanding blood, straining at their leashes to reach Hanoverian throats, guilty of usurping the God-given position of his family. Leo felt liberated; he was in new territory, the foothills of the mountain range to be conquered, at the top of which lay a crown that had slumbered for centuries, waiting for a handsome Stuart brow to grace. The Stuart Agenda was born, fanned into life by the gale-force wind of a vengeance that demanded satisfaction. Nothing less than a reversal of history would do to satisfy its loud clamouring resonance inside Leo's head.

"Go for it, Leo," said the Cardinal, putting his left hand over Leo's right in a gesture of friendship and commitment.

Chapter 3

Scotland, July 2035 - Culloden Battlefield

Leo and Françoise set off from their home near Fontainbleau, south of Paris, on the long journey to Inverness and Culloden. They had been warned that a few days of bad weather were in store. They made a very elegant couple, Françoise wearing a coat that suggested leopard skin but was far enough away from nature to appease any eco-warriors. Leo wore a light-brown camel coat with darker collar, over a dark wool suit.

Leo had been told by Robert about the confrontation with Prince Henry. Leo's feelings of concern and guilt hit a low point on the plane from Paris to Inverness. It was a service that had been started recently to accommodate the needs of the rapidly increasing population of the much warmer Highlands and increased number of tourists.

"It's my fault that Robert's in Scotland; my obsession to get even with the Hanoverians. The irony is that poor Robert doesn't really know what we're planning for him yet," said Leo.

"You can't blame yourself, Leo. Nobody at Gordonstoun knows who Robert is. Whatever's happened must have been something between boys and nothing to do with your Stuart Agenda."

"It would be such a pity if we had to throw in the towel now. Things are going so well for us on the political front in Scotland, with Bernard and Peter leading the charge, although Peter doesn't know about us yet."

"For me, the most important thing is Robert and how he's turning out. Even when I held him as a newborn baby, I sensed something beyond the sweet preciousness of a new life. The feeling was something like looking at a famous painting or sculpture, imbued with a history of its own and with its place in posterity guaranteed."

"You're right about that; he's a very special boy. Remember when we took him to see Cardinal McKerran in Rome when he was only six? The Cardinal was so impressed with him that he took us all to meet the Pope. I still recall the way the Pope looked at him. I think he saw something, too. And I suppose I was feeling something similar when I intervened to suggest that his parents call him Robert, the name of the first Stuart King, and not Maurice as they were planning."

"Don't get depressed about this, the trouble with the Prince will blow over," said Françoise turning towards him and putting her hand on his. Leo was warmed by the dark, hazel-flecked pools of her eyes and tried to shake off what she called the "Stuart melancholy" that afflicted him from time to time. He marvelled at the classic beauty of his wife. She had the kind of face that many of the great film stars of the past had. Her nose was chiselled to angular perfection above full scarlet sensual lips. He was always amused when French people refused to believe that his wife was English; she was surely too chic to be *une anglaise*. She did have a French mother however, who met her English father working for IBM in Paris as a young expatriate.

As the plane turned over the sea to land at Inverness, Leo looked down on the panorama below, picking out the Culloden battlefield to the south. From several thousand feet, the killing ground looked benign in the morning sun although rain clouds were approaching on the horizon.

From the airport they took a short taxi ride to the Culloden Hotel, a fine Georgian Palladian mansion, standing on the site of the earlier Culloden House that was used by Bonnie Prince Charlie as his field headquarters before the Battle of Culloden and burned down by the Hanoverians in an act of vengeance. The weather was forecast to continue wet and windy.

****

Robert left Gordonstoun in a taxi to join his uncle and aunt for dinner. He was very excited at the prospect of seeing them; he desperately needed Stuart company where he could talk more openly about the ideas that were buzzing around in his head. He was thrilled when they complimented him on how grown up he looked. He seemed to have reached manhood overnight, they said.

"Why didn't the Prince just take Scotland and settle for that?" asked Robert, as they sat down to a dinner of Scottish fare in the Adam dining room, still displaying original ornate cornicing and plasterwork. Only the tartan table linen hinted at a Jacobite connection; the rest was pure Georgian.

"That's a good question Robert, and with the benefit of hindsight, it's clear that he should have done. Taking on England was a step too far without popular support there and more commitment from the French. On the other hand, his grandfather had lost the British throne, so you can understand why he wanted it all back."

"What a big tactical mistake he made."

"Yes, we mustn't make the same mistake again," said Leo, glancing up at the sparkling chandelier as the gamey smell of venison wafted up from their plates.

"What do you mean?" asked Robert, looking intently at his uncle.

"I was absolutely delighted when you asked us to join you at Culloden. It's the perfect backdrop for introducing you to our Stuart Agenda. We're sure that at some time in the not too distant future, Scotland will become independent, breaking away from England, and we're secretly helping the Scottish Independence Party to achieve that," said Leo.

"You amaze me. I've read about the Scottish Independence Party in the newspapers. Most people seem to think that Scotland will become a republic."

"We think that's because the Scottish people don't like the Hanoverians, or the Windsor family as they call themselves now, and they don't know about the Stuart option yet. Once they do, we think that they'll want their own king back again."

"Their own Stuart King?"

"That's you, Robert. You are the rightful King of Scots. It's what I've been working on for more than ten years. We can make it happen," said Leo.

"What do André and Mother think?" asked Robert.

"Well, at first they were sceptical, but they're convinced now, if you're committed." Robert was reassured by the report of his parents' support. He would not have wished to go against André, his stepfather, who had loved and nurtured him as his own.

"So what's the plan now?" asked Robert, who was anxious to put some real images into the dark corner.

"Let's visit the battlefield first," replied Leo, as the Athol Brose arrived, a dessert concocted from oatmeal, honey, whisky and cream.

On the way back to school in the taxi, Robert realised for the first time that he was part of a bigger picture. He began to appreciate the full extent of Leo's ambition for him and the lengths he was prepared to go to achieve it. He felt a light tap of destiny on his shoulder. Sweetened by his spat with Henry, it added to his moral certainty that his cause was just. He felt like a strong young stag anxious to get on with the rutting battles that lay ahead.

The following morning saw them in front of the storyboards at the Culloden Visitor Centre. They told a truly ghastly tale of killing and maiming, followed by genocide and eventual ethnic cleansing on a Herculean scale. A doubly humiliating ethnic cleansing, where the new occupants of their land were not a rival tribe or clan, but animals, sheep. It was quite the saddest place that Robert had ever visited.

The Highlanders had stood opposite Cumberland's army on the bitterly cold morning of 16th April 1746, hungry, exhausted and dispirited after the long and painful retreat from Derby. The battle commenced at 1:00 p.m. to the accompaniment of the bagpipes. Hanoverian cannon soon provided the base notes.

Robert and Leo then went out into the driving wind and rain, leaving Françoise under cover. They walked across the killing ground, to the spot, marked by a red flag, from where the Prince had directed his troops. To the north, the haunting outline of the Black Isle was just visible through the thin mist that hovered over the Moray Firth.

They relived the details of the battle. The Prince's troops, exhausted after the long retreat from Derby, faced a disciplined professional force, superior in numbers and weaponry. The unsuccessful Highland charges were cut down by grapeshot; it was all over in less than an hour before the Prince escaped and the Highlands were put to the sword by the butcher, Cumberland.

Robert was transfixed by the monumental injustice of what had happened beneath his feet all those years ago. A righteous anger welled up within him and erupted in tears running down his cheeks from his overflowing heart. His head demanded vengeance and accepted the challenge.

"Don't torture yourself," said Leo.

"As you are my witness and before God, I pledge myself to recover the throne of Scotland for the Stuarts," said Robert, in a strong, emotion-charged voice.

The two of them stood silently, frozen by Robert's historic declaration, a team now committed to reverse the history that confronted them on Culloden Moor. The relentless rain pounded them as the Black Isle disappeared into the mist, just as it had on that fateful day in 1746. Looking into the mist, Robert could almost imagine a ghostly figure retreating on horseback leaving the baton of history in his hand, willing him to victory.

As they left the field, Robert thought of the Prince's eventual escape as he spent several months traversing the Highlands and Islands, often narrowly avoiding capture by the Hanoverians. He eventually boarded the French ship *L'Heureux*, ironically meaning "The happy one," on September 20th at Loch nan Uamh, the place where he originally landed in July 1745. That period added a final romantic twist to the Jacobite legend, rather like Dunkirk in a later era. Despite the odds, the Prince escaped, helped along the way by many loyal Highlanders, most famously, the beautiful Flora MacDonald who disguised him as her maid for a sea passage across the Minch from North Uist to Skye, a journey immortalised in "The Skye Boat Song." Many more songs and poems were penned in the aftermath. For Robert "Will ye no come back again" was to have a special resonance, as an open historic invitation from the Scots.

Chapter 4

France, August 2035 - Fontainbleau,

Back in France, still on a high after his emotional declaration at Culloden, Robert changed his plan for the school holidays to spend time at his great uncle Leo's *Manoir* at Fontainbleau dipping into the extensive collection of papers on the Stuart family. He was determined to plant his feet firmly in the family history to strengthen his personal Stuart credentials, and begin the transformation of a Stuart nobody into a Crown Prince. He was also looking forward to spending a lot of time with Leo and Françoise; he had so much to learn from them, as instigators of the Stuart Renaissance.

Robert came down to a beautiful summer morning, with bright sunlight filling the conservatory in contrast to most of the other rooms in the *Manoir* which tended to be old-fashioned and gloomy. The three of them sat around a table, covered with a Provencal tablecloth decorated with grapes and olives. Françoise wore a bright-green summer dress that perfectly complimented her auburn hair while the unshaven Leo still managed to look elegant and handsome in his gardening clothes. The smell of hot croissants filled the air. Outside the garden was at its vibrant summer best, with the old chapel visible through the trees at the end of the garden. Over breakfast, Robert took the opportunity to begin his questions starting with Leo's motivation to think of recovering the throne of Scotland for the Stuarts.

Leo retold the story of his fateful meeting with Hervé Dubois at the French Justice Ministry. Françoise remembered going to lunch afterwards in a restaurant in the Rue de Rivoli. It was full of loud Americans.

Robert was impressed by the passion of Leo's story which backed up his own emotional engagement with the spirit of Bonnie Prince Charlie. He also had the added spur of having already crossed swords with the Hanoverian Prince Henry. There was a continuity of family angst over the role of the Hanoverians that made their cause in Scotland not only justifiable but in urgent need of being implemented. He was particularly intrigued by the idea that the book that his grandfather, David Stuart, was supposed to have written might still exist.

"We don't know about the book. If it exists, it's in Marbella with your Grandma," said Leo.

"Your Grandma's a problem," said Françoise.

"Why does nobody ever mention her? It's as if she never existed. All I know is that she still lives in Marbella, but that's all mother will say about her."

"Believe me, there are plenty of memories," she said, getting an old photograph album from the sideboard. "The family had a holiday home in Perthshire, on the banks of the Tay. The men were all keen salmon fishers."

"She was very beautiful but I didn't like her from the start," said Leo, as he recalled David and himself in Scotland, climbing, swimming and fishing together before Monica appeared on the scene to spoil everything.

"Monique, or Monica as she was then, was the daughter of the local estate owner. That's David and her before they got married. He's not much older there than you are now," said Françoise, with the open album on the table between her and Robert.

"She was very pretty, wasn't she?" said Robert.

"Yes, and she used it. She pursued David from the first moment she saw him. He quickly became besotted and carried her back to France like a war trophy," added Leo, who remembered his confusion when he had to share the hero of his youth with the pushy Monique.

"So what went wrong?" asked Robert.

"She didn't seem to settle in France. She was fine for a while after your father was born but it didn't last. David and she were part of the fast crowd. Lots of drink, drugs and worse," said Françoise, shaking her head.

"We might as well tell you. She wasn't faithful to your grandfather. That's what your aunt is saying."

"And then the last straw was her leaving to live in Marbella with a lover, immediately after your Grandfather's death, more or less abandoning Alexander, your father."

"We looked after Alexander until he married your mother and of course, tragically, we lost him in a car crash not long after you were born. I truly believed that we were cursed," added Leo sadly, until a happier memory intruded. It was of Alexander calling him "Uncle" for the first time, allowing him entry to a new cosy class of manhood.

"You saved us, Robert, there was something about you from the start that we could believe in. That faith, plus Leo's anger and the opportunity of Scotland becoming independent became the three pillars of the Stuart Agenda," said Françoise.

"I have one more question. Can we prove our descent from Bonnie Prince Charlie?" asked Robert.

"Yes. David did a lot of work to establish the family tree and I got Cardinal McKerran to check. The Vatican has Bonnie Prince Charlie's wedding contract in their archive. I'm told the papers were deposited there by Henry Stuart, Charles' younger brother. He was a very influential Catholic Cardinal."

Françoise was delighted with Robert's progress as a student of Stuart history but even more pleased with his personal development. He was turning from a youth into a handsome young man. He didn't have the cool feminine good-looks of a male model. His nose was perhaps too long on its own but it was a "Stuart nose" that fitted perfectly into the frame of his face. The imperfection of a small rugby scar on his chin added a touch of worldly wear that gave him age beyond his years. However, she saw his greatest strength as his ability to engage with either sex. He made them all feel at the centre of his whole attention, a part of his space, fixed in the gaze of his big brown eyes.

Chapter 5

France August 2035 - Southern Rhône Valley,

Bernard Frank's wife, Angelique, slept for most of the car journey south from Paris towards their holiday home in the Southern Rhône valley. The temperature rose relentlessly as they passed Lyon and entered the throat of the Rhône valley where the sky began to turn a deeper blue, promising the perfume and sweetness of Provence to the south. Bernard was excited about the next few days as he tried to put the last of the foundation stones in place beneath his friend Leo's Stuart Agenda. He had just been told by Leo about Robert's adult commitment to his destiny, the signal for Bernard to proceed to the next phase. Bernard still remembered his first meeting with Leo and his astonishment at the scale of his ambition: getting an unknown French boy onto the Scottish throne. He had stressed how Robert needed to become a celebrity in his own right and insisted that the boy would have to be educated in Britain, something that the family was initially uncomfortable with before settling on Gordonstoun.

To progress the project in Scotland, fate had provided him with a front man, the famous actor, Peter Christie. The long term intrigue of the Stuart Agenda was the perfect antidote to the fast shallow advertising business that Bernard dominated.

"I can't believe that it's ten years since we got Peter involved," said Bernard, to Angelique, as she woke up and rubbed her eyes, looking out on the uninspiring industrial landscape of the middle part of the Rhône Valley. They were already well south of the landmark Hermitage and Cote Rotie vineyards and the temperature continued to climb.

"He's changed a lot since then. It's not every Scottish film star who becomes Chairman of a political party and drives his country towards Independence."

"It all hangs on tonight though. Peter's handled the political situation in Scotland brilliantly but knows nothing about the Stuart family and our ambition for Robert. Either I turn Peter into a kingmaker or we're bust."

"Have you ever failed, Bernard?"

"Thanks for the vote of confidence, but this isn't the same as advertising perfume you know." They pulled up at the *péage* booth, before leaving the A7 *autoroute* at Bollène and turning west towards Nyons.

"So, with hindsight, it's a good thing that we welcomed the Christies as neighbours, rather than behaving like snooty Parisians."

"I have you to thank for that," he conceded, glad to be driving through the vines at last, near to their holiday home. "The funny thing is that the locals are equally disdainful of Parisians and foreigners, so we did need each other."

"There's a car at Peter's house so they must be there already," said Angelique, as they turned down the track through the vineyard towards their own large farmhouse, which they had been gradually restoring and extending for ten years.

"I'm looking forward to seeing them tonight."

"The vines look good," said Angelique, as they got out of the car.

"Yes, the grapes are swelling nicely. The new irrigation system is helping. This place will be a desert soon," remarked Bernard, as he went over to inspect his small parcel of vines which were tended by a local *vigneron*. Bernard loved everything to do with vines, from the annual cycle of pruning, tying in and thinning to the joy of the harvest and the miracle of vinification that turned the fruit into wine. Little wonder the Greeks and Romans had gods of wine, he thought, and that the liquid could even stand in for the precious blood of Christ. He wondered whether his Stuart project would turn out to be a fine long-lasting noble red, or a pot of vinegar to be used for making salad dressing then forgotten.

The Christies arrived for dinner at eight and the two couples sat outside on a vine covered terrace, overlooking the swimming pool, as the sun gradually set over the mountains to the west. One of the walls was covered with a magnificent purple bougainvillea and the air was filled with the sweet scent of citronella from an anti-mosquito candle.

It was some time since they had met face to face and Bernard had almost forgotten the scale of Peter's magnetic charisma. Peter had the features and body of a Greek god, with twinkling blue eyes and an easy charming manner in contrast to Bernard's own weedier frame and thinning hair. Bernard could see why Peter was a star and so attractive to women, although it was rumoured that he did not exploit this bounteous natural advantage. It was something that the horny Bernard could not understand. "A starlet a day keeps the old man at play," would have been his motto in Peter's position. At first, Bernard used to wonder why a star like Peter bothered with Angelique and himself, but over the years it had become clear that Peter liked relationships with what he called "real people" outside the film industry. And then there was the wine. Peter and he were soul brothers in exploring the endless joy of the different wines which surrounded them in their beloved corner of Provence.

"Hey Peter, I've got a new one for you here," he said, handing his guest a glass. He was pleased that Peter seemed to be in a good mood. He needed that to build on.

"It's the colour of piss, Bernard, after a heavy night,"

"Any idea what it is?"

"Well, it's sweet and tawny, not as elegant as Muscat though, but otherwise I haven't a clue," he added, causing Bernard to smile with triumph. He was pleased that Peter had not been able to identify it.

"So what are we drinking, Bernard? Come on, put us out of our misery," said Peter's Swedish wife, Astride, now filled out comfortably from her former starlet winsomeness. A plain white linen dress showed off her deep tan and a large mother of pearl pendant hung in the throat of her ample cleavage.

"It's from Rasteau, just over the hill. It's made like Muscat de Beaumes de Venise, but the grape's Grenache," replied Bernard. He rather liked Astride. He found her very attractive and worldlier than his prim, pale *Parisienne,* Angelique, who sheltered from the sun below large hats. Despite that, he was pleased that the two women seemed to get on well together.

"So, what about films, Peter?" asked Angelique.

"Nothing at the moment. I'm being very choosy about scripts. We're determined to spend more time in Scotland and France, away from the Hollywood zoo."

"I remember you saying that you were born in Scotland, Peter."

"Yes, I was born in Glasgow in a tenement. I suppose you would call it an apartment block. The males in my family all worked in the shipyards as platers and riveters, trades like that. It's nearly all gone now though, all the slums cleared."

"There are some left," added Astride.

"Yes, a few are gentrified as they say, so the ghosts of my

ancestors have to share the place with IT experts and energy consultants, people like that," said Peter sadly, a strand of his swept-back black hair falling over his tanned handsome face as he leaned forward to pick up his drink.

"I can't believe that it's ten years since we started funding the new Party, Peter, and got you on board to front it," said Bernard, vividly remembering the night when he had concocted the Margaret Baird legacy cover story to explain the source of the money. At the time, he had ducked the monarchy issue, not sure of Peter's stance and anyway, the boy was very young then, it was all so theoretical at that stage.

"Well, we're a lot nearer to Independence now, I can tell you that and we're eternally grateful to Margaret Baird." replied Peter.

"Are you ready for office then?" asked Bernard, swirling the amber liquid round his glass as the evening chorus of cicadas began.

"In strictest confidence, I have to say not quite yet. Still too many lefties in the leadership and that wine cork has more charisma than the whole of them put together. But we've some promising young people coming along."

"When you do win, what happens to the monarchy?" asked Bernard, steeling himself to look Peter in the eye.

"No idea, the Windsor lot are very unpopular so I imagine the Scots would want a republic."

"What do you think yourself, you're a bit of a Scottish romantic aren't you, Braveheart and all that, Kings of Scotland? I imagine that you would have made a terrific King of Scotland, if your films are anything to go by."

"Oh, I would love the job, but I think a lad from the slums of Glasgow would lack the necessary breeding," replied Peter, chuckling at his gentle self-deprecation.

"Well, how about being the next best thing? Be a kingmaker."

"A kingmaker? What the hell do you mean by that?" asked Peter testily, sitting up straight to confront the word. Bernard was clear that he had opened the door but was in danger of having it slammed in his face.

"I mean that you could present the Scots with something new, a new option for a monarchy that's been there all the time but forgotten about," replied Bernard, inching his way through the door towards the crown.

"A new option for monarchy…what are you talking about, Bernard?" demanded Peter, setting his glass down.

"I mean that we have a boy of Royal Stuart blood who is ready to serve as King of Scotland. He wants to reclaim the crown removed from his ancestor's head in the seventeenth century and he's already in Scotland, preparing himself," replied Bernard, relieved that at long last he was confronting the last link in the chain.

"I had no idea there were any Stuarts left. I thought that they had all disappeared into history. So who is this boy?" asked Peter, clearly curious.

"He's a direct descendent of Charles Edward Stuart, better known to you Scots as Bonnie Prince Charlie. His line is legitimate but was airbrushed out of history by the Hanoverians," replied Bernard, with a sweep of his hand, delighted however, that Peter's initial reaction had been one of curiosity and not rejection.

"So, you think that I could be the Stuart kingmaker, when the Independence Party is elected and Scotland becomes free," concluded Peter, in a slightly menacing tone that suggested a negative position.

"Something like that," replied Bernard, his heart sinking at Peter's apparent stance.

"You know, if I'm honest, I'm a reluctant republican. Like me, most people just don't like the Hanoverians as you call them. But a young Stuart monarch might be an attractive option that could even boost our electoral prospects. The other parties in Scotland would represent either the status quo or a republic. It could be good for the tourist industry as well."

"I'm pleased to hear you taking the idea on board, Peter."

"Oh, I'm just thinking aloud. You wouldn't be taking candy from babies though, there would be a hell of a fight over this. The Hanoverians won't give an inch, we would have to take it from them."

"Not an open fight, surely, dirty tricks perhaps," replied Bernard, who quite fancied himself in the dirty tricks department.

"They'll try every trick in the book," said Peter, nodding grimly.

"So, we would have to be prepared."

"Anyway, we're getting way ahead of ourselves. What's he like, this Stuart prodigy?"

"We can have a late lunch with the Stuart family tomorrow if you like, but it would mean us driving up to Fontainbleau in the morning."

"So, you've already set me up, have you? I can't wait, but I'll have the bar set very high, believe me."

"Dinner's ready," called Angelique, who along with Peter's wife, had already withdrawn into the house to escape the boy's talk about wine and Stuarts. Bernard went into dinner absolutely delighted with the progress made. The only secret being kept from Peter was the real origin of the funds that he was dispensing. Bernard couldn't really tell Peter that he didn't know where they were coming from so he decided to let the issue lie. The subterfuge had worked for ten years, so why worry?

****

Overnight, Peter slept fitfully, disturbed by the unremitting Provencal heat which filled the top storey of the house. The Stuart Agenda was also troubling him, working its way through his subconscious. Peter's mulling usually resulted in the emergence of the practical thing that he wanted to do, the balance between his heart and his head, the dream balanced by the art of the possible. The Stuart Agenda, however, refused to be neatly processed and his heart and head battled for most of the night.

In the morning, he was clear. He found himself profoundly attracted to the idea of a Stuart monarch returning to claim his throne in an independent Scotland. He delighted in the prospect of such a neat reversal of history that had so many life enhancing sub plots for the Scots. In his mind's eye he could see the film: a handsome Prince storming across the country, sweeping all before him and reclaiming his birthright. But, he reminded himself, films were made by actors and the script only had to be plausible. Could the Stuarts really produce a Prince who would be a sure certainty for the role? He would have a better idea by the end of the day.

Even more worrying for Peter were the internal politics of the Independence Party, dominated by republicans who would gladly choose to appoint one of their own beached and dried out elder apparatchiks as President of Scotland. How could he possibly overturn the hostility that he would encounter from them?

As they left for Fontainbleau, Peter was still unsure of his approach; he would just have to wing it and trust his intuitions, which didn't normally let him down, but a lot more was at stake here than normal. For the first time in years, he actually felt nervous.

"That's Leo Stuart, outside the front door," said Bernard, as they swept up the drive. Peter thought that Leo looked uncomfortable and nervous, just like himself. Added to that, the *Manoir* looked a bit gloomy and forbidding, even under the bright August sun.

"Leo, this is Peter Christie," said Bernard, making a formal introduction.

"I'm intrigued to meet you after all that Bernard's been telling me," said Peter, shaking Leo's hand warmly.

"It seems as though I've known you for years. I'm sure you understand the difficulty of our position," replied Leo, ushering Peter into the oak-panelled hall, where Robert was waiting alone, standing in front of a portrait of Bonnie Prince Charlie, his handsome face a picture of pre-Culloden optimism.

"I'm Robert Stuart. I'm very pleased to meet you. I've so much enjoyed your films and it's a privilege to have you here today," he said to Peter, his six foot frame graced by Highland dress, worn with complete confidence.

"The privilege is mine. You look more the part than I ever did in any of my films," replied Peter modestly, taken aback by the sheer presence of the young man before him. He had expected to meet a hesitant half-grown boy but was instead confronted by a tall, handsome figure who radiated a commanding easy charm and spoke perfect accent-free English. Peter was filing away that all important first impression when he realised that he had been catapulted onto the slippery slope of approval, almost before he was inside the front door.

"You're very kind and now I'd like you to meet the rest of the family," replied Robert, leading Peter into the salon, adding to his sense of being processed. Peter stepped into the elegant half oak-panelled room. The upper portion of the walls was covered in heavy flock wallpaper of the sort that had become deeply unfashionable since appearing in up market Chinese restaurants.

"I've been looking forward to meeting you all," he said, scanning the eager faces of the Stuart family.

"May I introduce my mother, Simone, and stepfather, André, my Aunt Françoise and my younger brother, Jacques." Peter shook hands with each in turn, taking his time and making warm eye contact, noting how classically beautiful Françoise was, the equal of any of his long list of co-stars. Moving round, Peter sensed the strength of the family, an important asset for Robert, if they did go forward together.

"That's an impressive looking medallion you've got there," said Peter, whose eye had been drawn to the rather opulent piece fixed to Robert's jacket.

"That belonged to the Prince himself," said Leo, who was now dispensing glasses of champagne.

"That's our ancestor, Bonnie Prince Charlie," added Robert, for clarification.

"Nice link to the past," replied Peter, who was comforted by the historical link created by the medallion, giving the family the credibility of history.

"Let's drink to the health of our visitor. Welcome again," said Robert, raising his glass.

"Thanks, I'm delighted to be here," he replied, now looking forward to lunch with a pleasant group of people and the enigmatic Robert.

"Let's go and sit down then," said Françoise, "I think that our guest is hungry." She smiled sweetly at Peter as she guided him into the dining room.

"So, Robert, I hear that you're at Gordonstoun. How do you like it there?" asked Peter, towards the end of the meal, after he had answered all their questions about his life and especially his films.

"Yes, I'm very happy there, even though I've been called a "frog", but only once," he replied.

"Well, I trust that you dealt with that, and I hear that you're doing well at rugby."

"Yes, I've just been made Captain of the senior team. It's a great honour," Robert replied, tossing an imaginary rugby ball to his younger brother Jacques, who scurried to catch it, almost knocking over a glass of wine.

"So, what kind of king do you want to be?" asked Peter. Every eye turned on Robert.

"I feel that I need to be the kind of king who reflects the times, the kind of king that people want…yes, a people's king, not a rich man's king. I'm sure that there'll be work for me to do, things that I can lead on top of what the politicians can do. I'm sure that I'll be able to do a lot for sport, for example," said Robert, looking around the table for support for his immature prospectus.

31

"Well spoken," replied Peter, who shot Robert a brief glance of apology, for putting him on the spot.

"We could do some work on an agenda for kingship," offered Bernard, who was beaming his personal approval at the boy.

"Yes, that might be helpful," replied Robert.

"Now, I want to thank you for a wonderful lunch with your family," began Peter, looking at Leo and Françoise. "I have two daughters myself and if Robert was a bit older I'd be trying to fix him up with one of them," he added, causing smiles all round at the intended compliment.

"We do hope that you will share our hopes for Robert," said Leo brightly.

"And now a toast from me. To monarchy," he said, standing up and looking at Robert and Leo, who nodded in understanding.

"To monarchy," they all repeated seriously, putting their glasses to their lips.

"To a Stuart Scottish monarchy," added Peter, loudly and with careless pride, still on his feet, raising his glass even higher.

"To a Stuart Scottish monarchy," they repeated, before clapping and stamping their feet, looking at each other with knowing looks of joy at Peter's approval.

"As you can see, I do share your hopes for the future and believe that Robert has the potential to fulfil his destiny. However, I cannot personally deliver that. So much is uncertain, not least the view of the Independence Party as a whole and then the Scottish people. Everything can be worked on but nothing is certain," counselled Peter, taking the edge off his earlier enthusiasm.

"Thanks Peter, we do appreciate the difficulties ahead. It won't be easy but with Robert's potential and the resources that we have behind us, I'm sure that it's the start of a partnership that's going to change the face of history," said Bernard grandly.

"Well put, Bernard, I couldn't agree more. I'd like to thank Peter on behalf of the family for what he has already done and we pray for Scottish Independence and all that may follow," added Leo.

Robert then announced that he wanted to show Peter around the *Manoir* garden.

Peter walked into the garden with Robert, silently convinced that he was with someone beyond the ordinary. He felt a presence in

Robert that he had only experienced before in a few gnarled Hollywood legends who had constructed their personas over a lifetime. To Peter, the young Robert seemed to have been born with it.

"It's awesome what you've done for us over the years. I'm very grateful, Peter," said Robert, pausing in the shade of a well laden pear tree.

"Yes, as you say, isn't it ironic that neither of us was aware of the true purpose," replied Peter, generously putting aside any sense that he had been led along under false pretences.

"Well, I suppose I was too young and then again, I might not have been suitable," added Robert, leading Peter out into the hot sun towards an enormous bed of large dahlias which were just coming into bloom.

"You don't have to worry on that score. I'm sure you have what it takes, Robert. I'm really thrilled about your rugby success. There's a lot to build on there," replied Peter, who was secretly delighted that sport might deliver a platform of fame from which the final assault on their target would be so much easier.

"After Gordonstoun, I'm going to Edinburgh University and I already have an offer to play rugby for Edinburgh Tigers."

"Without doubt, a good choice" replied Peter, only on the basis of the rugby potential as they completed the circuit of the garden to be confronted with the whole Stuart family lined up at Bernard's car for their departure.

As the car set off, Robert remained with them waving in the wing mirror, causing Peter's minor discomfort to surface. He felt as if Robert had cast a spell over him, drawing him inexorably into supporting the Stuart Agenda, almost powerless to resist. Peter sensed an almost mystical element, like an invisible crown on the head of the young man. He did not share this view with Bernard, whose appreciation was normally confined to the very obvious.

"He's definitely got star quality," said Peter, as the car accelerated around the bend in the drive, removing Robert from the wing mirror.

"He's good, isn't he? And I'm particularly delighted that he's doing so well at rugby."

"In fact, he looks so good that I'm now wondering how we could make this work to the advantage of the Independence Party. I doubt if the republican leadership would tolerate Robert, even to get their hands on real power."

"Can't you change the leadership?" asked Bernard with a laugh. The question was so obvious that Peter had never thought of it but in that instant he realised that Bernard's quip contained the seeds of the answer, and he did have a young protégé who was on the cusp of leadership. Nervousness returned as the need for a political *coup d'état* within the party added to the pressure of his kingmaker role.

"That might be the answer Bernard. I'll have to cast around in my Lomond group for a candidate."

"Is that your collection of bearded protégés?"

"Yes, although the beards have gone now. We started out very informally as a group of students and young councillors, all committed to Independence. We used to go for long walks in the hills and drink lots of wine, my wine," replied Peter, who had fond memories of the period, despite the sore leg muscles and the hangovers.

"And no doubt you all talked a lot."

"Yes, only it was the kind of wild heady talk that sounds good at the time, but next morning nobody can remember what was said. Not very serious or politically grown up, but it did forge a group of people who are capable of changing things fundamentally," replied Peter, who had happy memories of fresh young eager faces in passionate debate.

"I suppose the name Lomond Group has the ring of a think tank about it, I'm sure that made them feel more important."

"Oh yes, particularly my star recruit, she's blossoming by the day." said Peter.

"Who's that?"

"Angela Brown," replied Peter proudly. Peter realised that he had never broached the subject of monarchy with her. She had to be his first convert but there was enough time for that, he comforted himself.

"Is there plenty of money left in the Margaret Baird fund?" asked Peter.

"Oh yes," replied a tired-sounding Bernard.

As they sped south, Peter felt elated, confronting the giant jigsaw that was the future of Scotland. Robert was the large new piece he had to play with, a piece that expanded the possibilities, enriched the brew if only he could make it fit. He knew that many of the other pieces would need to be reshaped for that to happen and he relished the challenge.

****

Back at the *Manoir* the atmosphere was charged up as the Stuarts celebrated Robert's success in winning over Peter. Leo opened an ancient bottle of Armagnac to celebrate the occasion. Robert felt that he had crossed a threshold into a more real world where Peter's engagement offered the potential for his Stuart Agenda to be built into the future thinking of the Independence Party, the key enabling step to meet his ambition. It was like a ship being launched after all the sweat and toil of the shipyard. He was now in the water, able to choose direction although still subject to the winds and storms of events beyond his control. He knew that he would also need a lot of luck and rubbed Bonnie Prince Charlie's medallion, just in case.

Chapter 6

Scotland, September 2035 - Loch Lomond

Angela Brown arrived at Peter Christie's house on the shore of Loch Lomond about an hour before the rest of the Lomond Group. The puppy fat of her school and early student days was long gone, replaced with a calculated elegance which added to the aura of latent power that surrounded her. She had remained faithful to her hair colour, even tipping the tone a few points further towards the red end of the spectrum, a warning sign to competitors. The cut was shorter and bouffant, a veritable lion's mane except that she was a lioness and much more dangerous. She was wearing a black dress with white collar and cuffs. Round her waist was a wide white leather gold studded belt which accentuated her hourglass figure.

She wanted a private word with Peter Christie, her political mentor, before the others arrived. She waited in Peter's vast study which had a mouth-watering view out across a very choppy loch towards the heather-clad slopes of Ben Lomond. She could see a line of tiny figures proceeding ant-like up the long gentle incline that tempts walkers up towards the much steeper slopes that access the summit and one of the best views in the world. She wondered silently where she was in the grand scheme of things—still at the bottom of the gentle incline? Surely not. Powering her way towards the steeper slopes and the summit? She liked to think so. She saw that the actual tip of Ben Lomond was shrouded in an ethereal cloud. Ah, they won't see me coming, she thought, smiling faintly.

She felt her customary flutter as Peter came into the room. It was the same flutter that she had felt when she first met him. He had been recruiting students to the new Independence Party at Edinburgh University Fresher's Week. Her teenage crush was now amplified by years of frustration at his indifference to her as a woman.

Sometimes she thought that he looked on her as a kind of political daughter, excusing his correctness, but that was wearing thin as she emerged as a fully-fledged politician in her own right. Peter was the only man who had ever declined her, although strictly speaking there had never been a transaction, never a blank refusal or put-down, just a complete lack of interest and it made him all the more desirable to her.

Angela was furious that sources close to the Party leader, Jim Robertson, were briefing against her and the ideas coming from the Lomond Group. She was quietly advocating a major shift in policy direction that was anathema to barely-disguised socialists like Robertson.

Peter seemed more serious than normal and Angela thought that he even looked older. There was no radiant smile or pleasantries, his customary charisma seemed dimmed by some undeclared burden.

"I've just heard that Robertson's coming to today's meeting," said Peter.

"He doesn't normally bother. He never even responds to our invitations. What's new then?"

"We should take it as a compliment that he's expressing interest. Give him the benefit of the doubt. However, try to keep your head down and don't provoke him. Don't give him any excuse. I've invested too much in you, Angela, for it all to go wrong now."

"You're right, we're not ready for a final showdown," she answered, thankful for his wise counsel which had already saved her from herself several times.

"I'm not always right. I once said to Robertson that the trouble with Scotland was that all the best Scots were someplace else. He didn't speak to me for a month."

"Thanks for the advice, Peter. What would I do without you?" she said wistfully.

"Let's join the others."

For the main meeting, the group was gathered round the large table in Peter's beamed baronial dining room, below a glistening chandelier. A magnificent pair of crossed claymores took pride of place on one of the walls. The room was filled with the sickly perfume from a huge vase of lilies that had been moved from the centre of the table to make way for them.

The presentation was given by a professor of statistics from Strathclyde University. Jim Robertson, the Party leader, arrived late as the presentation was finishing. Robertson was a big man and seriously overweight. He was of a size where he had to back into a car, place his bottom firmly on the seat, then swing his legs in, usually carrying something to eat at the same time. Like Angela's nostrils, his large ears reacted to stress, wiggling perceptibly at low levels, before rising in amplitude to fold back against his head when the going got really tough. Between the ears he had a permanently shiny oiled-looking face, dominated by a large nose. The overall effect, according to one of the Party wags, was that he looked like a cross between an elephant and a sunbeam, always charging about, but only occasionally casting a weak light on anything. Angela thought that his nickname "The Elephant" was an insult to these lovable creatures. However, she also knew that elephants could be unpredictable and dangerous and on that point the nickname was fully deserved. In the ageing Party politburo of nonentities, he was the only one with balls. He grunted a sweaty general greeting to the group before sitting down, breathing heavily.

"Sorry you couldn't make it for the talk, Jim, it was very interesting," said Peter brightly. Angela thought it disgraceful that the leader couldn't be bothered to arrive at such an important meeting on time.

"Could I just have a re-run of the conclusions, please?" asked Jim.

"Professor, can we have them again, please?" asked Peter patiently.

"OK, I've been doing a statistical analysis on the long-term polling results for the Independence Party, as requested by the Chairman," said the professor. "The bottom line is that the forward projections do predict another breakthrough for the Party, but this time to a working majority."

"Well, that's excellent news. So when can we expect this miracle to happen?" asked Robertson pugnaciously, sticking his big nose forward.

"It's difficult to say, and there are some caveats."

"So what's the use of a prediction if you can't tell us when it's going to happen?" demanded Robertson impatiently. Rude bastard, thought Angela.

"Let me try to explain," said the professor. "The optimistic assessment of the trend is that it is somehow natural, built into the way that the Scottish psyche is moving, the Zeitgeist if you like, inexorably taking us towards the promised land of independence as a small country within the European Union. That would mean you could keep going exactly as you are and ride that wave to power."

"I like that, you all know it's my clearly stated position," said Robertson, looking round as if to challenge dissenters. "So what's the pessimistic assessment, Professor?"

Naïve idiot, thought Angela.

"It's not really pessimistic, it's just different. The other interpretation is that you'll only get so far up the curve with your existing policies and will have to develop a radical new platform for the final push towards power," replied the professor.

"So which camp is the Lomond Group in?" asked Robertson, looking round the table questioningly as he began to sweat from the heat of the afternoon sun which had tracked round to stream in at the large dining room window.

"We'll no doubt keep a foot in both camps, but we were just about to start the discussion when you came in, Jim," replied Peter, exercising his chairmanship.

"So what do you think, Angela? Do let us have your pearls of wisdom and tell us what we need to change," asked Robertson, in a sarcastic tone, delving into one of his ears with his pinkie.

"I'm not sure that we should pay too much attention to the analysis of the trends. This is weaker than direct opinion poll data and we blithely ignore that when we don't like it," she replied, undermining the basis of the question so that it was not worth answering. She was furious that Robertson had trapped her in front of the group.

"So, should we continue as we are?" he persisted.

"We need to be constantly monitoring the developing political climate, public opinion and the activities of political opponents. But above all we must give the people a vision of what a free Scotland would be like, what all the positive differences would be," replied Angela. She saw Peter looking straight at her as if willing her to get it right. His expression signalled satisfaction.

"I like that, "A Vision for Scotland"," said Robertson, "why don't you work that up into a paper that we could draw on?"

"That's a good idea," added Peter enthusiastically, nodding at Angela to encourage her acquiescence.

"Yes, of course, that's something we will have to do," she replied, without enthusiasm. She was indeed working on a vision but would not wish to present it until she was sure the time was right, when she had the bull elephant in the sights of her loaded rifle.

Chapter 7

Scotland, October 2037 - Edinburgh

Robert was well settled into student life based in an upmarket apartment in Morningside, a posh Edinburgh suburb. The accommodation was more young-professional than student. The lounge was large, with elaborate original Victorian cornices and a slightly vulgar black and white marble fireplace. A big bay window looked on to the garden bounded by a secure high wall behind which he could park and charge-up his BMW-E series. It was the height of luxury after the spartan Gordonstoun and nobody tried to get him to eat porridge for breakfast. He was studying History and Politics. His flatmate, Andrew MacDonald, a friend from Gordonstoun, was studying Law.

Robert often walked around the city. In the Old Town, the narrow streets and grim dark closes and wynds fascinated him. He was astonished at the density of Stuart memorials, street names and other reminders of his family's long reign in Scotland. He found this strangely comforting, as if the Hanoverians had only borrowed the Stuart crown, looking after it until he was ready to take it back from them. He felt very much at home.

Walking up the Royal Mile from his imagined home in Holyrood Palace, he saw himself in the state coach accompanied by a troop of cavalry, the grating of the coach wheels and the urgent clip clop of the horse's hooves struggling for friction on the greasy cobbles, echoing eerily around the High Street. He could almost smell the animals, the clean leather alternating with the pungency of horse piss. Up the narrow street towards the Castle, he imagined the cheering crowds filling the pavements and hanging out of every window below the banks of chimneys that clawed at the sky above the steep pitched roofs. Then onto the castle and a glittering reception…

He checked himself; he was getting too far ahead of reality. So many imponderables lay ahead, not least the question of his own Catholic upbringing. Would the Scots accept a Catholic as King? His Catholic ancestor, James II, had insisted upon his "divine right" to rule, directly under God without the intervention of Mammon's parliament, adding greatly to his unacceptability. Robert sensed at least a "right to reign," if not rule, but nothing divine.

In the Edinburgh New Town, on the other side of Princes Street, the physical reality was different. On George Street, the massive statue of George IV sitting on a horse reminded him that this part of town was a Hanoverian construct, built after Culloden and populated by a largely Hanoverian-leaning middle and upper class.

Striding along Princes Street he longed to stop some ordinary Edinburgh folk and ask them what they would think of a Stuart restoration. The same question would perch on his lips in student bars and rugby clubs, but could not be asked. He was more than aware of the surreal nature of his position. The passionate emotion of Culloden was his refuge in moments of self-doubt, reinforced by his antipathy towards the Hanoverian Prince Henry.

One day, when he was in his second year at university, Robert happened to be in Fleshmarket Close when his phone rang. It was the call that was to change his life. After the call he closed his phone, completely stunned, and walked like a zombie into the Half Way House pub. He hardly dared believe what he'd just been told. He was being called up to play in the Scottish Rugby Team. It was the happiest day of his life. He had always sensed that he had rugby greatness in him and had read encouraging comments in the press, but now it was real. He thanked God for his Scottish granny. Monique may have been trouble for his grandfather, but it was thanks to her genes that he was now getting the chance to play rugby for the country that he loved.

The news of Robert's elevation to the Scottish Rugby team was greeted with delight by his inner circle. Bernard, ever the marketing man, was particularly delighted that such a vehicle for "celebrity" had presented itself, giving Robert a way of developing a positive public profile ahead of any launch into the royal market. Robert was a bit concerned about telling his stepfather, André. He knew about his ambition for Robert to play for France.

Chapter 8

Scotland, October 2037 - Glasgow

Piers Ross sat at his desk in the Scottish Cable newspaper office in Glasgow. It was a big friendly barn of a place that was home to a small group of staffers and a constantly changing mass of students, advertising people and freelancers. He thought that he could just about smell the heavy dull end of whisky from the exhalation of his colleagues who had just returned after the weekend.

He was of the freelance community, whose main brief was Scottish independence politics. During his student days at Edinburgh University, he had been prominent in independence politics as one of Peter Christie's first new blood recruits and took some credit for recruiting Angela Brown, now the rising star of the Party. Piers still had the boyish looks of his youth and the same lightweight physique. He had, however, given up on the trademark white jacket and polo neck that Angela Brown had torn from his back in their student days, in favour of normal business suits, which he had difficulty filling.

For his honours thesis at Edinburgh he had written naively on the history of nationalist parties. A few years in the jungle of journalism had convinced him that lust for power and the role of money in obtaining that ultimate political commodity, were the keys to outcomes. He kept his cynicism warm by closely following Party funding, having discovered that he who pays the piper calls the tune, even in politics. His zeal to uncover shady funding deals, in the public interest, of course, overcame any scruples he had about using semi-illegal methods of data collection. He regarded such white collar crimes against inappropriate privacy, as the end justifying the means. His small crime was aimed at shining light on an even bigger one; what could be wrong with that? And anyway, he wouldn't get caught.

He was looking into the funding of the Scottish Independence Party, which was mainly in the public record and looked to be coming largely from the film star, Peter Christie. Piers was aware of the star's legendary stinginess, which seemed at odds with the largesse being dispensed in his name. Piers had stumbled on an easy way of resolving such questions in the shape of a computer hacker who was delighted to take on sensitive assignments, mainly for the challenge and the price of a few pints in a Glasgow pub.

Piers excitedly opened the brown envelope that he had just received from his hacker. The data was raw from the innards of the Party computer, unmassaged for public consumption. He ploughed through each year's contributions, making a list of those from Christie. The first two contributions after Christie joined the Party were for three thousand pounds each, paid as a cheque from a Bank of Scotland branch in Glasgow. The third payment which arrived around the time of Christie being made Vice Chairman was much bigger at two hundred thousand pounds. The money had come in the form of a cheque drawn on a Swiss bank. The notes column recorded the name of an agency in Paris, Agence Frank. For all subsequent years, the money came straight from the Swiss bank by electronic transfer. Piers was intrigued at the wall of foreign money coming in under Christie's name. At face value, it looked as though Christie was using money which had been squirreled away outside the UK tax system, a grave offence on that scale. But would he be so naïve or stupid? Or more cynically, was he operating as a front for somebody else, with a less acceptable face? And what was Agence Frank?

A few days later, Piers invited Jamie Scott, an old pal from university, out to lunch in a smart Rennie Mackintosh inspired brasserie near the Clyde. In the aftermath of the 7/7/2005 bombings in London the government had insisted that the Security Service set up a series of regional offices throughout the country, both to recruit more locals and to keep an eye on potential troublemakers. Political correctness demanded that an office be opened in Scotland and this was done in Glasgow, which had the largest immigrant population north of the border. Jamie worked for the Scottish office of MI5, dubbed Tartan Park by the superior London cynics who were reluctant to yield up their monopoly on secrets. To add insult to injury, the occupants of Tartan Park were referred to as the MacSpooks, second class spies at best, barely a cut above ordinary plods on the beat.

"Jamie, how's the MacSpook business going then?" asked Piers, teasing his old pal. They were having their occasional catch-up Friday pub lunch together: a posh sandwich and a pint, or sometimes two. Jamie's brown waxed Barbour jacket was draped over the back of his seat, an uneasy cover for his pinstripe suit.

"Actually, it's not very busy at the moment," confided Jamie,

"Glasgow's immigrants are more interested in making money than bombs."

"So, you're not using your Arabic much?" Piers asked, leaning back in the Rennie Mackintosh tribute chair. He marvelled at Jamie's competence in a language which he himself found impenetrable.

"Not as much as I did working in Saudi, but I monitor stuff, you know."

"I don't think you've ever told me how an ordinary Glasgow Rangers supporter like you ended up speaking Arabic," said Piers.

"Well, I was always going to study languages at university so it was a toss-up between Russian, Mandarin and Arabic. I couldn't be bothered with the obvious European languages. I chose Arabic because it was warmer in countries where they speak it, but I think I got it wrong, Mandarin's the thing now."

"I bet it was warm in Saudi," said Piers, imagining the Lawrence of Arabia desert scenes, rather than the air conditioned offices.

"It was, but cold at heart. I really missed Glasgow life: the pubs, the football and the girls, so I came back to work for His Majesty. So, how about you?"

"Oh, the usual political reporting, and I'm still plodding away on my tome about the independence movement."

"You've got plenty of time yet. As long as you have it ready for the big day, when independence arrives, that's when it'll sell like hotcakes," said Jamie, already half way down his pint, which he held balanced on the bulge of his not inconsiderable stomach.

"Yes, I could do with it to kick start my pension fund."

"Or, get that flat in Marbella," said Jamie, looking out of the window towards the big cranes on the banks of the Clyde, relics of the mighty river's past, when the pubs had no connection with Rennie Mackintosh.

"I did stumble on something last week, though. It seems that there's something fishy about Peter Christie's funding of the Scottish Independence Party," said Piers, hoping that Jamie would not ask him to define stumble.

"What evidence have you got for that?" asked Jamie, who involuntarily twitched his nose and sniffed with interest.

"The money's coming from a Swiss bank in Zurich via an agency in Paris," replied Piers, lowering his voice.

44

"That's a very unusual route," replied Jamie, drawing heavily on his pint.

"Yes, before Christie became Deputy Chairman of the Party, the money was coming from the Bank of Scotland in Glasgow." replied Piers.

"How did you find this out?"

"Pass. A journalist doesn't reveal his sources, even to you, Jamie."

"Christie looks squeaky clean. What do you think's going on?" asked Jamie, finishing his pint with a wide swallow, as if he needed to drink faster when his brain was working.

"You tell me, Jamie. I suppose it could be entirely innocent or, at worst, Christie's using money on which he hasn't paid tax. The word is that he's a bit of a miser."

"Or perhaps he's acting as a front for someone else's money—foreign money."

"That would be much more serious, wouldn't it?" concluded Piers, "although, there is a tradition of foreign businessmen putting money into UK political parties."

"Businessmen, fine. We understand that and it's tolerated, but we know that money's starting to leak into parties from some very undesirable overseas quarters, particularly the Chinese mafia and even groups with links to terrorism."

"So is the Service looking at this?" asked Piers, who immediately realised that he should not have asked such a direct question.

"We look at all sorts of things," replied Jamie, gazing into the emptiness of his beer glass.

"So, what about Christie?"

"I'm pretty sure that we'll want to take a look," replied Jamie, whose eyes were flashing back and forth, trying to catch a waiter to order his second pint.

"I've looked up the agency on the net. It's called *Agence* Frank, mainly in advertising. It's privately owned by a Frenchman called Bernard Frank, that's as far as I took it myself."

"OK, we'll take it from there."

"Well, feel free to have a look at the case, as long as I get the story when it goes public—usual rules?"

"So, have you got any nearer to bedding the lovely Angela Brown that we both used to dream about?" asked Jamie, as the waiter delivered their sandwiches and his second pint.

"Well, I think I got a bit nearer than you, but on the fateful night, after pulling my clothes off, she fell asleep on me, dead drunk. She was a wild one. She wouldn't go out with me again. I think she was embarrassed. Who knows what goes on in women's heads?"

"Well, never give up hope."

"No chance, she's getting further away from me by the day. She's an MSP and shadow minister now. How can I compete with that?"

****

Back in his office after lunch, Jamie relayed the information to his boss, who was more special branch plod than spook. He was only too pleased to pass what looked like a hot potato involving the French, all the way down to London.

Chapter 9

Scotland, November 2037 - Murrayfield, Edinburgh

Robert's first cap for Scotland was in the Calcutta Cup match against England. The first choice centre had been injured in a club game and the decision was taken by the selectors to blood Robert. Scotland had enjoyed a mixed season up to that point. There had been good heroic defence but not enough points scored, a not untypical pattern for them. But against the Auld Enemy, the formbook could be thrown out of the window. That fixture was about passion.

Robert was delighted that most of his family were there. His parents and younger brother, Jacques, along with Leo and Françoise, had somehow managed to find a hospitality package at the last minute. Cardinal McKerran was in the stand with a small coterie of priests in tow, and Peter Christie was there with some of his rugby friends.

Coming out onto the pitch, the atmosphere at the game was friendly enough but Robert sensed the underlying tension that characterised games against the Auld Enemy. There were lots of national stereotypes on show, from kilted highlanders with plastic claymores to John Bull complete with dog. The teams were presented to the President and Patron of the SRU and the anthems sung. God save the King was something of a dirge, but manfully sung by the visiting supporters. There was some rude whistling from the small Scottish element that makes a point of cheering for Germany in England vs. Germany football matches. Then came Flower of Scotland, building up from the slow rolling start, as the English Prince Edward was sent "homeward tae think again."

The game started well for Scotland, who got a penalty almost immediately following some English indiscipline. That set the pattern for most of the first half, and with Scotland defending and kicking well, they went in at half time with a 9-0 lead.

The English stepped up several gears in the second half. Something must have been said at half-time, and a converted try narrowed the gap to 9-7 still in favour of Scotland. Ten minutes later, the heavier English pack broke through with a series of mauling runs that released the backs into a good position to steer the wing over to touch down behind a defeated Scots defence. The Scots now trailed 9-

14.

The crowd went quiet, beginning to fear a late rout by the now rampant English pack. A few minutes later a third try for the English looked inevitable and it fell to Robert to make a desperate crunching tackle on the English wing to propel him into touch within a yard of the line, a carbon copy of his tackle on Prince Henry at Gordonstoun but without the messy aftermath.

This act of resistance lifted the crowd, who began to sing Flower of Scotland again, beginning softly as the sound picked up round the stadium, rising all the time towards its demanding crescendo. From the next set piece Robert received the ball from the fly half well inside Scots territory. He dummied the first Englishman, feigning a pass down the line. He was sprinting very hard and with deft twists and turns, he weaved his way to the English twenty-two yard line as Flower of Scotland reached its emotional climax. Crossing the English twenty-two, Robert lost contact with the words and was seized by the sound of the pipes. He was back at Culloden. The sound seemed to slow down and Robert's vision broke into a series of quick frames.

He looked up for an instant. Through the cannon smoke of the English pack's hovering sweat cloud, the camera flashes searched him out but the bullets bounced off his flesh of steel. The Hanoverian banners on the terrace behind beckoned, inviting the charge. He put his head back and yelled something primeval. English hands were outstretched like bayonets trying to pierce him. He fended them off with the shield of his pride. Faces screwed up with hate and fear screamed as he passed them, unseeing. The last defender between him and the line was swatted aside as if he were made of cardboard. Robert crossed the line between the posts, and to touch down, stabbed the earth with the end of the ball, a mighty sword thrust. Victory would be his after the conversion.

He remained on his knees for a few seconds, humble before the tumultuous din of his compatriots and the memory of Culloden. His teammates ended his private homage, hauling him back to the present, onto his feet to face their adulation. The crowd was still going mad and the Royal Patron of the SRU was still on her feet cheering. She had just witnessed one of the greatest tries ever scored for Scotland. The deflated English went through the motions for the remaining three minutes before the final whistle and the ensuing pandemonium of victory for the Scots. Robert, the newcomer was an instant national hero.

After a shower and the changing room celebrations, he wished above all that he could see his family, but the schedule did not permit it. After several receptions there was the President's dinner, attended by both teams. Following a tradition started many years before by another royal Hanoverian Princess, the hostess was the young and attractive Princess Victoria, who was known to value the office of Patron of the SRU above all her other commitments. At the reception before dinner, Robert was sought out by the Princess.

It was a surreal moment for him, confronted by the second in line to the British Hanoverian throne and yet another representative of his natural enemy. This triggered unpleasant memories of his dealings with her brother, but a slight reserve on his part was all that showed. However, he was seduced by the geniality of the raven-haired Princess, whose most striking feature was her intense blue sparkling eyes. She managed the difficult balance between being regal, yet empathetic and in touch, unlike her charmless elder brother. She congratulated Robert personally on his magnificent performance. She was well informed and seemed passionate about rugby. After the dinner, Robert went back to his apartment, where his parents and aunt and uncle were staying for the weekend.

Next day, Peter would meet the Stuart family for lunch in a private room at a local restaurant. It was an Italian restaurant, chosen more for convenience than anything else. It had tiled floors and a low ceiling, the kind of place where the noise on a Saturday night would be deafening as tables of young females screeched at each other loudly over their large glasses of wine.

****

For Sunday lunch, however, it was quiet and civilised. As a sign of things to come, Robert was asked for his autograph by one of the staff on the way in. Peter was in ebullient mood. It was the first time that Peter had met them all together since his introduction to them at the *Manoir,* and he insisted on buying champagne to celebrate the success of the earlier meeting and all that had happened since, especially Robert's match-winning try.

In sharp contrast, Robert was feeling strangely subdued. He was worried that the opening of a door into the public arena would put a time limit on his secret. It now seemed much more likely to him that he would be uncovered, so he aired his concerns halfway through lunch.

"Peter, what will our opponents do when they find out about us?" asked Robert, thinking of his meeting with the Princess but having difficulty seeing her personally, as an opponent.

"They'll dig for dirt, I should imagine."

"What kind of dirt?" asked Leo, with a disgusted edge to his voice, as if no such material could possibly adhere to a Stuart.

"They'll be looking for anything that could show Robert in an unfavourable light. So, if there are any skeletons in the family cupboard get rid of them or hide them very deep," answered Peter with a smile.

"Uncle Leo, you've got the key to the skeleton cupboard," added Robert, giving a trace of a wink to his aunt.

"If they attack our legitimacy the Cardinal assures me that the Vatican has the papers that prove our case," Leo blustered, coughing.

"What else might they do, Peter?"

"They might go public on you and leak the whole thing as a kind of conspiracy story, hoping the Independence Party might tear itself apart once it becomes clear that they were being invisibly led towards a monarchy."

"That would create problems for you, Peter," said Leo.

"Yes, that's a risk I have to take."

"We need to keep it all secret for as long as possible," said Robert who was all of a sudden hungry as the smell of cooking parmesan wafted through from the kitchen.

"Robert's right; he needs more time to build his position and the politics are tricky. The monarchists among the independents have to get control soon," replied Peter.

"That's in your capable hands," said Leo, as the main course arrived.

****

That evening, Cardinal McKerran joined Robert and his family for a light supper after which the two of them went into the lounge for a private chat. The Cardinal looked tired to Robert. He was certainly overweight and his complexion was tending to the florid. Too much eating for God, thought Robert. After listening to another round of congratulations, Robert got to the point of his meeting with the Cardinal.

"Remind me, Cardinal, how you got to know Uncle Leo?" he asked. He sensed that the Cardinal's role in his life had been critical but hidden, like an iceberg.

"I ran the Vatican Constitutional Committee and your Uncle Leo was a member. Don't forget, he's a very well-known lawyer," replied the Cardinal.

"I'm very grateful for your support over the years. The meeting with the Holy Father was especially important. With hindsight, I can see that it was the act that got all the family on side facing the same way. While I've got you here, can we talk a bit about religion?"

"I should be qualified to help you with that."

"I don't mean any disrespect but it does seem to cause a lot of trouble. If I were ever to be crowned King of Scotland, who would put the crown on my head? A Catholic priest because I am a Catholic or a Church of Scotland minister because this is Scotland?"

"And a wedding would be even trickier. I don't have an easy answer to that Robert, just to say that if, and we pray when, the time comes, you'll have constitutional advisers who'll keep you right."

"We must talk more often," said Robert as he left the Cardinal.

****

That night, Robert lay awake, brooding on the religious question, not for the first time. So many of the other aspects of the plan were moving forward but his evident and unchangeable Catholicism remained a potential stumbling block, capable of snatching defeat from the jaws of victory. Any attempt to change his religion would surely seem shallow and calculating and alienate his closest supporters; he would be robbing Peter to pay Paul, literally. He had believed that in these more secular times Scots would be more tolerant but now he wasn't so sure. Perhaps he had underestimated the cultural dimension. He was beginning to realise that people were still cultural Catholics or Protestants long after belief had evaporated and the attitudes and prejudices attached to these labels still ruled how they saw themselves and others. Sleep finally released him from the endless recycling that always failed to produce an answer.

Chapter 10

France, November 2037 - Paris

The head of the MI5 office in Glasgow was obliged to agree to the temporary deployment of Jamie to Paris where he would work on the illegal political funding case with the local MI6 team. Jamie arrived at the *Gare du Nord* by Eurostar from St Pancras in London. He had been told to prepare himself for a stay of about a month and was booked into a small hotel not far from the centre.

The detail of his story had been sent ahead, so mercifully, he didn't have to repeat it again in the cramped, windowless office in the bowels of the British Embassy. Jamie was surprised at the old-fashioned painted metal desks and filing cabinets that furnished the place, a far cry from his smart new office in Glasgow.

His temporary boss, John, head of MI6 in Paris, was a rather blunt Yorkshireman in his mid-fifties, who sounded as though he would like to retire as soon as possible, to spend his summers watching his beloved county cricket team. A photograph of the legendary twentieth century cricketer and Yorkshireman, Freddie Trueman, stood on top of a book case. John had an unkempt look, exaggerated by dark bags under his eyes and unruly eyebrows, which curled up at the edges, almost forming question marks. It was the kind of old-fashioned face that seemed incomplete without a pipe.

His second in command, Mark, was a lot younger, almost prematurely bald, and had a face which seemed set in a semi-permanent scowl of disbelief.

"We've got the details of the case so far here, Jamie, so we don't need to go over all that again," said John.

"Yes, what a coup for Tartan Park," added Mark, with a touch of sarcasm, "and what an opportunity to catch the Frogs with their trousers down," he added, as he doodled incessantly on a sheet of paper in front of him.

"Now Jamie, the only lead we have at the moment is Bernard Frank. From public sources, he's chairman and owner of a large PR agency. They do advertising, mainly cosmetics, that's big in France. They also seem to represent celebrities. The accounts look good and the business is very profitable. From our own files, all that we have on

Frank is membership of the Paris Ring," said John.

"What's the Paris Ring?" asked Jamie, who involuntarily gave the wedding ring on his finger a few turns.

"As far as we can see, it's a harmless-looking semi-occult group. Virgin shagging in the woods on Midsummer's Eve dressed up as knights, that kind of thing. With a whiff of drugs as well," replied Mark cheerily, as though he coveted membership.

"Good fun if you can find it," replied Jamie, "but how do we know about this?" he asked, suppressing the lurid thoughts that had intruded.

"An important Brit who shall remain nameless got involved and was done for drugs by the French police. It was a bit messy and we had to rescue him," replied John, untangling the verdant end of his right eyebrow and letting it spring back into its questioning coil.

"Do we know who else is in the ring?" asked Jamie.

"Our British friend didn't know any of them by their real names but recognised Frank. He'd seen his picture in the financial press," replied John, pushing a photograph of Bernard across the table.

"Surely he knew where they met then?" pressed Jamie, picking up the picture.

"He said not when we debriefed him. He claimed that he was always driven to the meeting locations and never knew where he was," said John, as Jamie pulled a face of disbelief.

"Our Scottish friend thinks that we're tossers, or is he just in a hurry to get back to see a Rangers game?" said Mark provocatively, adding a final flourish to his doodle.

"Let's leave Rangers out of it please," replied Jamie, who instantly promoted Mark to his arrogant shites gallery.

"Yes, yes, Jamie, I agree it sounds thin, but we had no reason to press him. We just wanted to get him out of France as quickly as possible," replied John, responding to Jamie's scepticism.

"Believe it or not, Jamie, I've come up with something very interesting from the French records. They show that Bernard Frank and your heart-throb, Christie, own houses next door to each other in Provence. It doesn't prove a conspiracy but they must know each other," added Mark.

"So, Jamie, that's all we've got I'm afraid. Let's begin by putting a tail on Frank. I see from your record that you haven't done much surveillance work so this will be good training for you."

"What about his phone?" asked Jamie, who had all the training on high-tech surveillance and didn't fancy plodding about.

"We'll get round to that if need be. You'll need to follow him around for a bit. Build up a pattern. Tag his car and follow him using the satellite monitoring system to keep out of sight. Give it a couple of weeks and see what you come up with. I'll give you a local driver."

As Jamie was leaving, he peered over the desk to see the final result of Mark's artistic endeavour. It was a cartoon of a man in a kilt, pissing in a river with what looked like the Eiffel tower behind him.

The next day, Jamie had a good look at Bernard's office and parking arrangements and at his house in the suburbs of Paris. The house was screened by a high wall with wrought iron electric gates behind which lay a large dog. Jamie could see security lights on the walls of the house, which would illuminate the drive and garage area if triggered in the dark. The office was easier. Parking was in a reserved section of a public multi-storey car park. There was some camera surveillance but none directly on the Agence Frank section. It took only a minute for Jamie to fit the transponder that would relay the car's position to a satellite and back down to his phone. He could now follow Bernard's car from a safe distance without fear of giving himself away.

The first two weeks of the operation were fruitless for Jamie as Bernard either stayed in his office or went to meetings with clients, often in the towers of La Defense, the main Paris business quarter. In the evenings, he either went home or out to smart Paris restaurants for dinners with what looked like important clients. It was the pattern of a busy senior businessman. Jamie was getting fed up and downright tired since he had no back up to spell him and Bernard had not flown out of the country on business to give him a break.

The breakthrough came at the end of the second week. It was Saturday at about 6:00 p.m. when the monitor on his computer bleeped into life, indicating that the target was on the move. They picked Bernard up on the *périférique* ring road and Jamie asked the driver to close in briefly to check the occupants of the car. Bernard was alone and after several miles took the turning towards the A6 heading south.

"This is different," said Jamie to his driver.

"He's going out to dinner."

"At 6:00 p.m. on a Saturday, without his wife? I think not," said Jamie, feeling encouraged by the pattern break. They followed at a discreet distance until the navigation system showed him leaving the *Autoroute.*

"He's heading for Fontainbleau," said the driver.

"OK, let's follow."

Before Fontainbleau, however, they turned off the main road and followed Bernard down a narrow D road. After a few miles Bernard turned up a dirt track.

"He's up there somewhere," said the driver, pointing into the rapidly falling darkness when they stopped at the end of the track.

"OK, let's park a little further along this road and then walk up the track for a look." The track led up to what they could just make out to be a small chapel. A lot of cars were parked nearby. The only light came from an opaque glass panel above the heavy oak front door. A scout round the building revealed that all the windows were blanked out from the inside, except for a small high window at the rear of the building. Putting his ear to the door, Jamie could hear chanting.

It was slow and repetitive, almost hypnotic, using the same phrase over and over again. It was unlike any religious chant he had ever heard. He surmised that they had stumbled on a meeting of the Paris Ring and was determined to observe the proceedings. Round the back they risked putting on their flashlight briefly, to plot a route to the high window, up some ivy and across a sloping ledge which projected under the dimly lit aperture. Clambering up the ivy, Jamie then had to hang on grimly with both hands to avoid slipping down the ledge and falling back to the ground.

As he drew level with the window, his eyes opened wide at the sight of Bernard, his white robe open down the front, astride a heavily built, naked female figure with flowers in her hair. She was spread-eagled over the trunk of what looked like an ancient olive bent by some quirk of nature to form a step capable of supporting the female posterior and at the same time permitting access to the honey pot. Her arms were outstretched, holding onto Bernard.

The chanting from the surrounding circle of white robed figures was synchronised to Bernard's rhythm and appeared to be speeding up to a climax. Anxious to photograph the fertility rite, Jamie let go with one hand to reach for the camera in his pocket, but in so doing gave gravity a decisive advantage. His feet slid down the slope and his camera fell to the ground as he scrabbled hopelessly to get a grip on the greasy, algae covered surface. He dug his nails in, slowing his descent, but with another fifteen feet to go he still hit the ground fairly hard, fortunately on soft grass rather than the gravestone which stood three feet away. With Jamie limping from a twisted ankle, they retreated to the parked cars and made a note of all the car numbers and other details.

Returning to the chapel, they hid in the bushes quite near the front door and awaited developments. After a rather cold ten minutes, the external light above the doorway came on suddenly, making them feel uncomfortably close. They retreated a few yards further into the bushes.

The front door opened and about twenty people trooped out, one of them a plump young woman, presumably the goddess. He wished he could be photographing them but that was impossible in the circumstances. As Jamie tried to scan the faces for Bernard, two men split off from the group and walked straight towards them into the bushes. Jamie's heart was pounding as they stopped just a few yards from his invisible hunched form. His relief was palpable when he heard the pattering sound of a urine stream hitting the ground. It was the French pissing alfresco. Perhaps there was no loo in the chapel, reasoned Jamie. The chapel door was still open as the two urinators withdrew to their cars. Jamie relaxed slightly as two more men emerged, locking the door behind them. He recognised Bernard from his performance inside but not the other man. They were talking, but from his vantage point, Jamie could not hear them very clearly.

Jamie and the driver let them get a safe distance in front and followed them around the chapel to see the lights of a house about a hundred yards away along the path.

Turning back, they retraced their steps to the chapel door.

"Can you open this door?" Jamie whispered to the driver, embarrassed that his high-tech training had not included traditional skills like lock picking.

"No problem, but the tools are back in the car."

"OK, you go back to the car and get your tools and I'll have a look at the house. See you back here in five minutes," said Jamie, who proceeded around the end of the chapel along the path towards the house.

There were plenty of lights on in the house but most of the windows were screened and he could make out nothing inside. He worked his way to the front of the property and could just make out the name of the house on the gateposts. Old iron gates hung in place but the weeds growing up around them suggested that they were never closed. The house name was the *Manoir des Trois Amouriers.*

When he got back to the chapel, the driver was already there and had the door open. They stepped inside, closed the door and switched on a flashlight. It was a one room building, the main feature of which was a complex circular design in mosaic on the floor, with the dead olive trunk fixed into the floor in the centre. Jamie noted that the posterior supporting step looked polished from prolonged contact with willing earth goddesses. His first thought was "lucky Bernard" until the reality of such public performance struck him. Around the walls hung white robes, some with red crosses on them, neatly arranged on hooks. Otherwise, the place was bare. There were no statues of saints or devils; it was more like a mini-theatre in the round. As they were withdrawing, Jamie spotted a waste bin just inside the door. It contained an apparently used condom.

"We'll certainly have that," said Jamie, picking it up with tweezers and sliding it into a plastic evidence bag.

"Has someone been a naughty boy then?" asked the driver.

"All in the name of pacifying the gods, but enough to nail him if it's his DNA."

The sight of the condom reminded Jamie of the enforced celibacy that the mission was inflicting on him, working day after day without a break. They then withdrew and closed the door, the driver relocking it, hanging around for another hour until Bernard came out of the *Manoir* and headed off back in the direction of Paris.

****

Monday morning found them back in the area, at the *Mairie* of the local village, trying to find out who owned the *Manoir*. The property records did not clarify ownership. The house was owned by an anonymous trust. However, the lady record keeper was quite helpful and told them that the *Manoir* was occupied by a Monsieur and Madame Leo Stuart. It was the biggest house in the Commune and Madame Stuart complained quite a lot as if she had special rights. In fact, gossiped the record keeper, Madame Stuart, when exasperated by the failure of the *Mairie* to respond to one of her complaints, once stormed out loudly declaring, "This is no way to treat people who are descended from the Kings of England."

This eccentric remark had of course greatly amused the French staff at the *Mairie* and Madame Stuart was now jocularly referred to as *"La Petite Reine d'Angleterre."*

Jamie returned in triumph to Scotland before Christmas and in good time for the annual New Year's Day "Old Firm" football match between his beloved Rangers and Celtic.

Chapter 11

Scotland, January 2038 - Isle of Skye

Not a day passed when Robert did not think of his famous ancestor Bonnie Prince Charlie. He often went to Holyrood Palace to look at the Stuart memorabilia and portraits. He had already followed in the Prince's footsteps on a virtual tour of the West Coast and a visit to Culloden with Leo when he was still at Gordonstoun, but now he wanted to do more, to tap into the energy of that heroic figure. High on his list was the Isle of Skye. Andrew MacDonald had already regaled him with tales of his boyhood there and agreed to take Robert home to Skye for a weekend to soak up the atmosphere and meet some MacDonalds.

Robert was anxious to retrace some of his ancestor's footsteps on the island in the aftermath of Culloden when the Prince went west to look for the French rescue ship. Robert began in the North of the island, on the beach at Kilbride where the Prince landed on the 29th July 1746 having crossed the Minch by boat from Uist where capture was inevitable if he stayed much longer. It was not a heroic arrival since the Prince was disguised as a woman, the maid of the legendary Flora MacDonald. On the road to the capital, the Prince had discarded his female garb and walked into Portree dressed as a Highland gentleman.

As he stood on the beach looking out into the grey murk that hid the Isle of Lewis, Robert could only compare the hope and optimism of the Prince's landing on Eriskay with the desperate struggle to avoid capture that brought him to that beach on Skye. Robert felt the pain of his ancestor's predicament stirring the righteous anger that drove him. And yet, throughout the three months of his stay around the west coast and the Islands, Charles avoided capture largely due to the loyalty of the local population. Nobody turned him in, nobody took the blood money on offer and in spite of all the indignities and privation he had remained a noble figure, a king in their eyes and hearts. This was a great comfort to Robert.

Before going back to Portree, Robert and Andrew visited the grave of Flora MacDonald at Kilmuir just to the north of where she landed with the Prince. Robert was impressed by the 28 foot high granite Iona Cross headstone, a fitting tribute to a very brave woman who survived capture by the Hanoverians to live to a ripe old age, eventually returning from North Carolina to Skye after the American War of Independence broke out. Needless to say, she did not meet her Prince again.

That evening a small dinner was held in Robert's honour by Andrew's family in a MacDonald lodge just outside Portree. Everyone was welcoming and supportive but for the first time, he was aware of deference. These people accepted him as a prince and he grew with that realisation. After dinner, the senior MacDonald made an emotional speech in which he explained the behaviour of the Skye MacDonalds in 1745. Their hearts had been with the Prince but their heads told them that without French support, Charles had no chance of winning a war against the Hanoverians. In addition, the loyalist government had put enormous pressure on the MacDonald families not to join the rebellion. The result was history. In the new situation, short of getting his claymore out from under the bed, he declared that the MacDonald family would support Robert in any practical way to get the crown back for the Stuarts in an independent Scotland. The family then proceeded to a large lounge decorated with antlers and portraits of past MacDonalds, for a short Ceilidh. A piper played a lament to the Bonnie Prince. A pretty young girl sang "Will ye no come back again," which finished with a tremendous cheer from the assembled company and nods of agreement with the sentiment expressed by the song, a sentiment now transferred onto the broad shoulders of a latter day Stuart. The party finished off with the piper playing a lively tune that he had just composed that very morning. It was called "Robert's return to Skye."

"Lochiel would like to meet you," said the senior MacDonald, as Robert was leaving.

"Cameron of Lochiel?"

"The very same. His ancestor did support the Prince."

"Yes, I know and I look forward very much to meeting him," replied Robert.

Chapter 12

France, January 2038 - Paris, La Defense

Jamie returned to Paris immediately after the New Year celebrations buoyed by his team's emphatic victory in the traditional New Year encounter with the old enemy, Celtic. The DNA results from the condom were available. Biological analysis confirmed by unofficial access to the French national database, now underpinned Jamie's direct observation of Bernard in action in the chapel. They had him quite literally by the balls. They decided that they should sweat him and John telephoned to initiate contact. Bernard was at first very reluctant to grant them a face to face interview and John had to bluff about his knowledge of Bernard's personal Swiss bank dealings, while stressing that he was not from the French tax authorities. This proved to be enough to get them into Bernard's office which was high up in Tour Manhattan, with a splendid view out over La Defense, the Paris business quarter, towards the city centre to the east.

"Monsieur Frank, we've reason to believe that you're conspiring with Peter Christie and possibly others to manage an illegal fund that's supporting the Scottish Independence Party," began John, seated beside Jamie on a white leather sofa. Large prints of scantily clad models decorated the walls of the room.

"It's no secret that Peter Christie and his wife have been friends of ours for many years, even before he was famous," replied Bernard warily, from behind his white leather covered desk, furrowing his brows and already regretting having let them visit. A very uncomfortable feeling was beginning to develop in the pit of his stomach. He had thought long and hard about the indiscretions that might have attracted attention to him but the Stuart Agenda wasn't even on the long list.

"Monsieur Frank, foreign support of UK political parties is now illegal, especially when the true identity of the donor is disguised, so we must clearly understand where the money is coming from. We're prepared to believe that you're being used as an innocent front man and are prepared to overlook your contribution," said John, deliberately looking straight at Bernard, his hirsute eyebrows raised in a double question mark.

"Now listen to me. I don't see why I have to answer your questions. I'm a French citizen and you have no jurisdiction here," blustered Bernard, standing up to emphasise his stance, scratching at his wispy beard, and playing for time since he had not been presented with a killer fact.

"We would urge you to cooperate," stressed John, "please, just tell us where the money is coming from."

"I don't know," replied Bernard, wringing his hands.

"Perhaps you would like to read this report on a recent Paris Ring meeting. I watched from the high window at the back of the chapel near the Stuart residence. Your stamina was impressive," said Jamie, handing over a piece of paper that described Bernard's leading role in satisfying the Earth goddess.

"This is a gross invasion of privacy," stammered Bernard, who was writhing in embarrassment at the sexual revelation but even more disturbed by the almost casual mention of the Stuarts. He wondered if they knew everything. "This is blackmail," he protested, beads of sweat forming just below his nose.

"I repeat, we just want your cooperation," said John, lowering his eyebrows this time.

"Very well. The funding is coming from a trust set up by the will of a Scotswoman, Margaret Baird. She was married to a French officer in London during WWII. She just wanted to support the independence movement. Peter Christie is ensuring that the money is well spent," said Bernard in desperation, getting up and going over to the window.

"Interesting, Jamie will check the records right now on his handheld," replied John, who used the ensuing silence to further discomfort Bernard. Bernard had not expected an immediate challenge to his lie and realised that he was on the edge of capitulation.

"I've been through the records," said Jamie, after interrogating his device. "There isn't a Margaret Baird of the right age and no record of a marriage. You're lying to us, Monsieur. Please try again and give us the truth this time," said Jamie, in a more menacing tone.

"You might as well know that we found this in the waste bin," said John, throwing the plastic bag containing the condom onto the table.

"I believe the DNA is yours," added Jamie, as Bernard gently banged his head against the window, wishing that he could open it and fly out, away from his relentless inquisitors. He turned away from the window and walked slowly back to his desk. His shoulders were hunched, his defences destroyed and his confession perched on his lips.

"The funding was set up by Leo Stuart, quite a few years ago. He met someone in Brussels, from the European Union I think," confessed Bernard, who was feeling physically sick at his betrayal of Leo, to save his own skin.

"We need more details. Can you go back through your diaries? Exact dates would be helpful and anything else you can remember."

"So let's get this clear. The Stuarts with support from others, perhaps the European Union, are funding the Scottish Independence Party, presumably with a secret deal to drop the current Windsor monarchy in favour of them if Scotland ever votes for independence. Is that what's going on?" asked Jamie.

"Something like that," replied Bernard, who looked as though he had just lost his biggest advertising account.

"The illegal funding will have to cease immediately. Can you make that happen?" asked John, pulling on one of his unruly eyebrows for emphasis.

"I think so. I can certainly pass the message back to Leo Stuart and I'm sure that under the circumstances he'll cooperate."

"The biggest mystery to us is why they think they have any kind of legitimate claim to the Scottish throne. They seem to have been written out of the history books as far as we can see," said John.

"They claim that Bonnie Prince Charlie married again late in life and had a son from whom they are descended, so it's a direct legitimate line. I understand that the Vatican supports their claim so it cannot be without merit," replied Bernard, who was now feeling a little better and already wondering how he could cover his treachery.

"The Vatican?" repeated Jamie, looking quizzically at John.

"The Stuarts can't have anybody to put up against the Windsors?" said John, casually.

"Actually they do. He's a very impressive young man, who'll make a great King of Scotland. I'm sure he'll destroy the Hanoverians in a fair contest," said Bernard, who in that instant decided to go on the offensive, to put their prodigy in play and move forward to the next stage of the contest.

"I doubt that very much," replied John wearily.

"You're wrong there. His destiny says that he can't lose and in the end, you'll both be ashamed of what you are doing today," replied Bernard, who felt a sudden flow of sap rising from a romantic moral streak buried deep within him under layers of neglect and modernity.

"Why are you so confident about that?" asked Jamie.

"You're a Scot aren't you? I know enough accents to place you. Your children and your grandchildren will curse you for the mistake you're making. Robert Stuart is a gift from the old gods to the Scottish people, a reincarnation of a god king, up there with the Pharaoh, Ramses the Great," said Bernard, shaking with emotion, on the offensive and threatening them and theirs with the wrath of history, turning their success into their undoing.

"So where is this Stuart prodigy?" asked John.

"He's at university, but that's only the half of it," replied Bernard, almost smiling now as he could see the British agents looking at each other, hooked into the mystery of Robert. Bernard was elated. He had deliberately pushed Robert's cause into the public domain, where he was sure it would prosper. At the same time, he reconnected with his deepest spiritual self, something which had been long buried under a slime of false pleasures.

"I'll have a look," said Jamie, picking up his handheld again.

"He's there under his stepfather's name, so he's Robert Lafarge."

"Not the Robert Lafarge who played for Scotland against England?" said Jamie.

"The very same. Were you there? Did you see that try? Now you know what you're up against."

"It was a good try. I've got him, he's at Edinburgh University."

"How did you find out about me?" asked Bernard.

"A Scottish journalist sniffed you out," replied Jamie, lulled by Bernard's confession.

"You will make sure the funding stops," said John, his final words to Bernard.

As they left, Bernard collapsed back into his chair behind the white desk, torn between guilt at his betrayal of Leo but certain that the time had come to go on the offensive and use the unique qualities of Robert to begin to build his personal claim to the Scottish throne.

****

"What a load of bollocks," said John, as they descended in the lift from Bernard's office.

"I'm not so sure."

"Snap out of it Jamie, one mystical Scot's enough. We need to find out if Christie's working alone, or is it a wider conspiracy?"

"I'll get my journalist friend to find out."

Chapter 13

Scotland, January 2038 - Edinburgh

That evening, Angela received a call from Piers who happened to be in Edinburgh. She was impatient with him when he asked for an urgent meeting without being prepared to reveal the subject matter. She was in a suite at the Balmoral Hotel working with Peter Christie and an aide, on her still private agenda for the Scottish Independence Party. Nevertheless, she agreed to take some time out and meet Piers in a downstairs bar on the hotel ground floor. They were well acquainted, going all the way back to her early days at university when Piers introduced her to the Party, so she did owe him something. He was one of a small coterie of friendly journalists that she trusted as far as journalists could be trusted.

She turned up decently late and found Piers deep in thought, nursing a whisky in a quiet corner of the bar. She was wearing a light-blue soft leather trouser suit that oozed femininity and power. There weren't many people around in the gap between the after work quick drink brigade and the crowd having aperitifs before dinner.

"OK Piers, why the panic?" she asked, stalking up behind him and sliding into a deep shiny leather chair before Piers could get up to shake her hand or peck her cheek. She added to the sense of impatience by waving away the waiter who came to take her drink order. She was conscious that she was making Piers uncomfortable, doubly so because of his obvious infatuation for her.

"Angela," he stammered, "I've discovered a possible financial irregularity. We need to talk."

"Financial irregularity? If someone's been fiddling their expenses, I'm not interested," she replied, putting out her hands and shaking her head.

"No, it's nothing as simple as that."

"What then?" she snapped.

"You know the donations that your president, Peter Christie, makes to the Party?"

"Yes," she said, stretching out the word, preparing for disbelief, no matter what was said.

"Well, I've found out that he's not the real donor. It's not his money. It's coming from someone else."

"Not Peter Christie's money?" She drew herself in to calm a cramping stomach, throwing him a thunderous look that was normally accompanied by flaring nostrils.

"I'm sorry, Angela."

"So what the fuck is going on? Who told you this?" she railed, looking at him as though he was a freshly passed, evil-smelling dog turd. She was momentarily confused, not quite able to process a fact that drove a stake into her sublimated lover. At the same time, her political brain registered alarm.

"Steady on, Angela, don't shoot the messenger. It's not my fault," he said. "I take it from your reaction that you didn't know about this?"

"No way," she hissed, shaking her head from side to side as her thoughts turned to Peter, sweet innocent Peter. What was he playing at? Some great game of his own? She found it inconceivable that he could be operating behind the Party's back.

"What about the others? The Party Leader, Jim Robertson, might he be involved?"

"I'd be very surprised. That lump of elephant shit couldn't keep a secret for a day, let alone conduct a conspiracy," she spat, recalling the image of her all-time, least favourite person.

"OK, so if you and Robertson don't know, Christie must be working alone,"

"I suppose so," she replied. "So where is the money coming from?" she asked, a little calmer, as she began to think about the political implications.

"We know that it's coming from France. There was a cover story about the will of a Scotswoman, Margaret Baird, leaving money to the Independence Party. Margaret Baird doesn't exist, however, I've established that much."

"Who else could it be?" she asked, as a vivid scene from one of Peter's films entered her head. He was strapped to a table and powerful laser beam was about to render him a eunuch.

"I don't know. I'm still working on it, though."

"I can't believe that Peter Christie's deceiving us. I would have trusted him with my life," said Angela, with an air of exhausted finality, followed by the beginning of a wry smile. There was clearly a lot more to Peter than he had shown her on the surface.

"Can I get you a drink now perhaps?"

"Yes, why not? I'll need one before going back upstairs," she replied.

As she relaxed with her glass of wine, she began to think about how to flush Peter out. Should she go in with all guns blazing or take a more subtle approach? Could she somehow use this to get closer to him? Suddenly, she was aware of Piers looking at her quizzically and realised that he would have to be kept onside.

"Piers, I'm very grateful to you for telling me this. I can see that your heart is still with us but I'm sure you're aware that this information could destroy us," she said.

"I'm certainly not in the business of destroying you, Angela, and there's no rush to publish at the moment," he replied.

"Thanks, Piers," she replied, taking his hand and smiling sweetly at the man she was confident she could control.

"Angela, please be careful, the security services know about it, they're very interested in foreign funding of political parties," he said, almost touching her with his sincerity.

****

Angela returned upstairs to the suite to find Peter still at the dining table surrounded by working papers, some of which had been arranged in small heaps on the beautiful tartan carpet that adorned the floor. The view from the suite spilled over the railway tracks leaving Waverly Station, rising to the grandeur of Edinburgh Castle in the middle distance. The walls were covered with prints illustrating the buildings of the New Town. While she was physically calm, the look she gave Peter betrayed her concern at his duplicity before she launched into the substance of the charge against him, debunking the Margaret Baird story. It was clear to her, however, from Peter's response, that he had been duped by Bernard Frank; he hadn't looked the gift horse in the mouth.

"You let everyone believe the big money was coming from you," she said, thumping her fist on the table, causing a precariously perched file to crash to the floor.

"You became Party President on a lie and you've probably committed a crime," she continued, pointing her finger accusingly across the table at him.

"I suppose I should make a clean breast of it and tell you about

68

the Stuart family."

"The Stuart family? Who the hell are they?" asked Angela, with a pained expression, racking her brains for Stuart acquaintances.

"The Stuarts, you know, Bonnie Prince Charlie's lot," he replied, taking a large draught of the wine that he had poured for himself.

"I thought they had all died out," said Angela, struggling to remember the detail of the Stuarts losing out to the Hanoverians. Most of all, the Stuart tangent was rushing her into unexpected and uncomfortable territory, rather like a previously unknown alcoholic uncle turning up at your front door.

"Not at all, they're real and very committed to helping the Independence Party. It's a lot of money."

"Have you met them?" she asked, now wondering where the story was leading.

"Several times."

"And the rest, by the sound of it. So it must be the Stuarts who are funding us. What do they hope to get out of it?"

"Angela, like us, they hope and pray for an independent Scotland. Their money's helping to achieve that. I can see it happening," he said, looking away from her out of the window towards the castle.

"The money will have to be stopped. This will come out sooner or later. The conflict of interest is too obvious. You've been pretending all along that you were giving the money, so perhaps you could start picking up the tab now. Put your money where your mouth has been for a long time," she said, reaching over and clutching his wrist.

"I've been thinking about that. I suppose I knew that it must come out sooner or later and I do accept a moral responsibility to take it on from here. I'll pass the message back when I get hold of that liar, Bernard."

"Thank God for that," replied Angela, giving up her hold on him, relieved that the immediate problem had been solved.

"You know, the Stuarts also hope that an independent Scotland might want to be a monarchy and have the old Scottish Stuart line as kings, instead of the hopeless lot that we have in London at the moment."

"A monarchy! Shit Peter, I always thought that we would be a republic, a plague on all royal houses, and all that," she said, with less than her customary venom for monarchy. Adding monarchy to illicit funding momentarily numbed her as she struggled to find levers to control the panic mounting inside her.

"That's what I thought at first as well, but then I wondered," replied Peter. "I've got Dan Miller, the American pollster, working secretly on it. How would the Scots actually respond to a Stuart monarchy if they were offered one? Dan will tell us if anyone can."

"Peter, what the fuck are you getting us into?" she exploded, as the realisation dawned of just how far Peter had gone behind her back and the tsunami of a potential Scottish monarchy washed over her.

"I haven't promised anything. We can't, can we? We may be able to turn it to our electoral advantage; a charismatic young Stuart king, a restoration."

"What do you mean, a young king, a restoration? Have you taken leave of your senses, Peter? Are you telling me that—?"

"Angela, there's someone I'd like you to meet," he said, cutting her off.

Chapter 14

France, January 2038 - Fontainbleau

Following his promise to John from MI6, Bernard had to approach Leo about the need to stop the funding. Despite his stout mystical defence of the Stuart's historic rights and his earlier confidence that the time was right to put Robert in play, his guilty confession had plunged him into unexplored territory of self-doubt. The message from Peter Christie was one of anger that he had been duped with the Margaret Baird cover story and Bernard had to make a grovelling apology for that falsehood. The news that Peter would now personally pick up the responsibility for continuing donations to the Independence Party was Bernard's wakeup call from the nightmare of his guilt. He decided to respond very quickly and made an impromptu visit to Leo the same evening.

"I've had a call from Peter Christie. It's bad news I'm afraid," said Bernard, with total confidence, as he settled into a comfortable armchair in Leo's snug at the *Manoir,* glass of wine in hand. He found Leo relaxed, wearing slippers and reading a copy of The London Times.

"Has a film flopped?" asked Leo, smiling to himself.

"It's more serious than that. A Scottish journalist has somehow found out that Peter isn't the originator of the funds coming into the Scottish Independence Party. The journalist has also worked out that Margaret Baird never existed and all that has now been put to Peter. Unfortunately, I never got around to telling Peter after he found out about Robert. Peter jumped to the conclusion that the Stuarts were doing the funding."

"But we're not; I don't have that kind of money," declared Leo, sitting up straight and widening his eyes.

"I didn't tell him that, I thought it best to let him continue to think that you are the source. Anyway, since I don't know exactly where the money is coming from I couldn't tell him anything else, could I?" said Bernard.

"I suppose not," replied Leo, who did not amplify.

"So Peter's position is that the potential conflict of interest for the Scottish Independence Party is unacceptable so he's asking that payments cease," said Bernard, looking deeply into his glass.

"Are we finished? Is the journalist going to publicise all this?"

"No, not immediately, anyway. Peter seems to have some sort of hold over the journalist."

"So we're still in business. It's just a question of where the money comes from is it?"

"There's good news on that. In the circumstances, Peter's willing to pick up the tab, so everything will become as it seems, the lie disappears, it's very neat," replied Bernard, in a sanctimonious tone.

"That's very honourable of him, even though he's very rich. I'll get in touch with him to express my appreciation. Meanwhile, I'll get in touch with my Brussels contact and ask them to stop payments."

"And Leo, Peter seems to think that MI5 in Britain may be involved and that they know about the Stuart connection, about our plan for Robert."

"If MI5's involved, we're in new territory, Bernard. We have no idea how the Hanoverians will react and Robert might even be in danger, especially when he's already fallen out with Prince Henry. We'll need to get proper security for Robert right away. And it's also time to be getting Sir Duncan Flockhart on board as well. Robert needs a senior advisor on the spot. I'll deal with that," said Leo.

Driving home, the sense of relief for Bernard was palpable, like being told that a cancer had been completely cured. His guilt at being trapped into informing on Leo had been bearing heavily on him but he had found a way of satisfying his MI6 tormentors without having to confess to Leo. He would be eternally grateful to that Scottish journalist who had provided him with a story that enabled him to cover his guilt. It could now remain hidden and deeply buried in his consciousness to wither quickly and die.

Chapter 15

England, February 2038 - London, Cabinet Office

Jamie was beginning to regret ever going to Paris. To the intense annoyance of his boss in Glasgow, London was going berserk over Jamie's report. John had forwarded it to a very secret section dedicated not to the physical protection of the royal bodies, but to the protection of the institution of the British Monarchy itself, in some ways a much more serious responsibility. The section was headed by Michael Underwood, a career spook from the hard Special Forces end of the business. He was a Jekyll and Hyde character who could ooze diplomatic charm when required, always shaking hands with a velvet-covered steel fist. He had a sceptical face which accurately reflected his view of the world.

The section's most famous event had been the death of Diana Princess of Wales almost forty years before. Diana's final behaviour had terrified the Monarchy and its advisers, and the whole affair had seriously weakened the institution. In the grim humour of the service, the section had been referred to as the DKs by the wags, because of the juicy conspiracy theories linking Diana's death to the British Secret Service.

Because of the implications for the monarchy, the King's private secretary, Sir Humphrey Grey, had been called in for an urgent meeting. This was a very unwelcome development as far as Underwood was concerned. He did not like being under the scrutiny of ordinary civil servants, especially haughty Mandarins, added to which he had been obliged to retreat from his high-tech palace on the Thames to appear in the dark gloomy warren that was the Cabinet Office behind Downing Street. The walls were half-covered in dark oak panelling above which hung oil paintings depicting fading triumphal scenes from the old British Empire. It was all so nineteenth century.

"It's been going on for years," bellowed Underwood, "a direct threat to the British Monarchy, and our Scottish friends didn't spot it," he added, delighted to have a stick with which to beat Tartan Park, a convenient whipping boy for all other unnecessary regional offices of the service. "And now they have Bonnie Prince fucking Charlie Mark II waiting in Edinburgh. It beggars belief," he thundered, thumping his desk menacingly with his fat fists, causing his jowls to wobble uncontrollably.

"Yes, yes, Underwood, but we are where we are," said Sir Humphrey, ever the pragmatist. "Well, first I should tell you that I had a message earlier this year from a private contact reporting the presence of someone, presumably this Robert Stuart, at a dinner in Skye. He apparently told them that he was the Stuart heir but nothing about a conspiracy to retake the Scottish throne. We didn't think it was worth reporting," added Sir Humphrey, a tall distinguished-looking silver-haired man with a pronounced Roman nose and a very old-fashioned plummy voice.

"Every little helps, sir."

"Let's get back to first principles. Legitimacy dear boy, legitimacy. Who are these Stuarts? They're certainly not the ones on the Official Pretender Stuart family tree."

"I understand that they claim to be legitimate descendants of Bonnie Prince Charlie, sir. They further claim that the Vatican has the papers to prove it," replied Underwood, who was dismayed at having to deal with the issue through the cautious Mandarin. He hankered after the days of his youth in the service when such threats could be eliminated by making a simple phone call.

"The Vatican and the Stuarts? Has that fiendish partnership been revived after three hundred years of slumber? Can we get someone into the Vatican to check the documentation?" asked Sir Humphrey.

"Yes, we have a Rome professor on the books. I'll get him to do that," replied Underwood, who had pleasant memories of being on station in Rome.

"Shouldn't we also be combing their cupboards for skeletons, Underwood?"

"I've been thinking about that. The immediate family looks squeaky clean. The only bad egg looks like the grandmother who lives in Marbella. She might be prepared to talk. She'll have an axe to grind. I've got just the man to interview her," replied Underwood, who wagged his finger in support of his suggestion.

"So what do we know about the source of the illegal funding?

"It's not very clear yet, but the Paris boys are working on it," replied Underwood.

"But can you confirm that the illegal funding has stopped?"

"We have an undertaking on that but the problem won't be solved. We think that Christie will simply pick up the bill that everyone believes he was paying anyway," replied Underwood, in a resigned tone. He felt that he was swimming in treacle, like a dog with a collar round his neck, attached to a lead held by his Mandarin masters.

"Can't we just leak all this stuff out? Christie would have to resign and presumably take his money with him. It would be very disruptive," suggested Sir Humphrey.

"That's an option for later if they turn out to be a real threat but at the moment, the Home Office is urging caution. Anything heavy handed will play right into the hands of the Scottish Independents. They're doing disturbingly well in the polls. What's the Palace thinking on all this?"

"The King's playing it cool. He just can't see what all the fuss is about. How could they possibly succeed? Unfortunately, His Majesty took Prince Henry into his confidence. The Prince's reaction was different. Apparently he knew Stuart at Gordonstoun and there was bad blood between them."

"So what are you going to do about it, Underwood?"

"I'm setting up surveillance to find out what they're up to. Maybe we've only seen the tip of the Stuart iceberg," replied Underwood, into whose mind appeared a Hanoverian Titanic steaming at full speed into northern waters, risking a metaphor that the Mandarin would have considered tasteless in the extreme, if not treasonable.

Chapter 16

Scotland, February 2038 - Edinburgh

It was Saturday night and the Edinburgh Tigers' bar was packed with people. It was a home win so most of the players were around and the mood was upbeat. A gender separation saw the girls together in a corner, while the boys stood up at the bar re-living the game, kick by kick. The team captain had already spread the word that he was having a party later at his flat. After the requisite number of pints, he signalled time and the exodus began. He went over personally to alert the lovelies that it was time to go. As usual, there were a few extra girls whom he vaguely recognised, so they were invited as well.

In Jim's flat, however, the gender apartheid was quickly reversed as most paired off with their girlfriends, wives, or dates. There were only a few unattached males and females present. Robert's eye fell on an unclaimed blonde who happened to be looking his way with a receptive expression. He responded to her call and within a few steps her features began to make sense. He recognised her as the new fitness trainer at the Tigers' Club.

"It's Tina from the club isn't it? I hardly recognised you," he said, completely bowled over by the vision before him. The rather dull female in the baggy tracksuit had morphed into a gorgeous blonde with a radiant smile. She was wearing a spectacular dress made from gold metallic-looking material, a little over the top for the Tigers' bar he thought. He remembered discussing her with Andrew after first seeing her in her new role in the training centre. They'd failed to look beyond the surface and erroneously dubbed her frumpy and butch, which, they laughed, sounded rather like a lesbian double act.

"I've got to keep a low profile at the club. You know, the rules discourage fraternisation with the members, so I dress down and play down, it keeps things simple," she replied.

"So what about tonight, have you got a free pass out? Time off for good behaviour?" he asked, intrigued by the transformation from dowdy to exotic.

"Well, a girl has to live a bit Robert, take the odd risk for a good cause," she replied, pronouncing his name the French way, stretching out the second "r" in his name and dropping the "t" at the end. He found that comfortingly familiar and sexy.

"So, how come you speak such good French?" he asked.

"That was only one word," she replied evasively.

"But you said it so well, just like…someone I know," he said, thinking of his mother.

"A French girlfriend perhaps?

"You know something, I've never had a French girlfriend," he admitted candidly.

As they danced and made small talk, Robert felt the walls of his self-imposed almost celibacy shake and begin to crumble. He had been warned by both Peter directly and Leo obliquely to be very careful with women and the baggage that might ensue. He had to be seen as squeaky clean when he finally emerged from the Stuart's long sleep.

****

The taxi took them in towards town and down the Royal Mile to Tina's apartment block not far from the Parliament. The intimacy of the party had dissipated on the journey and he felt a little nervous going up the stairs, not quite knowing what to expect. Under the apartment lights he got a good look at her for the first time. She had an intelligent face, despite the heavy makeup, with full lips all framed by long blonde highlighted hair. She was beautiful without any trace of bimbo but above all she had a feline physical presence, which excited him. Although he couldn't be sure, he suspected that she was older than him, perhaps in her mid to late twenties. The apartment was tastefully furnished in post minimalist style with bang up to date infrared controlled personal space heating. It all seemed a bit grand to Robert for an entry-grade fitness trainer.

She made him a strong coffee from a micro-machine and they sat down opposite each other in leather armchairs joined at floor level by a silk oriental carpet.

"So, I can't imagine that fitness training and picking up young rugby players is your whole life?"

"You're very perceptive, Robert, I'm only a part-time fitness trainer. I'm really trying to be a writer and I'm one of those very fortunate people who doesn't have to work for a living."

"A trust fund writer?"

"Something like that. Historical romances but nothing published yet."

"How did you get into fitness training?"

"Through keeping very fit myself. I'm a gym addict so it wasn't a big step."

"You play squash?"

"I'll give you a game anytime. But Robert, I want to hear about you. You're the enigmatic hero. You seem to have come out of thin air to set the rugby world on fire. I've seen that try in slow motion from several angles. I'll never forget the look on your face. For an instant, it was the face of a killer. You seemed very angry, not elated, and did you pray after you touched down?"

"Are you a fitness trainer or a psychoanalyst?" he asked, startled by the acuteness of her observation, putting him on his guard. He was not going to reveal the Jacobite vision that had driven him to make the score.

"I'm at Edinburgh via Gordonstoun. My family are in business in Paris and wanted me to have a more international education, although that's taking second place to rugby."

"Prince Henry was there, wasn't he?"

"Yes, I played rugby with him; he was pretty useless. Good at Maths though and school chess captain. Our first egghead king in the making," said Robert trying to put the best possible spin on his view of the Prince.

Robert then gave her a potted history of his earlier life in France without mentioning the Stuarts. When she turned the conversation towards Scottish independence, Robert announced that he had an early training session the following morning and would have to leave. He could see the look of disappointment on her face.

"You're welcome to stay."

"No, I must go and anyway, I don't have my tin opener with me," he replied, still dazzled by the metallic dress.

Chapter 17

Scotland, March 2038 - Glasgow

Jamie was astonished when John from MI6 in Paris appeared unannounced at his office in Glasgow. He was writing the report on his visit to old Mrs. Stuart in Marbella. It felt like a dawn raid, a spot inspection to catch them off guard. Jamie collected him from security and welcomed him warmly nevertheless. He liked John, who had treated him well and taught him a lot. Jamie had an extra swagger to him in the glow of his successful operation in Paris, despite the fuss made by Underwood, and Rangers had won their game on Saturday. He also had the surveillance up and running in Edinburgh, although nothing of value had materialised yet. Jamie thought that John seemed very tense indeed and clearly had a problem.

"You seem to be comfortably housed," said John, looking at the state of the art offices and equipment as they walked through the building. "As you saw in Paris, we're in a veritable rabbit warren compared with this."

"Yes, we can't complain," said Jamie, leading him to a free conference room. "Well John, this is an unexpected pleasure, a bit like a visit from my mother-in-law," he added, as they sat down in a room with views to the north, over the Clyde towards the mountains. Jamie was wearing his pinstripe suit while John sported a tired looking tweed jacket and casual trousers.

"As good as that," snapped John. "I'm finding that there's more to this case than meets the eye and I've never been to Glasgow."

"Well, that's a good enough reason on its own. It's a pity Rangers aren't playing tonight; I could have given you a real experience. Anyway, what about the case, is there anything wrong with my conclusion?" asked Jamie, a little defensively.

"There's been a new development. Mark's been working hard on Leo's reported meeting in Brussels at the European Union. We got all the archive CCTV footage from the Brussels buildings and eventually found Leo Stuart and the contact we think he made," said John.

"So, do you know who the contact is?" asked Jamie, who now wished that he had followed it up himself.

"Yes, it was one Albert Delavarenne, a retired French Secret

Service officer, at least the French insist that he's retired and that the conspiracy has nothing to do with them," replied John.

"Can we safely believe that?" asked Jamie, who instinctively distrusted the French.

"I think so. I'm inclined to believe them. They would have blamed it on rogue elements if we'd really caught them with their trousers down," replied John.

"So our Albert has a little part-time retirement job to eke out his pension, freelancing for someone else," said Jamie, thinking bizarrely of the old guys who help out at supermarket checkouts.

"Yes, Jamie, we really need to know who his employer is."

"I don't suppose that they gave you a forwarding address for Albert?" asked Jamie, noting that John's eyebrows lacked the animation of the interview with Bernard.

"I tried that without success. They probably do know where he is but still owe him that protection. I've looked for him in the French domestic data bases but can't find him. He's disappeared without trace."

"Could we search for him through Interpol?"

"Too obvious and we would needlessly upset the French. Listen to this though, I've managed to establish that Albert flew into Brussels on a flight from London and went out the same evening on a flight to Rome after his first meeting with Leo. Mark's also found out that Leo Stuart serves on an important Vatican committee,"

"Have we been looking in the wrong place, I wonder?" asked Jamie, scratching his chin.

"And didn't Bernard tell us that the Vatican supported the Stuart's claim to the throne of Scotland?"

"The Vatican, does that make sense?" asked Jamie, for whom the mention of that place in Rome raised all the negative stereotypes of Catholicism ladled into his Protestant psyche since childhood.

"Historically yes, they were strong supporters of the Stuarts, but I can't imagine them meddling like this in the middle of the twenty-first century."

"Do we really need to know? Surely the key thing is to get the funding stopped," added Jamie, as he followed the track of a jet as it approached along the river before descending into Glasgow airport.

"Well, you know that Bernard is supposed to be making that

happen."

"Anyway, I have something of a breakthrough to report as well. You know that Underwood asked me to go and interview the Stuart granny in Marbella. She's a bitter old alcoholic, with a nasty tongue in her head, but what she told me was dynamite. She claims that Robert's father, Alexander, was the son of her lover, not her husband, which means that Robert isn't a true Stuart at all, and therefore has no claim whatsoever to the throne."

"That is good news for us. We could use that to force them to withdraw. Well done, Jamie. Underwood will be pleased," replied John, his eyebrows perking up at the news.

"Yes, but first we have to be absolutely sure about the facts. We need to gather DNA from the main characters in the cast to check out who really is related to whom," cautioned Jamie. I presume you can use your contacts to get it from the French national database."

"Would it be possible to get hold of a sample of Bonnie Prince Charlie's DNA? That would be the ultimate test of Robert's claim."

"That's a brilliant idea, John. There's certainly a sample of his hair on display in the museum at Holyrood Palace. The provenance might not be one hundred per cent but it'll give us something to attack with. I'll deal with that."

"On a more cheerful note, how's the surveillance going?"

"The plods have found the Stuart boy for me in a very posh apartment in Edinburgh. I've just set up the team to do the business there," replied Jamie.

"Anyone interesting?" asked John.

"Underwood found me an experienced officer who's just come back from Ireland, as well as a technician," replied Jamie.

"I can't believe that we still have to bother with the Irish after all this time. It just keeps erupting every few years, although I suppose it's as much organised crime as terrorism," said John.

"Well, weaponry *put beyond use* was always a convenient euphemism. We know that they've been doing a bit of modernising, buying in new stuff on the *just in case* principle," replied Jamie, who had been heavily briefed on the situation in Ireland but in the end not required to go.

"Anyway, be careful with Underwood, don't forget that he's in business to eliminate threats to the Crown," said John.

"Eliminate?" queried Jamie, uncomfortable at the use of such an extreme term.

"Oh, not in the physical sense, of course," clarified John. "Let's just say, neutralise."

"Can't the Windsors look after themselves? They've got a vast PR machine at their disposal," replied Jamie, overcome with uncertainty. Despite his academic credentials and being an agnostic Protestant, he had not dismissed Bernard's lyrical presentation of Robert as a reincarnated god king. Or was he simply subliminally favouring a Scottish David against an English Goliath, a metaphor that had supported several famous victories for Scotland over the Auld Enemy. And what about his own position? If Scotland did go independent where would he end up? He would most probably be in the Scottish version of MI5. But if the Stuarts prevailed, his current activity would brand him a traitor. It was the beginning of a gnawing uncertainty. It began to eat into the bones of Jamie's hitherto unquestioning commitment to the Union that had its deepest expression in the Hanoverian Monarchy.

Chapter 18

Scotland, March 2038 - Edinburgh

Robert left the David Hume Tower after his Politics lecture and went around the back to the car park to find his BMW. As he turned the corner of the building, three hooded men pounced on him. He managed to lash out with his fist at one of them and saw a flash of blood, the red droplets that spouted from his assailant's nose slowing down and freezing in the last frame that he saw before he was struck on the head.

He wakened to complete darkness, in agony from a splitting headache, and feeling sick from a combination of the irregular motion and the atmosphere of car exhaust fumes. He struggled to move but quickly realised that he was bound hand and foot.

With all the strength he could muster, he tested his bonds but to no avail and tried to calm himself until the situation clarified. Desperate thoughts prevailed. He imagined that he was about to be shot and his body dumped in a ditch. Or perhaps he would be put on a boat and taken out to sea and slipped over the side, or more simply driven onto the Forth Road Bridge and thrown over into the concealing waters of the estuary below. Every option involved Hanoverian agents committed to eliminate his challenge.

He slipped in and out of consciousness and after what seemed an eternity there was silence, at least no throbbing exhaust just below his head. The engine had been switched off. He heard the car doors opening and then the lid on his dark world lifted briefly only to be quickly reinstated as a hood was thrust over his head and he was lifted bodily out of the vehicle boot and dragged painfully into what he assumed was a building from the feel of wooden floors beneath his feet. Another door creaked open in the blackness before him and his head struck a wall as he was thrown bodily into another small prison. He heard a key turn in the lock behind him as he lay on the floor listening to the excited cries of his tormentors and the click and fizz of beer cans being opened.

Next time he awoke he was dimly aware of a slight difference in light level, it was almost certainly morning. He was starving and also had a raging thirst. The key rattled in the lock of his prison door and he was lifted roughly to his feet, which were then unbound. He was dragged out and along what seemed to be a stone floored corridor into a cooler freshness. The faint rustling of leaves in the gentle breeze told him that he was outside, beneath his feet a softer carpet of grass. There was no birdsong; that would have been a mockery. He heard his tormentors laughing and wondered what degradation lay in store for him.

"Run, you Stuart bastard, run," he heard a familiar voice shout.

"We're coming to get you," said another, at which point, he was hit with enormous force just above the knee and bowled over, with someone on top of him. He had been rugby tackled, bringing back the memory of the day when he had brought down Prince Henry on the field at Gordonstoun, and the acrimony that followed. Clearly this was some kind of payback.

"You didn't score there did you?" taunted the voice, now menacingly clear to Robert as he was hauled to his feet. The voice belonged to Simkins who had planned to beat him up at Gordonstoun.

"Try again, the line's there, just there, ten yards away," taunted Simkins. Robert tensed, expecting another tackle but this time he grunted in pain as an elbow smashed into his cheek, pole-axing him to the ground, the wet morning grass penetrated his hood as his left eye closed, driven by the swelling creeping up his tortured face.

"A bit high, that tackle," said Simkins in a mock caution.

"Next exercise," shouted Simkins, as Robert's hood was removed and he was dragged to his feet, the sudden brightness blinding him. His arm bindings were adjusted to free his left arm and a rapier thrust in his unfeeling maw. Robert's first sight of Simkins was not promising. He felt the evil in the fixed stare from his heavy distant eyes. A second acolyte of Prince Henry stood by.

"I seem to remember that you fancy yourself as a swordsman, Stuart," taunted Simkins.

"Only with my right arm," protested Robert grimly, as he tottered on senseless legs around the tiny lawn at the back of the stone building.

"I don't want to hear any lame excuses," replied Simkins, who approached Robert with a series of sword thrusts that caused minor flesh wounds to his forearms before he backed off.

"Come on, Stuart, I'm expecting a fair fight here," said Simkins laughing, as Robert lunged back only to be kicked to the ground. Simkins moved in above him and plunged his rapier into the ground near enough to Robert's ear to provoke a feeling of terror. Looking up, over Simkins' shoulder, Robert briefly glimpsed the figure of Prince Henry, watching the proceedings from an upstairs window.

"Right Jacobite, it's time for the trial," announced Simkins, as they pulled Robert upright and marched him towards the building, an old barn. Robert searched desperately around but could not see a way out.

They dragged him upstairs to the hay store where bales had been used to furnish a make-believe courtroom. The walls were playing a vast computer battle game which was paused while the participants dealt with their prisoner. Robert, both arms bound behind him again, was placed on a bale of hay in front of a judge's bench consisting of four bales stacked two high. Prince Henry was sitting behind the bench gravely, one acolyte standing on either side. The proceedings were illuminated by a large window behind the judge's bench.

"Robert Stuart, you are charged with treason against His Majesty the King's person in plotting to steal the throne of Scotland. How do you plead?" asked Simkins.

"I'm not playing this game, Henry. You must have some kind of mental problem and a fanatic like Simkins isn't helping. Stop this before it's too late," pleaded Robert, looking at each of the acolytes in turn.

"You're trying to undermine the authority of the court, so that's the end of it. Let's proceed to sentence," said Simkins, looking to Henry and his acolytes for confirmation.

"Aye, sir," they chorused, as Prince Henry put the small black cap onto his head.

"Robert Stuart, you are hereby sentenced to death by beheading. May God have mercy on your soul," he said, as the acolytes pulled back the four bales of the judge's bench to reveal a large rough wooden block with an axe leaning against it, not a wide sharp butchering axe but a crude, blunt woodcutting instrument.

"This is crazy, you've got to stop, it's murder," yelled Robert, as the acolytes manhandled him towards the block, forcing him into the prone position with his neck exposed, ready for the blow. Robert tried to summon the spirit of Bonnie Prince Charlie to help him but it was all going too fast.

"Does the condemned man have a last wish?" taunted Simkins.

"That you'll all rot in hell," shouted Robert, as Simkins lifted the axe and gave it a few practice swings to the side.

"You're supposed to be nice to me so that I'll finish it with one blow. Imagine the pain of your head being cleaved off with a blunt axe," said Simkins, swinging the axe high above Robert's head. As the axe came down, Robert thought of his mother, then Leo, his life's work wasted and closed his eyes tight, waiting for the blow.

"That's enough Simkins," he heard Prince Henry shout as he felt the wind of the axe passing his head and the loud jarring thud as it embedded itself in the wooden floor. Robert realised that Henry had intervened and pushed Simkins sufficiently to upset his aim. Simkins turned angrily towards the Prince and the acolytes moved to prevent an altercation between them, releasing the pressure on Robert's arms. The reprieve stirred Robert to action as his enemies were distracted.

Robert looked up and saw the sunlight beckon through the window in front of him. With his shoulders now only lightly held Robert twisted free and thrust himself up, head butting Simkins under the chin, causing him to scream as he bit through his tongue. Robert lowered his head and charged forward towards the light, almost knocking himself out as his shoulder shattered the wooden window structure that held the small panes in place. He exploded into the sunlight in a shower of glass and hit the soft coolness of the lawn outside rolling over several times, sustaining a myriad of small cuts. He ended up on his back among the shards and picked a large one up between his bound hands as he rose to his feet to flee.

He headed as quickly as he could for the cover of the trees fifty yards in front of him, relieved that none of his assailants had the courage to leap after him from the upstairs window, onto the carpet of glass. After he had run a hundred yards along the uphill track, he stopped, backed himself against a tree and sawed awkwardly through his wrist bindings using the shard that he had picked up. He then heard the sound of a Land Rover coming around the end of the barn building, heading in his direction. He decided to leave the track, darting into the trees on his right. After running painfully for about ten minutes his sense of direction deserted him and he realised that he was completely lost. Just then, he scented wood smoke and began to move against the wind along the slope in the direction of the smoke, finally coming to a cottage on the edge of grassland beyond the wood.

As Robert surveyed the scene, a man carrying a rifle came out of the cottage, glanced around, jumped into a truck and roared away. A second vehicle, a small van, was also parked there. Robert approached it hoping that the keys would be in the ignition.

"Looking for something?" said a woman's voice from behind. Robert let go of the door handle and swung round from the van to see a pleasant looking brunette in her mid-forties, pointing a shotgun at his chest.

"I need help," he replied, with a pleading look, praying that the face was as kind as it seemed.

"Are you the killer my husband's just been called out to look for?"

"It's just the opposite, they tried to kill me; I've just managed to escape from Prince Henry and his friends."

"Did they do that to you?" she asked, pointing at his face with the end of her shotgun.

"Yes, they were torturing me but I managed to escape," replied Robert, who sensed that he may have found an ally.

"He's a bit odd, young Henry, but that Simkins is completely unhinged. He's no good for the Prince. He tortured a dog once," added the matron, pursing her lips and shaking her head to reinforce the seriousness of that particular crime in game keeping circles.

"They're out looking for me now. If he catches me again, he'll kill me. Can you help me to get away?"

"You look familiar. Do I know you?" she asked, ignoring his plea.

"Rugby, you've probably seen me on TV."

"Yes, you're Robert….. I remember my husband going mental when you scored that try against England in the Calcutta Cup. I can't see you being a killer. Come in and I'll clean you up a bit. You can't go into the village looking like that, can you?" she said, lowering the shotgun and pushing him in front of her into the cottage.

"This is very kind of you," he said, looking back to make sure they were unobserved.

"Oh, your poor face," she said, as she washed the blood from his swollen face, then his forearms, applying sticking plaster liberally.

"Right, into the back of the van with you and I'll take you to the village," she said, bustling him back outside.

"The village? Where are we?"

"You're on the Balmoral Estate."

"What's your name?" asked Robert, thinking about how he would eventually thank her properly for her kindness.

"It's Margaret MacKenzie, I'm the head gamekeeper's wife."

****

Back at the barn on the Balmoral Estate, Henry was relieved that Robert had escaped and impressed at how he did it. Despite the threat to lose part of his future kingdom, he did not wish Robert or anyone else any harm. He'd been assured by his mother that the Stuarts couldn't possibly win, although there was a risk that his family would lose out to a republic. He was being told by his father that being the king of anywhere was very difficult these days. He'd be better off with a proper job.

Henry agreed. He didn't have a lot of time for meeting people and shaking hands. He really wanted to be a computer game designer, but that didn't fit the family plan for him. He'd been obliged to join the Army, alongside his friend, Simkins, but couldn't seem to focus on the leadership he would need to demonstrate as an officer. He was fascinated by all the technology behind up to date weapons systems but because of his status, he wasn't allowed to go anywhere near the engineering regiments. When he left the Army, Simkins came with him to be his equerry. He knew that Simkins hated Robert Stuart after what happened at Gordonstoun. That way he agreed to his suggestion that they invite Robert to Balmoral to sort things out. They played a lot of games together. Simkins liked very aggressive games where lots of people got killed and there was blood everywhere. Henry hated blood and couldn't stand seeing animals shot for pleasure. He knew he was a disappointment to his father, who wasn't impressed by chess victories or computer skills. He knew that Victoria was his father's favourite and that he wished she'd been a boy. He didn't know what to do. He heard Simkins come back in after the fruitless search for Robert.

"Right Henry, let's play the Battle of Culloden again. You can be Cumberland this time."

Chapter 19

Scotland, March 2038 - Edinburgh

Robert took the bus from Morningside into Princes Street, getting off at the west end of the gardens. It was a typical Edinburgh spring day with just enough sunny periods to balance the cool east wind and encourage the first leaves to abandon their winter buds for the green miraculous joy of photosynthesis. Chattering rooks busied themselves in the higher trees, squabbling over nest sites and flying twig sorties from the depths of the gardens to build precarious platforms for their annual rebirth.

Robert had just about recovered from the attack by Henry's henchmen, but still had a black eye to remind him. He was also very curious about the Prince's mental state. He seemed to condone Robert being teased and tortured but did not have the stomach to finish him off and remove him as a threat.

Despite the Hanoverian threat, he walked with an added sense of purpose, since his campaign was moving into a new phase where his claim could be tested and asserted. Leo had quickly moved to appoint Sir Duncan Flockhart, the disgruntled ex-British Ambassador to the Gulf States, as Robert's senior advisor and potential Chief of Staff.

Halfway along Princes Street, Robert turned left towards Sir Duncan Flockhart's apartment in the New Town. Robert was excited about his first meeting with Sir Duncan, who was to be his advisor and political mentor. It represented a step change in the effort being applied on his behalf and the beginning of a more planned approach to his as yet undeclared candidacy as King. Leo and Françoise had rushed over urgently after the attack to accelerate the installation of Sir Duncan and get the working relationship with Robert set up. With immaculate timing, Leo and Robert arrived together, Leo having walked from the Balmoral Hotel at the other end of Princes Street.

Sir Duncan welcomed Robert at the door with an oriental sweep of his hand, bidding him and Leo to enter. Robert was astonished to find himself seated in a Middle Eastern oasis within the Georgian splendour of Sir Duncan's sitting room. The walls were covered with pictures of Bedouins with camels, turbaned Sheikhs sporting long curved swords, oil wells and opulent palaces, illustrating the rise of the

Middle East from medieval barbarity to obscene riches, in a few generations. Every corner of the room was packed with Sir Duncan's collection of artefacts and mementos; in one corner a water pipe sat in front of an elaborately tiled mosaic panel, illustrating a Moorish battle scene. Mozart's Piano Concerto No 23 played soothingly in the background.

"Welcome, Gentlemen, to my little corner of Arabia in Edinburgh. I'm really looking forward to this new challenge. It looks much more interesting than the offers I've had to go on the boards of security companies," said the silver-haired Sir Duncan, wearing an immaculate silver grey suit with a slight sheen. A pink tie with blue spots completed the elegant picture.

"I'm glad that you're relishing the challenge, Duncan. We're lucky that providence made you available at the right time," replied Leo.

"Providence, my arse; it's those bastards in the Foreign Office you have to thank."

"Oh, was there a problem?" asked Leo, who was unaware of the exact circumstances of Sir Duncan's departure from the Diplomatic Service.

"I'm afraid there was. I was a bit keen on pointing out human rights abuses and got shafted by a Sheikh as you might say; actually it was an Emir. Early retirement they called it, just a couple of years really, but I did object to being pushed out."

"Well, it's our good fortune," replied Leo who then left the two men together.

Robert then spent two hours describing the Balmoral attack in detail followed by a potted history of his life to date. It was clear that Leo had already briefed Sir Duncan on the political steps that had been taken and Sir Duncan had a good sense of how the independence issue would play out.

"I really want advice on what I should be doing at this stage," said Robert as he got up to leave.

"Not much yet. I'll give you seminars on how constitutional monarchies work, what the models are and then we can do some work on what we think might be the best model for Scotland. In the end, it'll be a negotiation with the politicians, but you're already well placed there I hear."

"I look forward to that."

"Don't forget that constitutional monarchs don't have any power, that's the whole point. Their job is to fill a constructive vacuum that prevents anyone else exercising absolute power."

"Could we expect any support from aristocratic quarters?"

"You may find some friends among the aristos in the old Jacobite regions in the North West but I wouldn't go down that road yet."

"I've already been to see some MacDonalds in Skye. They knew who I was but not the bigger picture. They were very supportive and told me that Cameron of Lochiel wanted to see me. I thought I would leave it until the Glenfinnan gathering in August."

"Yes, that's quite a Jacobite fest."

"And Lochiel's the Chieftain this year," said Robert who was interrupted by the ringing of Sir Duncan's doorbell.

"That'll be Birnie," said Sir Duncan looking at his watch.

Sir Duncan rose to answer the door, welcoming Jack Birnie into the apartment and introducing him to Robert. Jack had a round sallow face with larger than normal teeth, giving him a mysterious oriental look. The scars on his face and his slightly bent nose bore testament to his lifetime of fighting.

"Jack's going to look after your security. He's ex-SAS. We worked together in Oman," said Sir Duncan, lifting a photograph from a table and bringing it over. It showed a group of figures wearing Bedouin head dress surrounding a jeep.

The three of them than got down to the details of what steps had to be taken to establish Robert's security.

****

After leaving Sir Duncan's place, Leo picked his wife up from the Balmoral Hotel and took her by taxi to the museum at Holyrood Palace. A cold east wind echoed around the cloistered open ground level and they cut fine figures walking into the quadrangle. He was wearing his favourite camel coat with a darker brown collar. She was wearing a sharply cut checked suit that suggested tartan. The swirling dragon on her silver brooch added to the restrained Celtic look.

In the museum, Leo felt strangely low, even allowing for the bombardment of echoes from the stalled Stuart history. He thought that it was probably a reaction to the position of Sir Duncan who would now replace him as Robert's chief mentor. Perhaps he was having difficulty letting go, although he fully recognised the necessity to do so and had, of course, personally selected Sir Duncan for the job. As he walked round the museum, questions rolled around his head. Why did they do that…? It seemed clearer than ever to him that Robert was correct when he said that Bonnie Prince Charlie had made a big strategic error in trying to take England. He should have stopped in Edinburgh.

Leaving Holyrood Palace he was cheered by the sight of the Scottish Parliament building opposite, an ultra-confident building worthy of an Independent Scotland.

****

Back at the Balmoral Hotel, Françoise decided that Leo needed cheering up and suggested that they join the afternoon tea brigade in the Palm Room for a glass of champagne.

"Nicole phoned from Boston when you were with Robert and Sir Duncan," she said as they boarded the taxi.

"How is she?" asked Leo, visibly cheered by mention of his daughter.

"Her research is going well, stuff about the brain. That was all she talked about really. Oh, and she's been to see Uncle Harry's grave. She thinks the gold lettering needs to be redone, so I asked her to arrange it."

"You liked your Uncle Harry, didn't you?"

"Oh yes, I've got very fond memories of him. He used to turn up at our house in London and spoil us with lovely presents from America."

"So did you manage to persuade Nicole to abandon Boston for a few days to come and see us?"

"There's a conference in London in the summer, so we'll see her then."

"Research is very competitive, I'm sure she's doing the right thing," said Leo, who was more than aware of his wife's doubts about her daughter's lifestyle, in particular the remote possibility of providing her with grandchildren.

"I wonder how Robert is getting along with Duncan. I'm surprised that you didn't stay with them."

"I thought about that. Robert has to learn to stand on his own feet, especially when the Hanoverians have declared their hand and attacked him."

"But could it be Prince Henry acting alone?"

"Yes, up to a point, but he must be getting information about Robert from someone in the Security Services."

"I hope our security man is good."

"He should be arriving at Sir Duncan's about now," said Leo, looking at his watch and draining his glass.

"Siesta?" she asked invitingly.

Chapter 20

Scotland, March 2038 - Edinburgh

Within ten minutes of looking round Robert's flat, Birnie was clear. He ushered Robert quickly out of the front door and round the back into the gathering darkness in the garden, with a protective hand on his back, as if he was in immediate physical danger.

"Your flat's been infiltrated by the enemy, sir, there's sensors everywhere, like lice on a rotten old prostitute," he declared, in the harsh voice that he reserved for foes.

"So what do we do about it?" asked Robert, wincing at Birnie's simile.

"It's like the lice, sir. We need to pick them off one by one. I've got a scanner that'll show them all up. I'll do your car as well."

"Who can be doing this?" asked Robert, who was astonished that he hadn't noticed anything.

"It'll be MI5, Sir."

"How can you be so sure?"

"They're the very latest type o' bug. MI5's the only ones that's got them. They're linked directly to a satellite. No vans parked in the street, that's old hat now, sir."

"But how did they get there?"

"They must have sent in a technician. Have you had any workmen visiting?

"The electricity company came around last week; something about new regulations."

"That'll be them, sir, no doubt about it. It's them head bangers from London listening in the comfort of their offices on the Thames. I went there once for a special operations briefing."

"But don't they have an office in Glasgow now?"

"Oh, that's just for monitoring Rangers supporters, sir. You're bigger stuff than that."

"We need to call Sir Duncan. We've got to respond to this."

Sir Duncan arrived within the hour as Birnie was sweeping Robert's bedroom.

"I hope you haven't been whispering sweet nothings in here, sir," said Birnie, with a twinkle in his eye.

"Only if I've been talking in my sleep, Birnie," replied Robert sharply.

"Well done, Birnie," said Sir Duncan, as he arrived slightly breathless, turning to Robert who anticipated what Sir Duncan was going to ask.

"I don't think we've been compromised. Nothing's happened here that would give them a clue."

"Good, excellent. This had to happen sometime and at least we're reasonably well prepared now to exploit it."

"How can we exploit it?" asked Robert.

"I'll write a strongly worded letter to the Home Secretary. The Government is very sensitive to the situation in Scotland, with the Independents doing well in the polls and won't want this publicised. I'll ask for official confirmation that they'll stop monitoring us. Perhaps Peter could do the same. That should have plenty of impact."

"We should mention the Balmoral attack as well," added Robert.

"Yes, perhaps obliquely, so that they can keep an eye on their loose cannon Prince," replied Sir Duncan.

Robert was now clear that his quest had entered a new and sinister phase. The enemy was aware of his presence and probably his intentions; the phoney war was over and hostilities had broken out at least against him. His team had no dirty tricks department to fight back with. All he had was the strength of his cause to keep him strong and Birnie to protect him. He was not afraid; he was excited and looked forward now to the next challenge. That was to persuade Peter's political *protégé*, Angela Brown, that he would be an asset in the fight for independence and the government of the Nation thereafter.

****

Peter shook Robert's hand warmly before introducing Angela Brown at the door of his suite in the Balmoral Hotel. The meeting had been scheduled to take place at Robert's flat in Morningside but the concerns over bugging made them change the venue. Robert shook her hand, and held her gaze, determined not to be the first to blink. He felt her piercing eyes on him, assessing him from the first glance. He sensed a formidable presence in the attractive female MSP and shadow minister. She was wearing a pinstripe trouser suit, and a white blouse and pearls, which made her look more like a high powered business woman than a politician. He had decided that he would let her dictate the agenda. She would have concerns that she wanted satisfied and he would have to respond.

"You could be Robert's father," she said to Peter, "you look so alike. Or should I have said brothers?"

"Thanks for the compliment," he replied.

"You do suit the kilt, Robert; we could certainly make you look the part," she said, lifting up the photograph of Robert in Highland dress that Peter had already shown her.

"Oh, I presume it's OK to call you Robert, is it?" she added.

"Please do; I want to be as informal as possible. Congratulations on becoming Deputy Leader of your Party," he replied.

"Thanks Robert, you might say that crown princes should stick together but for the whole of my political life I've been a republican. I've always thought of monarchy as a deferential system that operated to the detriment of the mass of ordinary people."

"Well things have changed since the tyranny of divine right of kings. We would have to agree a role for me, wouldn't we?"

"It's all about what kind of Head of State we want, isn't it?" added Peter.

"Do you really want old washed up politicians as Heads of State?" asked Robert.

"Don't forget, Angela, that a lot of everyday Scottish Republicanism is partly a reaction to Hanoverian unpopularity," added Peter.

"I believe that a fresh monarchy, Scotland's own, along with a new dynamism from your political party, would galvanise the country. Together we could redefine what it is to be Scottish, replacing the current confused identity with a new one," said Robert, standing up with his back to the fireplace.

"But what actual role could you play?" asked Angela sceptically.

"I believe that governments are beginning to see the error of trying to nanny every aspect of their citizen's lives and often failing at great expense. Government intervention's often the problem, not the solution. Much used to be done by the charitable and voluntary sector. I'd like to lead the revival of that in Scotland."

"That's an interesting idea, but we can't go back to locking up unmarried mothers in institutions and getting their babies adopted; the moral tone would have to be different this time round."

"I agree with you there, but you will have a once and for all opportunity to zero base the social contract."

"Well, let's see how it goes. We'll need to do a lot of work on a new constitution. That would have to include the role of the Head of State," answered Angela coolly.

"There's a lot to think about there, Angela," said Peter.

"Do you think that your religion might be a handicap?" asked Angela.

"Well, of course, there is no hiding the fact that I've been brought up as a Catholic. I do have a spiritual side and I am a believer. However, my policy will be to keep my private beliefs just that, private. As a monarch, I would try to somehow find mechanisms to reach out to people of all faiths and of none, who are of course the majority," replied Robert, without enthusiasm. He realised that his Catholicism was probably his Achilles heel and he didn't yet have a really convincing way through.

"That sounds fine as far as it goes, but being all things to all men won't be easy. Bigots will set traps for you," she replied, testing his weak thesis further. "And you would have to come off the pot when it comes to marriage or coronation."

"I'm thinking of a way to handle that."

"It'll be part of the PR, won't it?" added Peter.

"Speaking of PR, I'm delighted that you're already in the Scottish rugby team," said Angela, rising to her feet to signify that the meeting was over.

"Thanks to my Scottish granny."

Robert formed an impression of Angela as someone of enormous competence and potential, overlaid with a coiled impatience, which would only be released by gaining power. He of course felt a similar impatience but his calculation on power was different. She was already well up the greasy pole and in a sound position to plot her future. He was in a quantum position; it would be all or nothing, played for much higher stakes. Despite Angela's calculated coolness, Robert was pleased with the outcome of the meeting and felt that he had established a position where monarchy was now an option for her. They were within negotiating distance of a role for him as Monarch.

Robert then left for the Club to have a game of squash with Tina. They were now well built into each other's fitness regime. Robert was beginning to see the enigmatic Tina as more of a sporting mate, than a conventional girlfriend. She was very enthusiastic about physical activity of every kind, including sex, which for her was mainly about noisily exercising the cardiovascular system.

****

"Well, what did you think of him?" asked Peter urgently, when Robert had gone.

"You know, I went in there planning to sort him out, to ridicule his impossible ambition. Somehow, I'm not really sure why, it didn't turn out that way. There's something about him. I haven't met anyone quite like that before."

"I know what you mean, I had the same feeling the first time I met him. He's a real charmer isn't he?"

"Yes, Peter, but it's more than charm. I'm pretty resistant to that by now and can spot the false side of that a mile away. No, it's something deeper and more powerful. There's a lot of integrity there and true belief in his destiny."

"Perhaps the bluest of blue blood does have something extra in it, some hereditary corpuscles that make them masters."

"His ideas sounded good. He's right about the role of the state, but doing anything about it is deeply political. You can't just hand over vast areas of social responsibility to a charity."

"Yes, he would have to understand the limits of his role."

"He clearly wants to be involved in politics and there could be problems for us there. Anyway, he's a terrific candidate, but I want to see the polling data before making up my mind. I need to see what he can do for us. We can't afford to harness ourselves to a loser, can we?"

"He's not a loser, Angela, I'm sure of it," replied Peter, who was very relieved that she had taken the first step towards coming onboard.

****

After the clandestine meeting with Robert, Angela looked forward to making a range of secret contacts with other stakeholders in the issue of Scottish Independence. With the deputy leadership under her belt, her self-confidence was at an all-time high despite the leader briefing against her. She took this signal for change as a remit to behave independently from Robertson and start developing her own agenda. The mechanics and terms of a separation from England were uppermost in her mind and she decided to secretly engage with the key players. Like the Independents in Scotland, the Conservatives in England were ahead in the polls but not far enough ahead to get a working majority. Angela was well aware that the heavy Labour vote from Scotland was a key factor in denying the Tories decent UK majorities. With Scotland removed from the political equation, the Tories would be the natural party of English government. If the Tories could swallow separation then they would have a vested interest in her success, which might even translate to help in one form or another.

She had already arranged a clandestine meeting with Morris Newbold, the latest in a line of power hungry, media savvy young Conservative leaders who were sacrificed in turn after each electoral defeat. Her only regret was that she couldn't take Peter into her confidence. She was sure that he would absolutely veto her plan.

Chapter 21

Scotland, April 2038 - Edinburgh

Sir Duncan switched on his phone after an evening meeting to hear a very worrying message. The caller, who had a strong Glasgow accent, was anonymous but nonetheless intimidating. He informed Sir Duncan that he was mentoring flawed goods. The Stuart claim was false and the evidence would arrive in the post the following morning.

Next morning, Sir Duncan waited nervously for the post to arrive. The caller had tapped into a deeply buried concern that somehow the Stuart claim was based on thin historical evidence. He opened the envelope carefully and withdrew several sheets of typed paper and some graphics. He read the typescript then immediately called Robert and Leo, who was still in Edinburgh, asking them to come to his flat for an urgent conference. The gist of the documentation was that Robert had a completely different DNA profile to Bonnie Prince Charlie, based on hair samples taken from the museum at Holyrood compared to Robert's profile obtained from the French National database.

"That's ridiculous, Sir Duncan. Tell him, Uncle Leo, that just can't be true," said Robert in response to Sir Duncan's summary.

"Well Leo, what have you got to say about this? Annoying as that prospect is, we have to answer the charge. If this is true we have a big problem."

"Putting my legal hat on, the first thing we need to do is challenge the authenticity of the Holyrood hair sample. Bonnie Prince Charlie locks are about as common as pieces of the true cross in medieval times. They can't all be authentic. Most Highland castles have samples in their museums. We need to gather as many as we can, clandestinely if possible. Birnie can you please arrange that? I'll give you a list of places to look. To be absolutely sure, however, we could try to get a sample from his tomb in St Peter's in Rome. I'll ask the Cardinal about that."

"What if the problem is more fundamental? A hidden break in the Stuart male line for example?"

"It pains me to say it, but David's wife was not a model of faithfulness. She did have lovers, so there is certainly a theoretical possibility that it's true. However, they were legally married, so in that sense Robert's father and Robert himself, are Stuarts," replied Leo, looking at Robert. Robert sensed an apology in the look, although he had already heard Leo mention Monique's infidelity.

"Well, thanks for that honest reply, Leo. I take your legal point but I'm sure you can see that if this were true and publicised, Robert's quest would be finished. So we need to check everybody," said Sir Duncan looking at Leo whose face darkened.

"This really is tedious," he whispered.

"Finally, someone from their side wants to meet us," said Sir Duncan.

"To receive our surrender he probably thinks. To see us off the field leaving the Hanoverians unchallenged," added Robert angrily.

"We need to be careful, it could be a trap," said Birnie.

"We'll have you watching over us, Birnie, just in case," concluded Sir Duncan.

Robert left the meeting with a deep sense of foreboding. To have come so far and then have such a fundamental question mark hanging over him. Was he a real Stuart? Did he have the right to be staking a claim to the throne? He would be letting down so many people who were taking great personal risks to help him achieve his destiny. But was it his destiny?

****

A fortnight later, Robert and Sir Duncan headed for the rendezvous in the Botanic Gardens. Robert had been obliged to insist on being present in the face of Sir Duncan's security concerns. It was a park bench behind the Palm House in a pleasant, sheltered corner dominated by a large camellia, which had finished flowering, leaving the ground strewn with the decaying petals from the dead flowers. It was a warm sunny day and many of the visitors were going about in shirtsleeves, although their contact, who was already there, was dressed in a uniform of pinstripe suit and Barbour jacket. Sir Duncan had his silver locks hidden under a cloth cap and Robert was keeping a very low profile in a dark blue tracksuit and trainers. Birnie was hidden in some bushes opposite with binoculars and a long lens camera.

Robert thought that their contact looked rather benign, like an old-fashioned bank manager or insurance salesman. His pleasant flabby features betrayed no hint of malice or threat. He did not live up to the image of the tense, honed spook that Robert had in his head.

"Thanks for coming, gentlemen. I'm assuming that you'll back off now that your Pretender is just that," said the contact, in his Glasgow burr. Robert was surprised to hear a Scottish accent. He somehow associated spooks with London. At the same time, he thought he detected a certain cockiness in the spook's expression. He clearly thought that he held all the cards.

"We've been around all the castles in the Highlands. We've got seven different hair samples purporting to come from Bonnie Prince Charlie's head. The details of the profiles are in here," said Sir Duncan, handing back the same brown envelope that had come through the post. "They're all different and different from the Edinburgh sample. One of the samples is actually dog hair, from a spaniel we think. So your exercise doesn't prove anything and we persist with our certainty about Robert Stuart's lineage."

"OK, I'll look at your stuff, but really guys, you just can't win this war. So far, you've won a few skirmishes but in the end, just like your famous ancestor, you will lose," said the spook, looking directly at Robert.

"Why are you pursuing us anyway? We're behaving legally and only the Scottish people can decide if they want us," added Sir Duncan, as a football rolled across the grass towards them, hotly pursued by a boy of about ten wearing a Heart of Midlothian football jersey. The spook got up instinctively and kicked the ball back towards the lad before turning back towards his opponents.

"Are you as naïve as that Hearts supporter? You know what you're tangling with. It isn't as simple as you put it," he said, with a shrug of his shoulders.

"You're trying to threaten us. We don't accept threats. We're very confident we can win."

"I'm not threatening you. The service has been told to back off. You've got some heavy hitters on your side who complained to the Home Secretary."

"But what about the unofficial service? The one that attacked me on the Balmoral Estate."

"Yes, you'll attract attention from elements beyond our control."

"Can you control Prince Henry?" persisted Robert.

"He's getting treatment in a private clinic."

"I'm very glad to hear that," said Robert, who was then able to see his humiliation at the hands of Simkins and Henry as a kind of victory.

"But he has a lot of friends."

"When we win, we'll need intelligence agencies in Scotland. So what will we think of you when we look at your CV? Will we see you as a friend or a traitor?" asked Robert.

"If I'm not your friend, I'll be an asylum seeker in England. Don't forget, they'll need spies to keep an eye on the Scots."

"Keep in touch," concluded Sir Duncan.

Chapter 22

Scotland, April 2038 - Edinburgh, Murrayfield

Less than a year after his first game for Scotland, Robert was unexpectedly made Captain of the Scottish rugby team. The appointment was a tremendous motivator for Robert and his small team of supporters. His first game as Captain was against France at Murrayfield. Scotland managed the exuberant French well and secured a narrow victory. The SRU Patron, Princess Victoria, hosted the post-match team dinner as usual. It was the team Captain's job to walk her around during pre-dinner drinks, as she complimented particular players on their efforts.

"I'd like you to attend a small party I'm giving after dinner, at Holyrood Palace," she said to Robert, at the end of her procession around the players. He stiffened slightly at both the invitation itself and the location. "That's a royal command, by the way," she added, her eyes sparkling. He sensed that she could see his reluctance from the way she finally averted her eyes with a questioning look. All his instincts told him to refuse, to tell the Hanoverian siren to get lost, but his head warned him not to snub the Princess and make an unnecessary enemy, especially in the rugby world, which held such promise for him. The invitation was also made in front of some teammates and a negative reply from him would be incomprehensible to them.

"Thank you very much, ma'am," he said formally, after too long a pause, with the tiniest inclination of his head.

"I'll take that as a yes then," she replied, widening her eyes in mock surprise. It was clear to Robert that her invitations were normally greeted with more enthusiasm than he had managed to demonstrate.

He was picked up from the restaurant at 11:30 p.m., suffering some ribald jokes from his teammates as he left. He was apparently not the first. It was very traditional. At the Palace, he was dropped inside the gates, taken through into the quadrangle and up the great staircase, through the throne room and into the evening drawing room.

Many in the assembled company turned as he entered. He smiled and nodded in acknowledgement; clearly everyone knew who he was. The Princess came forward and shook his hand.

"Welcome to Holyrood Palace, Robert. Now, come and meet everyone and get yourself a drink."

Sensing the warm ambiance of the event, a reflection of the bubbly and informal personality of the Princess, Robert relaxed and began to enjoy the company. Everyone wanted to ask him about his last minute try in his very first game for Scotland; it had certainly made an impression and had not been forgotten. He had a particularly good chat with Alex Douglas. Mrs Douglas, Emily, was a companion of the Princess when she visited Scotland. When Robert had finished his chat with Douglas, the Princess appeared at his side. This time he smiled back normally, although somewhere inside him a kind of guilt and embarrassment welled up, but not the anger that the presence of her brother would have provoked. It was more a case of him letting his side down; what on earth would his uncle Leo think if he could see him now? Leo would consider him a traitor, dealing with the enemy and would strongly disapprove.

"Have you ever visited the old Royal Apartments in the Palace?" the Princess asked.

"Oh, a long time ago," he lied, covering up his status as a frequent visitor. He often felt like asking for discount at the pay desk.

"Would you like a private guided tour?"

"Only if a Princess is to be the guide," he replied, as he took a further step into the world of the beautiful Hanoverian Princess. He thought it might be fun to have her off guard, to observe her closely from his hidden sanctuary; he might even find a skeleton or two.

"Let's go then," she said, leading him out through the other end of the evening drawing room and around past the King's rooms.

"This line of rooms was the King's private quarters built by Charles II after his Restoration," she said rather formally. "Apparently the bed's not very comfortable, not that I've slept in it myself," she added hastily. Of course, Robert knew that Charles II had never actually slept in the bed, or indeed set foot in Holyrood after its construction. As they continued, a squall of heavy rain spat hard at the windows on their right and a peal of thunder caused the lights to flicker momentarily, reminding Robert of his delicate position.

She then led him to the next arm of the quadrangle, which was occupied entirely by the Great Gallery. Robert stiffened as he entered. He had been in the gallery many times but the impact of seeing nearly one hundred portraits of real and legendary monarchs of Scotland, most of them his own ancestors, always made him stop.

"These were all painted by the same artist, De Wet, in the 1680s," said the Princess, with a sweep of her arm. As they strolled down the gallery, Robert recognised the face of Charles II. Half way down he was stopped by the Princess.

"That's Mary Queen of Scots, one of my ancestors," she began, looking up admiringly at the portrait.

Robert looked up at the portrait of Mary, perhaps his most controversial ancestor. Her tired eyes were on him. He looked into the intelligent sad pools, a sadness that seemed to reflect not only her own tragic life but the demise of the Stuarts that followed her. Her witnessing gaze began to make him slightly uncomfortable in Hanoverian company. As he took another step, changing the angle of her gaze, it seemed to soften and he sensed that he had her support; was she too willing him to claim his birth-right? Would that bring her peace? Robert was then aware of the Princess looking at him rather than Mary.

"An ancestor of yours, was she?" he replied, disengaging from Mary, "and a very attractive woman, too," he added, looking back at the Princess, complimenting her by association.

"Yes, she was."

Robert smiled at Victoria and shook his head in wonder. They were both descendants of Mary. Victoria much more distant, but both of them were drawing legitimacy from the blood tie. At that moment, Robert realised that he was a very distant cousin of his beautiful Royal tour guide.

"Now you must tell me about the try that you scored in your first game for Scotland. That was something else. As you crossed the twenty-two you seemed to be possessed," she said, as they arrived in front of a portrait of Bonnie Prince Charlie.

"Have you ever visited Culloden Battlefield?" he asked her.

"Yes, but I was very small."

"My great uncle took me there a few years ago. We finished the tour on the exact spot from where the Prince directed the battle. I stood there for a long time as the Prince himself did before ordering the Highlanders to charge. I went with them all the way to the Hanoverian lines, facing the flashes and roaring of the cannons, through the smoke and the grapeshot, past the bodies of dead and wounded comrades." He paused, sensing that he was going too far.

"Go on," she said tenderly.

"When I hit the twenty-two that afternoon against England, I was somehow back there again at Culloden. I think the camera flashes and the flags set me off. I just went mad. Nobody could have stopped me."

"We must get the whole team to visit Culloden," she replied, laughing.

"I don't know why I am telling you this. I've not said it to anyone else."

"Is it being in this place, standing in front of the Prince himself?" she asked. "In fact, he held a ball in this very room in 1745."

"Or maybe it's the company," he replied, lulled by her allure.

"We could have a quick look at Mary Queen of Scot's Chambers," she said, as they reached the end of the room.

"Not tonight, thank you," he replied, his need to keep the exciting Victoria firmly in the enemy camp just winning out over his desire to take her in his arms there and then.

"We'd better go back then," she said, taking his hand. They walked back slowly, each with their own thoughts, under the watchful eyes of his ancestors. The physical contact with Victoria excited Robert. Was she going to drag him into Charles II's bed on the way back, he fantasised? As they passed that hurdle without incident, she let his hand go and speeded up, walking faster as if she had come to a decision about something. Before they turned the corner to re-join the party she stopped and turned towards him, taking both his hands in hers.

"Who are you, Robert?" she asked, her face now grave and mildly questioning, looking up into his eyes. Had he given himself away, blathering about Jacobite tries and communing with Mary Queen of Scots in front of her?

"I'm looking forward to you finding out," he said cheekily, to be struck by a solid pang of guilt, as he hoped that he would see her again.

Chapter 23

England, May 2038 - London

In London, the Queen was having one of her regular meetings with her daughter.

While they did formally live in the same Palace it would have been easy to lose touch if contact was left to serendipity. She had been aware of the Stuart challenge in Scotland for several weeks and like the King had dismissed it without giving it any serious thought. However, the private report from Douglas House that Victoria had invited the Stuart Pretender there for the weekend forced her to take a more active interest in affairs north of the border. In addition, it was the first time that Victoria had ever done such a thing, indicating a more than normal interest on the part of her daughter.

The Queen was very concerned about her daughter's future. The constraints of security and the need to protect the reputation of the Monarchy kept her on a very tight rein in a claustrophobic set of fast people. The Queen was appalled at the thought of Victoria choosing a partner from among them. Neither did she look forward to her daughter spending a long period as a singleton, becoming a playgirl and degrading her reputation. After all, she was the second in line to the throne, the spare in a situation where there were doubts about the first in line. The Queen longed to marry her off, safely but happily, as soon as possible. So far the attention of the press and the glamour magazines had been positive but celebrity given by them could just as easily be taken away; they were waiting for the golden Princess to trip up.

"You look very nice today, Victoria."

"When you say that, Mummy, it always means trouble."

"Tell me about this Robert Stuart that we're trying to ignore."

"The enigmatic Robert! I'm finding him difficult to ignore."

"That's why we're having this conversation."

"Before we knew who he was, he'd been presented to me often at rugby matches and I've seen him at all the dinners. He was always reserved and distant with me, as though he didn't like women but now of course I understand. I was the enemy. When he became Captain, I followed the tradition and invited him to the Holyrood party. I was intrigued to know how he would react to me inside Holyrood Palace. He was a bit stiff at first but eventually he opened up. I took him on a tour of the museum. He gave himself away a bit in front of the Mary Queen of Scots portrait.

"So what did you think of him?"

"He's an incredibly attractive man. Physically he's an Adonis. He makes you feel the centre of the world when he talks to you with his big brown eyes. It's more than charm and politeness, it's pure charisma and he's got it."

"Do you think that he likes you?"

"I sensed that he does but he was reluctant to show it. If someone asked me to describe a Prince Charming, I would describe him. I've never met anyone like him."

"So you're arranging to see him at the Douglas Estate to find out if he's as smitten as you?"

"What do you think, Mummy? Am I doing the right thing?"

"My heart says yes, but my head isn't so sure. Just be very careful."

"Thanks Mummy, you're so wise."

When Victoria left, the Queen began to calculate. The bookies were telling her that they were going to lose everything in Scotland, as it became an independent republic following the next election. As a passionate horse racer she took more than a passing interest in their opinions. Would the fresh charismatic Robert fare any better? Was there a strategy in this for the Windsors to retain a half share in Scotland? Was it time for Robert's claim to be subjected to public scrutiny to see if he was a horse worth backing with the hand of her daughter? She telephoned Sir Humphrey to arrange a meeting with the King to get an agreed family position.

The Queen also had to face the awkward fact that Victoria's description of Robert would have been her own prescription for a Prince of Wales, her own son. Sadly, there was a world of difference between the two. She had absolutely forbidden the use of the term "autistic" to describe her son but in her heart she knew that he wasn't quite normal. He was good with animals and brilliant at maths but had little empathy with people. As a boy, he developed an obsession with computer games and wanted to do little else but play them. As he grew up, he seemed unable to graft a sense of right and wrong onto his behaviour.

Eventually, she came to realise that her own denial had prevented early intervention that might have improved his condition. He was being treated with the latest drugs which offered only minor short term improvements. A further complication was his dependence on an old school friend, Simkins. The Queen had initially been grateful when Simkins became Henry's social eyes and ears, but over the years a kind of merging of personalities was taking place, where the fantasist Simkins was assuming too much of Henry's role.

****

The following weekend, Robert arrived at the Douglas Estate at 7:00 p.m. after the game. He was still wearing a tracksuit and trainers and had his Highland dress in a suit carrier. It was a fine evening with a risk of a late frost following a still bright day. The place looked quiet although there were a few shooters' vehicles in the parking area and a dog barked at him hopefully from one of them.

The centre part of the house looked very old, with vestiges of fortification. The wings leading from the centre looked Georgian and comfortable. The enormous outer oak front door looked original on its massive hinges but its practical function had been replaced by a modern construction of new oak and glass, a few feet further into the expansive hallway. The butler showed him up the impressive central stone staircase lined with portraits of Douglas ancestors.

The next staircase was accessed through a small door, which led into a much plainer world. It was an unadorned servants' access, leading up to the bedrooms and down to the kitchen. He was lead up to a corridor of rooms in the top storey. Robert's old servants' room was surprisingly well appointed, with sections of oak panelling. It even had an en-suite, created by cannibalising part of the adjacent room. The butler informed him that aperitifs would be served at 7:30 p.m.

Robert changed into his eveningwear and wandered downstairs, encountering some other guests on the way down. A waitress at the bottom of the grand staircase offered glasses of champagne and directions to the dining room.

Alex Douglas was already there with a few people, mainly other local farming gentry who were still talking about the shoot. Robert could hear one old buffer blaming the dogs for not being able to find the bird he was sure he shot. Other guests trickled in, mainly

Edinburgh folk; lawyers and financial people. Most of the assembled group recognised him immediately and he was soon the centre of attention answering questions about his rugby career, especially the internationals.

At 7:50 p.m. when most of the guests were present, the dining room door opened and Princess Victoria floated through, looking spectacular in a plain white dress with a tartan plaid. Every head turned to see the royal apparition. Aged only twenty-one, she was a great beauty, with long dark hair and vivid blue eyes. Robert was surprised that his anti-Hanoverian instinct was more than balanced by an inward elation. At Holyrood he had felt very comfortable in her company, as if he had known her for a long time.

The Princess had been on the shoot and had already been introduced to most of the company, so Alex confined himself to introducing her to the few guests who were not present earlier in the day.

"Ah, Captain Robert, pity you couldn't come today, you missed a good shoot."

"The demands of the game ma'am," he replied.

"Did you score today?"

"I'm afraid not."

"Never mind…," she replied, not finishing her sentence and giving him what he thought was a "the night is young," look.

At dinner he was placed well away from the Princess next to her friend, Emily, the wife of Alex Douglas. The table was sumptuously laid with silver cutlery and decorated with silver candelabra and flower vases, making it difficult to see the guests sitting opposite. Robert took an instant dislike to Emily, finding her overbearing and altogether too conscious of her position. She also asked far too many questions, and was clearly trying to find out about his background. It was more of an interview than a conversation. He obliged with his now standard sanitised version of himself. Her questioning had depressed him slightly and he caught the waiter's eye to have his wine topped up.

On Robert's other side was a farmer's wife who talked of nothing but horses, severely testing his powers of concentration. At the other end of the table he could see the Princess keeping her listeners highly amused, awarding marks out of ten for shooting. He did make eye contact with her several times during the dinner but he could read nothing in her face.

After dinner, the guests moved on into the ballroom, a large room with an impressive beamed ceiling. The musicians sat up in a box, clipped to the wall like a pulpit. Robert was an accomplished dancer, able to put into practice all the Scottish dancing training that he had received at Gordonstoun. He was soon in the thick of it, swept up in the whole swirling sweaty melee of the set dances. He danced a couple of times with the Princess; a Gay Gordons and a Barn Dance. They had little opportunity to talk and as soon as each dance finished, she was whisked away from him.

At the end of the evening, the Princess disappeared quickly with Emily, and most of the other guests retired or went home, leaving Robert talking to Alex about the forthcoming rugby fixtures, including the next international, over a whisky nightcap.

Alex finally declared that he was turning in, so Robert headed for his staircase feeling sheepish that he had misinterpreted the Princess's "the night is young" look. After a shower, he was arranging his Highland dress back into the suit hanger when a part of the wood panelling slid open to reveal a staircase built into the wall. His first reaction was irrational fear, and thoughts of ghosts. However, the emerging apparition had long dark hair and was clearly alive and of Robert's world. She was still wearing the long white dress making Robert feel uncomfortable in his pyjamas and dressing gown. She had two glasses on a small tray.

"This is extra time. Just a little nightcap. I've nicked some of Alex's vintage stuff."

"I've never seen anything like you come out of the tunnel. I'm glad you've come though, we didn't get much opportunity to talk earlier."

"I hoped you would say that."

"And thanks for inviting me. I wondered whether I would see you after the Holyrood party."

Victoria was immediately conscious that both of them were parked behind their respective walls of genial politeness and family loyalty. Perhaps it had been a mistake to blunder into the lion's den, an action that went beyond her mother's call for her to be careful.

"Why didn't you ask me for a date?" she asked, trying to flush him out.

"Do Princesses do dates?"

"Of course, with the right person, especially if he's a Prince," she said, stressing the last part of the sentence and raising her eyebrows in a quizzical smile.

"You know, don't you? Yes, you must, the Secret Service knows. This whisky isn't poisoned is it?" he asked with a smile, setting his glass down.

"Robert, trust me, the women in this family see it differently," she said, moving towards him into his responding opening arms. The first touch of their lips was a tentative puckering, perhaps fearing that a thunderbolt might strike their forbidden liaison. The second touch was searching and urgent.

When eventually Victoria went back downstairs to her room, she had the answer to her question.

Chapter 24

England, May 2038 – London, Cabinet Office

With MI5's hands tied by the politicians and the Stuart bandwagon making steady progress, Underwood was becoming increasingly frustrated. His discomfort was aggravated by his sweat from the exertion of walking to the cabinet office in the warm stickiness of an early summer London day to meet Sir Humphrey.

"I assume that you've backed off, Underwood," said Sir Humphrey.

"Into the deep shadows, sir," replied Underwood, who was appalled at the weakness of lily-livered politicians, terrified of losing a few votes.

"So, what's the answer to the Stuart legitimacy question?"

"We've got a photo reproduction of the Bonnie Prince Charlie wedding contract from the Vatican. It looks correct for the period but we really need to examine the document scientifically to be sure about its authenticity."

"They'll never agree to that."

"It's unlikely, so we've asked if our expert can at least see the parchment for himself. They're considering that request."

"So the jury's still out there, then. What about Granny in Marbella?"

"Well, at first she came up with gold dust. She told us that Robert Stuart's father was one of her French lovers so not a blood Stuart. It isn't the case, however. We got all their DNA profiles from the French database. Robert Stuart is kosher."

"I think it's time for action, Underwood. We need to leak the conspiracy. The politicians are being too careful," said Sir Humphrey, faithfully implementing the Queen's secret instructions.

"About time, too! The Independence Party will surely turn on their President, Christie the film star fellow. There'll be a hell of a row and a good chance of a Party split. They'll never get elected."

"How would we do it?"

"There's a freelance journalist in Scotland. Ross, I think his name is. He tipped us off in the first place and we promised him a scoop someday, in return for the information and keeping his mouth shut. A day's lead is all he needs. Then we can rely on the tabloids. They'll finish the Stuarts off within a week. I can set Ross up to go whenever you like," said Underwood.

"Yes, as soon as possible."

"So, exactly what are we going to leak, Sir Humphrey?"

"Well, the storyline should be that the Scottish Independence Party has for years been funded secretly by the Stuarts, plotting to recover the throne of Scotland. The President of the Party, Christie was the key agent in the deception. Quite simple, that's the bones of it."

"To be strictly factual, sir, we don't know who was doing the funding, but we can assure you that it's been switched off."

****

Underwood immediately contacted Jamie at Tartan Park, passing on the core of the message agreed with the Mandarin's.

Piers was ecstatic when he got Jamie's call. He'd already drafted and redrafted his story a dozen times. He trembled as he heard Jamie's instruction, overawed at being the mouthpiece of history. The Mandarin's core message about the funding was easily passed on. However, it would not be possible to write Robert Stuart off as a mere rugby player. He was now Captain of the Scottish rugby team with a big public profile. He was handsome and squeaky clean so far and very popular, a fantastic TV performer with star quality, a real people's Captain. Adding on the Crown Prince title projected him into open *Braveheart* territory, satisfying a deep felt need among Scots for contemporary heroes to stand alongside those of the past.

Robert was the story, not the funding. Who cares? He thought; perhaps a few political geeks. The editor at the Scottish Cable was only too pleased for his publication to be the platform for such an historic article, which would go down in the annals of newspaper publishing. Piers was commissioned to write follow-ups every day for the following few weeks and given a team of researchers to help. He was delighted at the improving circumstances for his pension fund and in the heat of the moment, careful not to forget to warn his idol, Angela Brown, of developments. The story was due to break on Sunday, to give everyone plenty of time to read it.

****

On hearing the news, Angela was stung to action. She already

115

had the Deputy Leadership as a springboard from which to attack the highest office and she was well prepared to use her "Vision for Scotland," demanded by the hated Robertson, to attack and hopefully destroy him.

She would try to use the furore caused by the publicity to mount a coup that would make her Leader of the Party in good time for the next election. As she imagined herself standing with her foot on a recumbent Robertson's chest, raising her standard on the flagpole of Scotland, she had a moment of reflection on the consequences of failure. If she failed, she would take so many people with her; her beloved Peter would be in the wilderness with her and although that had a certain attraction, she wanted him with her at the top of the mountain, surveying their kingdom together. And then there was Robert. Her failure would certainly confine him to a very short footnote in history, perhaps just half a line: "another failed romantic Stuart." Bulldozing these negative thoughts aside, she called Peter.

"It's happening; I've just had word from Piers that he's going public with the story on Sunday. He has a day's exclusivity and then, of course, everyone will have it on Monday," she said.

"Shit, we're not really ready yet."

"Yes, we are, Peter. I have the whole thing drafted out, all the new policies we need, and we still have time to do a bit of polishing tomorrow or tonight even."

"Thank God for that, we might just make it. We can set out our stall to the Lomond Group on Saturday and then deal with Robertson on Sunday. You're right, Angela, we can turn this to our advantage, so come tonight as soon as you can."

"Can you get your polling guru, Dan Miller, along as well?"

"That'll be a tall order at such short notice but I'll try."

"And Peter, you will phone Sir Duncan, so that the Stuarts know as well?"

"Of course," he replied.

Before reaching for the card with Dan's number on it, Peter paused to take stock. The press article on Sunday would present him as the lead conspirator in the affair, funding the Independence Party clandestinely and leading them against their natural constitutional leanings towards a monarchy, all on his gut feeling that the Scots would go for it. He desperately needed Dan Miller to tell him that he

116

was right. And even if he was right, he had probably flouted Party funding rules and perhaps even broken the law. However, he was confident about the obfuscation potential of parliamentary enquiries to delay and bury any major concerns on that front.

"Dan, it's Peter Christie here."

"Oh, Peter, I'm a bit tied up at the moment."

"Where are you, Dan?" asked Peter, with the singsong of a parent calling a hiding child.

"I'm in Paris, and absolutely not available. I thought I'd turned this phone off."

"Are you with anyone special, Dan?" asked Peter, sensing the reason behind Dan's reticence.

"Special? I'll say. It's taken me three months to persuade this English goddess to come to Paris with me, and it's costing me a fortune, pal."

"You can afford it at your rates."

"So why are you calling me on a Friday night? Is there an emergency, an abdication or something like that?"

"Not quite that but you're in the right area. You know I have you doing some polling research on the acceptability of a Stuart monarchy."

"Yes, but it's Friday Peter. I charge double, or to you, triple at the weekends."

"Dan, this is deadly serious, I haven't called for a chat. Our enemies are going public this weekend so we need to act now or we're dead, sunk without trace. We need you to come over and help us with whatever data you've got," said Peter, with a steely authority.

"This weekend?"

"More specifically, tomorrow morning Dan, at my house on Loch Lomond."

"But how will I get—?"

"I'll send a private plane for you early tomorrow morning."

"Early?"

"Very early, I'll phone back with the details."

"Very early it is," acquiesced Dan.

"And, Dan, don't worry, the world is full of goddesses."

Peter's next call was to Sir Duncan who would have to get the PR machine moving and ensure that Robert was well protected from the media storm that would engulf them. Sir Duncan was thrilled that the action was about to begin and immediately called Robert.

"Robert, where are you? It's Duncan."

"I'm just leaving the training ground in Edinburgh."

"What about tomorrow?"

"I'm playing in the Borders, why?"

"And afterwards, what then? Where will you be on Sunday morning?" probed Sir Duncan.

"I'll be with friends in the country. Is anything the matter? Why all the questions?"

"Robert, I'm afraid I've just heard that our cover will be blown in the Sunday papers. We need a few days to put the PR plan in place."

"We're not really ready, are we?"

"No, we're not, Robert, and of course we're very dependent on political developments but Peter sounds confident that he can deliver that side of it. So I want you to disappear until we get ourselves ready to present you to the world. Can you do that? If you come back to Edinburgh you'll be torn apart in the media scrum."

"Yes, I think so," replied Robert, who was already thinking of a remote holiday cottage on the Douglas Estate.

"OK, keep your head down and I'll keep you informed on progress."

Robert made his way back to Morningside deep in thought. It seemed an impossible dream that he had come this far but now the guerrilla skirmishing with the Hanoverians was over. Everything would be out in the open and he would be at the centre of a public relations war for the hearts and minds of the Scottish people. He was confident that he had already won a kind of place in their hearts but what would their heads make of his final ambition to be their King? And then there was Victoria, and their burgeoning love. Might that be forbidden by the dynastic competition that would make him a traitor to his own side and even more unacceptable to the Hanoverians who would see him as a throne stealer?

He dreaded the prospect of having to tell his family. Thoughts of giving up haunted him, a kind of pre-abdication for the woman he loved and the woman he could not live without. Would she be happy as a professional rugby player's wife? Since meeting Victoria he had dwelt less on the injustices meted out to his ancestors. He rummaged in the Stuart file seeking inspiration but saw only clouds. Not even a vague shade appeared, to comfort him in his dilemma. He felt alone and abandoned.

Chapter 25

Scotland, May 2038 - Loch Lomond

That evening Angela arrived at Peter's Loch Lomond house, at 7:30 p.m. Peter could see the change in her. She was upbeat, on a high and charged up to fight her way out of the impossibly tight corner that they found themselves in as a result of the bombshell that would be dropped in Sunday's press revelations. She already had a first draft of her "Vision for Scotland" paper, which she was due to present in front of the Leader at the Sunday morning session of the Lomond Group. Peter read the document quickly under the steely gaze of his *protégée*.

The paper started with a detailed analysis of Scotland's strengths and weaknesses and went on to propose the transitions and policies required to push an independent Scotland to the top of the international league tables within a generation. It covered all the policy areas but particularly taxation, energy, healthcare and social policy.

Robert's ideas on expanding the charitable and voluntary sectors were shamelessly borrowed and the need for a zero based monarchy outlined without specific mention of the Stuarts. Entrepreneurship was the most frequently used word in the document and the Nationalist drum beaten with a remarkable pledge to take Scotland's seas back from the lunacy of the European Union's Common Fisheries Policy.

While Peter had already discussed individual parts of the document with Angela, he was not quite prepared for the impact of the whole drawn together. It was an epic piece of political thinking, which made him deeply proud of her. He had no doubt that the ideas expressed were a good basis for turning the country round to fulfil its potential. He also had no doubt that its radicalism would be completely unacceptable to the current Party high command.

"This is excellent stuff, Angela. My only thought is that most of these policies are unsupported. Where are you going to get the money from?"

"It's confession time for me now. I've been having secret talks. The English Tories need us to take Scotland independent for them to get a good majority in England. I've got a promise of help and a good transitional payment plan to tide us over," began Angela.

"Angela, I can't believe that you took the risk of speaking to outside politicians."

"That's only the start. I've also had secret talks with the Norwegian Deputy Prime Minister. They feel very lonely, if successful, outside the EU and would like an independent Scotland as a friend and ally. They love my proposal to take our fishing back and would invest here from their Sovereign fund. But most important of all, they'll give us a huge medium term gas contract on favourable terms, until we can get our nuclear policy in place."

"That's exactly what we need. Between them and the EU you should be able to finance the gap, although you might need to sacrifice Sterling for the Euro."

"But you wouldn't believe what the Minister said under his breath and in the strictest of confidence, just as I was leaving. They have a spare Prince. We're welcome to him if we need a king."

"God forbid that we should need him."

"What do you think, then?"

"It's an awesome manifesto, Angela. It should win hearts and heads. I'm very proud of you," he replied, thinking ahead to the meeting with the rest of the Lomond Group.

For him, Angela's analysis and proposals had swept away any remaining doubt that she was ready to lead the Party forward to independence. However, there wasn't a vacancy at the top, so during the weekend ahead, they had to engineer a coup, to remove the existing leadership. It was a daunting prospect for Peter but he now had full confidence in Angela's ability to pull it off.

At 8:30 p.m. Peter received a long communication from Dan Miller, his private pollster. It went into great statistical detail about the opinions of Scots when asked a series of different questions about their attitudes to independence and preferences for different kinds of Head of State.

It stressed how monarchy in Scotland was not seen as culturally defining, in sharp contrast to England. On the straight question of a Scottish Republic vs. the Windsor Monarchy, there was a substantial majority preferring independence under the republican option. Adding in a hypothetical third option, a return to the old Dynasty with a fresh young Stuart monarch, some switching of republicans and wholesale desertion from the Windsors put support for the Stuart option on a par with the republicans. Peter comforted himself with the certainty that

Robert would make the difference and charm many more Scots into their camp, assuring them of victory.

Peter sat back in his chair and breathed a huge sigh of relief that his gut instinct was being backed up by respectable polling data. That evidence would be needed to persuade cynical self-seeking politicians to adopt the Stuart monarchy as the Independence Party's preferred constitutional option for a free Scotland.

****

Next morning, Angela and Peter got down to work with renewed enthusiasm on the detail of "The Vision for Scotland" Paper, for presentation to the Leader the following day, and were finished by the time the Lomond Group returned from their afternoon walk. At dinner Peter announced that he was going to make them work late. He was afraid to move earlier in the day for fear of leaks. When the table was cleared, he began the most important presentation of his life.

He honestly reviewed the details of his role in building the Party including how he acted as a front for the funding from Margaret Baird's legacy, which he had innocently passed off as his own. He told them about eventually meeting the Stuart family and his own thinking on monarchy.

Swallowing hard, he announced that everything he had just summarised was going to be made public the following morning in the press. He stifled all their questions and added the polling data which cast a potential Stuart Monarchy in a favourable electoral light. At the end of the presentation most of the group had got the point but it still seemed finely balanced and theoretical to them.

"But we don't have a king," said one of the exasperated participants.

"Ah yes, but we do, and he is already well known to you," added Peter, switching on a projection of Robert in full Highland dress.

"But that's Robert Lafarge, the rugby captain," gasped one of the female MSPs.

"It's Robert Stuart," replied Peter, to a hushed calculating audience, "he's the head of the Royal Stuart line and one of the most recognised and popular figures in Scotland," said Peter.

"He's fantastic," said the same MSP.

"I'm sure that with him as the candidate for the monarchy, we'll win the election and independence at last," concluded Peter.

There followed a flood of questions about Robert and his background, his authenticity and much more, which Peter dealt with patiently and in great detail before turning to the next part of his agenda.

"But Jim Robertson won't back this; he's a confirmed republican," pointed out one of the group.

"Of course, we understand that, but we're also fairly clear that a much more positive policy agenda is needed to fuel that last heave towards power. That's where Angela's "Vision for Scotland" comes in," replied Peter, inviting Angela to take the floor.

She made it clear that, like many in the gathering, she wanted a new start. Many other parties had done the same in the past. It did not require an entirely different name but the "New" in "New Independence Party" would signal a change. Her second point was her desire to move the Party onto the centre ground of politics, which they had abandoned to other parties. She then went through each new policy area in detail, giving many examples. Her third and final point was hastily updated to take account of Peter's polling data. It was a clear recommendation to re-establish the Stuart monarchy in an independent Scotland.

Peter could see that her colleagues were stunned by the audacity of the presentation and fell silent for a few seconds, before a spontaneous outbreak of applause. There then followed a full hour of question and answer, which seemed to satisfy the doubters.

"Are you with us?" shouted Angela, at the end of the session, raising a fist.

"Aye," replied the group.

"Are you with us tomorrow when we confront Robertson?" she added, looking around them. She could see that most had not thought that far or deep, perhaps fearful of Robertson's notorious republican left wing orthodoxy, and his vicious streak.

"Remember, the basic story about the funding and about Robert Stuart will be in the press tomorrow, so we need to be clear about your support tonight if we are to confront the Leader tomorrow," warned Peter.

"We'll talk to you all individually before midnight," added Angela, looking forward to the tawdry negotiation of the price of political support.

Some gave it freely, emotionally, on the case. Others traded it for promises of office and power, the politician's ultimate commodity. By 12:30 a.m. she had the support of the group without making too many rash promises but had sworn them to secrecy. She then started a long round of external phone calls. At least people should be at home in the middle of the night, she thought.

When she finally got to bed, too tired even to think about Peter, she found an envelope on her pillow. The card inside read:

"There is a tide in the affairs of men,
Which taken at the flood, leads to fortune.
"Your flood-tide cometh, be ye bold."
Love, Peter.

Chapter 26

Scotland, May 2038 - Douglas Estate

Robert had a lacklustre day on the rugby pitch at Galashiels. He normally loved playing there in the small town atmosphere with a good intelligent crowd, but on that day his mind was elsewhere. After a drink with the teams he headed off to the Douglas Estate for his last weekend of freedom. He had asked Victoria to arrange for him to stay in the holiday cottage deep in the woods, away from the main house and prying eyes, who would become aware of his position on Sunday.

As he drove down to the cottage, he felt a curious mixture of elation at the prospect of seeing Victoria and concern about the reaction of her family. On top of that was a gnawing apprehension about the reaction to the following day's press revelations. He felt as though life as he had known it was ending. Tomorrow he would be someone else, a plaything in the hands of history, with little control over the immediate run of events. He was clear about one thing. His feelings for Victoria had crystallised since their last meeting.

The old stone built cottage was no palace, but it was functional. It had two bedrooms, a bathroom and a small kitchen. The rooms were wood-lined and furnished mainly with cast outs from the big house. It had a small garden which had not been cultivated for many years. Only the stubborn stalks of rhubarb stood witness to the gardening skills of an earlier generation of occupants. Victoria and Emily Douglas were already there making dinner. Emily had over-reacted to Robert's impending status by bringing some silver cutlery from the big house. She took Robert's arrival as her cue to leave.

"I've missed you terribly," said Robert taking Victoria in his arms.

"I'm so glad, Robert. You're the man I love, the man I want to marry."

"Oh Victoria, I'm so relieved to hear you say that because I feel the same way."

"Could we call it the Treaty of Douglas Park?"

Over dinner, Robert turned to his immediate concern.

"What about your family, they're never going to accept me are they?"

"I wouldn't say that. Mummy's sitting on the fence. She wants to see how the Scots react to you. But I'm sure that she likes what she's seen so far."

"What about the King and your brother?"

"Daddy doesn't seem to care one way or the other. He thinks the whole idea of Monarchy is well past its sell by date; we're relics he says."

"Your brother? I can't imagine him being very pleased about it."

"Actually, we're very worried about Henry, he's not very stable."

"I know. I was at Gordonstoun with him. Looking back, I would say he was on the autistic spectrum somewhere."

"I agree, but Mummy won't hear that word mentioned, she's in denial."

"How was he as a child?"

"Very withdrawn and clumsy. Other kids seemed a bit scared of him. But he did have strengths. He was good at puzzles and remembering numbers. He had a party piece reciting lists of numbers from the phone book."

"Clumsy, that sums him up on the rugby pitch."

"Henry wants to go for Scotland himself, hoping that he can somehow keep both Scotland and England. Pity the Scots if he made it, is all I would say."

"We'll just have to make sure that he doesn't."

"We need to be ready, Robert. When he finds out about us, I'm sure he'll do crazy desperate things."

"He already has," said Robert who then recounted the details of the spat at Gordonstoun, the kidnapping at Balmoral and the surveillance by the Secret Service.

"Oh, you poor darling," she said, clutching him and pulling him closer. "What did you do?"

"We complained privately to the Home Secretary. The heavy surveillance was called off and we eventually got assurances that the Prince was out of harm's way in an institution," replied Robert.

"I wouldn't put much faith in that. Henry's out now and back with his old cronies from the regiment."

"I'll have to be careful then."

****

Next morning, Robert rose early and switched on the TV news.

The cottage had an ancient free standing TV which still worked well. He was the top story of the day and as he suspected he had become someone else, a construct of the press. Just then, Alex arrived with the Sunday News, much of which was taken up with Piers' long polished article about Robert and the political conspiracy.

Robert read it out loud to Victoria over breakfast. It was an ode to a hero that Robert barely recognised. It portrayed a picture of a latter day saviour, a second coming of a Stuart, but this time there would be no defeat and ignominy, no Culloden cross to be nailed upon, no retreat in women's clothes. Piers had stolen the New Jerusalem from the English and robed it in tartan. Victoria was moved to tears.

"There's a lot to live up to there," said Robert, feeling the burden of expectation descend on him. He thought it was an impossibly heroic pair of shoes to fill.

"You can do it. We'll do it together."

After breakfast they decided to get some fresh air in the woods. Victoria put on a pair of boots loaned by Emily. They set off at a brisk pace, both of them relishing the exercise after the trauma of his exposure in the press. They walked hand in hand through a plantation of conifers, which gave them protection from the blustery wind, laden with the scent of pine resin.

"What will your family think of me?" she asked.

"The big problem for me will be my Uncle Leo. He's very anti-Hanoverian, it's been his motivation since the start. He'll see this as treachery on my part. You'll have to charm him and win him round. Aunt Françoise will think it's very romantic, the stuff of dreams, Robert marrying a beautiful Princess. There won't be a problem with her or my parents."

"Hopefully, I'll meet them all soon," said Victoria as a small family of roe deer crossed the track a hundred yards in front of them, causing them to stop for a moment. Something in Robert almost envied the freedom of the little family to roam at will, until he thought of Alex and the shooters.

In a silent moment when each of them was absorbed in their own thoughts, Robert realised that the anti-Hanoverian obsession, shared with his Uncle Leo, could no longer be the basis of his motivation. He was not above calculation, and wondered what the Scottish people would think of him marrying Victoria in the unlikely event of her parents' approval. He knew that the Princess was personally popular for her down to earth character and lack of stuffiness and people everywhere liked weddings, especially fairy-tale ones, and eventually babies.

The thought of babies wakened him fully with a jolt. Royal babies were not just warm, pink, and cuddly expressions of joyous parenthood. They were strategic symbols of the future, recognised by the State and blessed by its religious institutions. Victoria was a Protestant. Should their children be brought up as Protestants? Was that the answer to the problem that had haunted him for years? Surely the Scots would forgive him his Catholicism for a single generation.

However, that would be yet another slap in the face for his family and supporters. What would the Cardinal think? He resolved not to tell his family about Victoria until he absolutely had to; at least not until he was clear about the signals coming from London.

Chapter 27

Scotland, May 2038 - Loch Lomond

Peter rose early on Sunday morning, desperate to read Piers' article. It was easy to get the paper since one of the small but growing group of journalists already camped outside his house was handing out free copies. He was delighted that the article made little of his funding sins and concentrated on presenting a heroic picture of Robert, all very favourable to their cause. Robert was the story, not the funding, not himself. He could see that the balance of the article would encourage the Lomond Group in their resistance to the orthodoxy of their Leader. His phone began ringing at 6:00 a.m. and he disconnected it and switched off his mobile.

****

Jim Robertson was woken by a phone call at 6:30 a.m. from a newspaper editor. He couldn't believe his ears as the editor ran through the summary of Piers' article. Did the Leader have any comment? The comment was unprintable; Robertson was a resolute leftist republican and the news was anathema to him. He was also deeply personally hurt by what he saw as Peter's duplicity. He would sack Peter for this. He immediately called Peter to find his lines engaged, in fact, off the hook.

Conveniently, he was going to the meeting of the Lomond Group that very morning, so he would deal with Peter there and reassert his authority. As he got out of bed he became aware of a commotion outside his bedroom window, which was just above the street. He looked out to see a gaggle of reporters and cameramen already gathered outside his front door. Going downstairs he noticed that several Sunday papers had been put through his letter box. They were all copies of the same paper with Piers' headline screaming, "Stuarts back Independence Party in bid for Scottish Monarchy."

Robertson was appalled and decided to go to Lomond early to confront Peter. He fought his way through the press scrum outside his door. They were screaming at him for a response to the article and were not willing to stand aside for him until he commented. He realised that he must say something.

"I don't have much to say this morning. However, I can say that this rubbish is not the policy of the Independence Party," he began, holding up the offending newspaper. "It's the work of rogue elements within the Party and they'll be dealt with. That's all I have to say at the moment but I'll probably hold a press conference later tomorrow."

Waving away the barrage of questions that followed he struggled to his car and set off to Lomond. On the way, he called his coterie of key supporters and aides. They reported that Angela Brown had been making nocturnal phone calls seeking support for new policies. Seeing that he might need help, Robertson asked his key aide, Terry Wilkinson, to join him immediately at Lomond. Followed by several press cars, Robertson eventually arrived at Lomond, to be confronted by another media scrum.

Peter's impressive security precautions held the pack back, and he was able to drive through the gates unhindered. The clear preparations, however, added to his unease as he approached the front door. He tried to calm himself for the inevitable confrontation. He was annoyed when a security man at the door asked him his name; he barged past, ignoring the request. The security man was about to tackle Robertson when Peter appeared.

"Jim, I'm glad you've come early," he said, as if Robertson was a close friend.

"What's all this?" asked Robertson, waving the offending newspaper.

"Let's go into the lounge, we'll get peace there."

"Peace, this is a declaration of war, Christie," he shouted.

"Would you like some coffee?" asked Peter, trying to control the enraged Robertson by feeding him something.

"Yes," he shouted, striding into the room as his Party President went into the kitchen to get two cups and the remains of the coffee pot, still warm after breakfast.

"There's some toast here, OK?"

"Yes, yes," replied Robertson impatiently.

Peter began by going through the Margaret Baird story again, citing the need for absolute confidentiality as his reason for not telling anyone, including the Leader. After all, leaders changed quite often, Peter reminded him, and this had been a very long term project. Peter swore that it was only in the last few weeks that he had heard that the Baird story was untrue and that the Stuarts appeared to be the source of the money.

"But what about all this monarchy stuff? Where did that come from?" asked Robertson, a little calmed by the sustenance.

"Well, that gradually grew as we realised that Robert Stuart was such a star and good monarch material; but the key thing, Jim, is that secret polling work is showing that the Independence Party could gain electoral advantage and power from an association with the Stuarts; it seems to be the key to independence."

"Bollocks, the Scots want a republic; I've always believed that. This is completely unacceptable," shouted Robertson.

"Just wait until you see the data before making up your mind."

"I've seen enough, Christie. You're a disgrace to the Party. I'll take your formal resignation now. If I can nip this thing in the bud it won't do too much harm."

"Jim, you're forgetting one or two important facts. First, the money; I'm now putting in the same amount as was coming from the Stuarts so the Party depends on me for funding. Secondly, my terms and conditions are exactly the same as yours; only the Party can sack either of us. You don't have the power to sack me," insisted Peter, who was now clear that war had been declared with the Party old guard. It was a war he was sure he could win with Angela's aces up his sleeve.

"We'll see about that," he answered, cold fury in his eyes.

"I'm certainly not going to resign. Look, Jim, you have every right to be very upset about this. Let it sink in properly, talk with your aides about it and we'll discuss it again. In the meantime, why don't you go to hear Angela's presentation?"

The Lomond Group had fallen into an untypical expectant silence as the Leader, with his chief aide, Terry Wilkinson, at his side, took his place before Angela spoke.

Peter marvelled at the composure of Angela as she let everyone settle down. He had never seen her look so formidably calm and confident. She was wearing a pinstripe trouser suit but not the usual one. This one had wider, bolder stripes set off by a white ruff at her neck. An interesting fashion combination or a subconscious Jacobite symbol, he wondered.

She made an impassioned introduction, which dealt with Scotland's history from the dawn of the Stuarts, speaking impressively without notes. She then projected one slide as the backdrop to her main presentation. The contents were simple; there were only three bullet points on it.

~The New Scottish Independence Party - Policy Highlights for a renewed Party

~A Centre Party devoted to Entrepreneurial Growth in an Independent Scotland

~Restoration of the Stuart Monarchy in Scotland

"Where did this crap come from?" exploded the leader, shouting at Angela, his ears flapping.

"Jim, this is the "Vision for Scotland", the future, this is what you asked for. Let me go through the presentation," pleaded Angela.

"I'm not listening to any more of this rubbish," retorted Robertson, getting to his feet, struggling to pull his trousers up, his ears now fixed down against his skull.

"Don't try to shoot the tiger, ride it for a bit," whispered Terry, to his leader.

"I have a lot of support for this vision," said Angela, leaning forward with her hands on the table, looking threateningly at Robertson.

"From the tenderfoots," laughed Robertson dismissively, at the rest of the Lomond Group round the table.

"Can you ask for an adjournment, a break? We must talk, Jim," whispered Terry to his boss, loud enough so that Angela could hear. "I need to have a private chat with Angela."

"Let's adjourn for ten minutes to let things settle down," announced Peter, who sensed that the moment of crisis was not far off.

Angela, Peter and Terry went out into the garden behind the house, hidden from the press pack at the front and the rest of the group melted away, leaving Robertson alone in the dining room.

****

Terry Wilkinson returned after ten minutes, ashen faced.

"It's not good, Boss. Angela's got strong support for her new agenda. They've also got polling data on a new monarchy. It looks like a winner; maybe we've got it wrong, Boss."

"It's a direct challenge to everything that I stand for, and my leadership; it's intolerable. What do you think we should do, Terry?" asked Robertson, who now realised that Peter and Angela were not merely trying to tweak Party policy. They were conducting a *coup d'état,* to take over the leadership for themselves, consigning him to the scrapheap of political history, just as power seemed to be coming within his grasp. He also didn't like the way Terry was looking at him. He thought he detected a trace of pity, or was it the beginning of doubt and potential disloyalty?

"We need to be careful. Politically there may be something in all this. We might want to cherry pick it for the manifesto. Don't forget we have an election in a few months' time," cautioned Terry.

"Why don't we call an urgent special Party policy conference? We can hang her out to dry there," suggested Robertson.

"And we can put up a motion of no confidence in Peter Christie and get him out as well," added Terry.

"Yes, we can sort the whole thing out at one Party meeting." Robertson was now confident that in the full glare of the Party headlights, Angela's ideas would melt down and drip away into the dust of failed challenges.

His final meeting with Peter was more business-like, if still very cold. To maintain a veneer of unity, it was agreed that they would hold a joint press conference the following day.

****

As Peter watched Angela's car leaving on Sunday night, he was still in awe of her performance over the weekend. He had never seen anything like it in his political life. Its power came with an attached force that pushed deep into his most private thoughts. Angela had blasted a way through to his inner emotions, recently disturbed by news that his wife was being unfaithful to him in France, blowing another hole in his armour. For the first time, he was able to see Angela as more than a political daughter.

He was then struck by a sense of time passing quickly, of missed opportunity, something he would need to redress quickly.

****

At 11:00 a.m. on Monday, Peter and Jim Robertson were sitting behind the microphones in the press room at the Independence Party HQ in Edinburgh. The room was full, something that Peter had never seen. In addition, there was unusual foreign interest with a European and American presence.

The statement was read out by Jim Robertson. It covered Peter Christie's innocent acceptance of the Baird money and the conditions attached to it. It dealt head on with the monarchy issue by saying that the Party was not yet ready with constitutional proposals for an independent Scotland but that these would be discussed at a special policy conference to be held the following week. It was brief and simple. The questions that followed from the journalists were not those that they expected.

"Where are you hiding Robert Stuart?" was the first question, to Robertson.

"Robert Stuart has no connection with the Independence Party. I can clarify that I have never even met him."

"Has Peter Christie ever met Robert Stuart?" was the predictable next question.

"Yes, I've met him a few times socially."

"Is Peter Christie going to resign over this?" was the following question.

"No, I am not going to resign. My future is in the hands of the Party."

"Would you accept Robert Stuart's girlfriend as Queen?" asked a naïve American reporter. This question was so outrageous that it gave Robertson the perfect pretext for closing the session.

"I think some of you would rather be at a Stuart press conference, so I'm going to finish this now. I look forward to seeing you all next week after our policy conference."

****

That evening, Peter asked Angela to come to his suite at the Balmoral. Having wasted so much time ignoring Angela, he now couldn't stop thinking about her. He was fully aware of her feelings from his own dispassionate observation as well as the nods and winks of others. He now understood his own feelings, blunted by years of artistic abuse, rescued from the brink of oblivion by Angela's obvious love for him.

"Angela, we need to have a serious talk about our situation."

"I'm listening."

"This isn't Hollywood crap, Angela, I'm serious. I think that we've been in love for a long time, it's just that I didn't realise it. I was blocking it out," he said taking her hand.

"Well, I haven't been making any great secret of it," she replied, slipping into his arms and kissing him on the lips for the first time.

"You don't think I'm too old, do you?"

"Don't be silly, Peter. Of course, you're not too old."

"I've spoken to Astride and we've agreed a formal separation. She has someone else in France and apart from visits to the dentist, I don't think we'll see much of her here, so the way's clear for us."

"Peter, I'm so glad, I've never been so happy. Did Astride ask for a divorce?"

"Not in so many words, but we'll get around to that later."

"What about your daughters?"

"One is in Hollywood and the other's a model in New York. They seem relaxed about the split. I suppose they see it around them every day. You'll meet them soon; I think you'll all get on."

Peter then took a ring box from his pocket and opened it to reveal a sapphire and diamond ring, the stones improbably and expensively large. He slipped it onto her manicured finger.

"Wear this for me."

Chapter 28

Scotland, May 2038 - Edinburgh

Françoise and Leo arrived from Paris late on Monday morning. They went straight to the offices of Sims Associates, a large Edinburgh PR firm which Bernard had previously worked with, promoting whisky in France. Sir Duncan was already there. The PR firm was delighted to get the work, despite the haste and lack of definition. A senior partner in the firm, Amanda Kennedy, had been allocated full time to the project, which could call on other detailed resources within the firm as necessary. The firm had managed to clear a fairly large room for them, with the necessary number of desks, phones and a conference table in the middle. Françoise handed over a large bag of photographs and video footage of Robert taken throughout his life. Françoise explained that Robert's parents were unable to help. Andre had a big business to run and Simone had her family to look after. Amanda immediately delivered these to the photo section of the agency. Over a sandwich lunch they got down to work immediately.

Leo was soon bored by the discussion that ranged from exactly how Robert should be addressed to what he should wear at the forthcoming press conference. He was amused when part way through the proceedings Amanda asked incredulously,

"Did someone plan all this?"

Late in the afternoon, he telephoned Robert to tell him to come to the Sims' office the following morning; they would be ready for him.

****

The following morning, Alex and Emily Douglas woke to find several press cars parked on their land outside the front gates. By 8:00 a.m. the press pack had swollen to completely block the entrance to the estate. The word was out. Someone somewhere had talked, but exactly what had been said and how much of the secret revealed, they did not know.

Emily immediately phoned the police, who arrived within ten minutes and got the press and other onlookers to back off, setting up tapes to control the crowd in the interests of public safety. The car arrived to collect Robert an hour later. Knowing that Robert was deep in the country they had sent a big estate car with Birnie glowering from the front passenger seat and an additional driver in the rear who was to take Robert's car back separately. The vehicle was ushered round to the back of the house out of sight of the pack to be met by Alex and Emily. Alex Douglas led them down the track to the holiday cottage in the woods, in his Land Rover.

Meanwhile, back at the estate entrance, some of the press were getting desperate and one vehicle shot forward through the police tape and down the drive towards the big house. Seeing no vehicle behind the house it carried on down the road, which led to the woods, hotly pursued by a police Land Rover with its siren going. Alerted by the noise, Douglas, thinking quickly, bundled Robert into the back of the estate car and ordered the driver to follow the track further into the woods. Douglas followed them in his vehicle to a gate on the edge of the woods. He leapt out and unlocked the gate, opened it and waved the estate car through, handing the driver an estate map through the open window. As Douglas was locking the gate behind the estate car, the press car drew up behind him, the driver punching the steering wheel in frustration as Robert's car roared up the track through the open moor.

"Who was in that car?" he shouted at a deaf Douglas.

****

In a little over an hour, Robert was delivered to the Sims' office without being recognised. He was wearing a waxed jacket with the hood up. Amanda and Françoise were there. Leo had volunteered to go out to get a list of Edinburgh sites with Stuart connections.

Amanda welcomed Prince Robert to Sims, gushing a bit nervously about his rugby performances. He kissed his great aunt on both cheeks, delighted by her reassuring presence at the centre of things.

"I am going to call you Prince Robert, you must get used to hearing that, OK?"

"So what's been organised so far?" asked Robert, who was relishing the action after so much waiting.

"We're overwhelmed by the level of press interest."

"What's the venue for the press conference?" asked Robert.

"The press room here's far too small. It's going to have to be held in one of the big hotels; we're working on that."

"What preparation do I need to do?"

"I've already seen you on TV being interviewed after rugby matches, and you have a good natural style. This sort of conference is different. The cameras are much further away but the questions are likely to be much nastier."

"Should we rehearse the nasty questions then?"

"Well, Françoise has already answered a list of difficult questions about the Stuarts, but there will be questions that only you can answer," she said, giving the Prince a knowing look.

"I can imagine, like *how did I lose my virginity*?" he said.

"I don't think they'll go that far, but you are in the right direction," Amanda said, nodding. They then set to work on how he should answer almost any conceivable question on girls, girlfriends, potential Queens, children. Later, they got to the key messages that he wanted to get over. Robert was thrilled by the sense of action that Amanda was creating and was looking forward to his first public performance off the rugby field.

****

After lunch, Françoise took a call. She was astonished to hear the plummy tones of Sir Humphrey introducing himself.

"Mrs. Stuart, we've not met. I'm Sir Humphrey Grey, the King's private secretary. Are you enjoying your stay in Edinburgh?"

"Yes, Sir Humphrey," she answered in a welter of confusion.

"I'd like to invite you and your husband to come down to London for an urgent meeting with me."

"What about?"

"I can't say on the phone," replied Sir Humphrey haughtily, "but I can assure you that it's very much in your side's interest that you attend. How about Friday around 2:30 p.m.?"

"Yes, we could manage that."

"Very well, and please Mrs. Stuart, could you keep this strictly confidential at this stage. Nobody else needs to know, do they?"

****

Robert was almost blinded by the camera flashes when he stepped onto the stage for his first press conference. He felt a surge of adrenalin that exceeded anything he had experienced running onto a rugby field, and very comfortable in the smart cool casual clothes that Amanda had insisted on. To his left and right giant screens projected details from his own life, including his rugby triumphs and that of the early Stuarts in Scotland.

He was astonished at the press turnout, much of it foreign, which packed the seating in front of the stage with a large bank of TV cameras at the back. He sensed a tension in the room that reflected the extra interest in the unusual and historic situation that he was in. As he took his seat between Sir Duncan and Amanda at the table covered with Royal Stuart tartan-edged fabric, he spotted a worried looking Leo and a radiant Françoise in the front row. He held her energising gaze until Amanda began the conference by welcoming everyone, then going through the basics of Robert's life and the Stuart claim to the throne of Scotland. Robert could sense the impatience in the room as Amanda reviewed the already well-known story. He knew that they wanted to hear from him.

Amanda then invited questions. The first few were polite and respectful. The next was trickier.

"The Prince has been brought up as a Catholic. Does he see that causing any problems for him?" asked a reporter, who represented one of the tiny religious magazines.

"I'm glad that you've asked that question. My view on that is quite simple," said Robert. "A king has to represent all his subjects, of whatever religious persuasion, and the majority who probably have none. For me, religion will be a private matter separate from potential duties as King."

"Does that mean that you, as King, would not become the head of the Church of Scotland, as the current UK Monarch is the head of the Church of England?" asked the same reporter.

"Exactly so," said Robert. "I would not wish to be the head of any church. It seems to me that church authorities should head their own denominations."

"If you become King, one of your prime duties will be to provide an heir. What will the religion of your children be?" he persisted.

Amanda expressed impatience with the question but Robert raised his hand slightly to calm her.

"That is a very important question. However, a responsible father would want to discuss that question with the child's mother before replying." The hacks allowed themselves a smile at the expense of the questioner.

"Does the Prince believe in the divine right of Kings?" asked a young American reporter. Most of the local hacks yawned.

"The historically minded among you will know that this question caused several of my ancestors to lose their jobs and even their heads. I see modern monarchy as constitutional with its powers carefully prescribed by Parliament."

"So following that up, what would you actually do as king?" asked a reporter, from a Glasgow newspaper thought to be hostile to Independence.

"Broadly speaking, I see a modern king as having three roles. The first is to operate as Head of State, welcoming appropriate visitors to our country and playing a constitutional role in Parliament. Secondly, there is a lot of charitable work to lead, especially if the State decides to delegate more work in the social field to voluntary agencies. Thirdly, the Monarch would be the focus for what I hope will be a Scottish Honours System. Parliament will decide on the correct model for our country," replied Robert.

"You have a girlfriend, Tina, who seems to have disappeared. Is she going to be Queen?" asked a Dutch reporter. Amanda nodded to Robert. She would take this one.

"I must stress that Tina was Robert's fitness trainer, not his girlfriend. I hope that answers your question."

It was time for the planted question from a friendly Edinburgh reporter.

"When did Prince Robert realise he wanted to be king?" he asked. Amanda nodded at Robert.

"When I was eighteen, I visited Culloden and stood on the spot where Prince Charles Edward Stuart ordered the Highlanders to charge against the Hanoverian forces. I was overwhelmed by the tragedy of that day and pledged myself to reverse that defeat, if the people of a free Scotland wish it. Beyond that, it will be my mission to be a people's king, not a remote figure in a palace, but someone who can make a difference to people's lives in a country that has given so much to the world but perhaps neglected itself for too long."

"Well, I think that was a very fitting closing remark for this conference," said Amanda.

"I would like to say one more thing. If the Scots vote for independence then I will ask them to vote for me in a separate plebiscite. I want to be a democratic monarch in keeping with the times," said Robert, completely off script.

The conference then closed to spontaneous applause, an unprecedented gesture from cynical hacks.

****

The following day, Sir Duncan called a meeting to review all the press coverage between the publication of Piers' article and Robert's press conference. It was attended by Amanda, Françoise, Sir Duncan and Robert, in the Sim's office. There was a long agenda.

"OK, let's look at the main press coverage. Amanda, give us a summary, please," said Sir Duncan.

"Well, the first thing to say is that there doesn't appear to be any backlash from the Party funding irregularity. There have been so many scandals about Party funding that the public doesn't really care. There will be a parliamentary enquiry that may slap wrists but we're not seen as being at the centre of some evil conspiracy."

"On the political front I can report that Peter and Angela have launched their coup and have everything staked on a special policy conference taking place next week. So far so good, especially since the latest polling data looks encouraging," added Sir Duncan.

"There's a rather funny article in The Times comparing Robert with Jim Robertson, leader of the Independents, as potential Heads of State. Robert scores well and the cartoon of Robertson as an elephant rampaging around doesn't do him any favours. There are lots of articles on Robert himself, his background, his rugby career and his thoughtful presentation at his press conference. All very positive," said Amanda.

"Anything negative?" asked Sir Duncan.

"Yes, we've seen quite a few articles about the history of the Stuart Monarchs. They come over as pretty despotic and arrogant, underpinned by the so called evil tyranny of Catholicism. I do believe that religion is still a problem for Robert," said Françoise.

"I'm very conscious of that myself. I'm thinking about what to do," replied Robert.

"We've got to vigorously promote Robert the man, not Robert the Catholic," said Amanda.

"Any lighter contributions?" asked Sir Duncan.

"Well, we have a quote from a German newspaper that the King of Bavaria is furious and is going to mount some kind of legal challenge. He thought that he was the inheritor of the Stuart claim to kingship," said Robert.

"We'll deal with the Bavarian King if he dares to enter the race," replied Sir Duncan.

"I was very amused to see that one of the channels is planning a mock reality TV contest between the houses of Stuart and Windsor. The Scottish public, voting directly by telephone, will select the winning house. That should be fun and stoke up interest at the same time," said Amanda.

"Can you try to find out how that's being organised? We need to be sure that we have at least a level playing field," replied Sir Duncan.

"There is one more thing I should raise. Tina, from the club, the girl who was mentioned in the newspapers as my girlfriend, she's disappeared. She didn't come to work on Monday and she's not at her flat or answering her mobile. The Police have been told but they're not treating it as suspicious at this stage."

"I'm sorry to ask you this, but is there any baggage there, any kiss and tell potential?"

"Not really, we enjoy playing squash together and walking in the hills. She's more of a mate than anything else, but I am worried about her."

While Robert could publicly declare his concern over Tina's disappearance, he could not share his nervousness about the new woman in his life and the strength of his feelings for her. He couldn't imagine the new relationship surviving the antipathy between the rival camps. He was also getting nervous about the silence from London. Victoria had still not got a response from her parents.

Chapter 29

England, May 2038 - London, Buckingham Palace

At the Buckingham Palace complex in London on Friday, Leo and Françoise arrived promptly at 2:30 p.m. for their meeting with Sir Humphrey. The Palace complex was no longer a residence. A small part was used as offices for the Royals, while the rest was a vast museum. They were shown into the private secretary's large office, where Sir Humphrey was waiting for them. After civil introductions he motioned them to sit on easy chairs surrounding a low table.

"Is all this a museum now?" asked Leo.

"It has been for the last ten years, but this firm is still very much in business. Monarchy evolves like everything else, survival of the fittest as Darwin put it. I needn't say anymore, need I?"

"Yes, but species can make a comeback when the environment improves for them," answered Leo waspishly.

"You must be wondering why I called you here today. As you would have expected, we challenged the legitimacy of your claim to the Scottish throne and you appear to have weathered that storm. I congratulate you on your skill in handling all that. However, looking forward there might be an opportunity for us to form a collaboration that removes the competition between the families."

"What do you mean?" asked Leo.

"Would you come with me now, please?" requested Sir Humphrey. Françoise looked at Leo and they both stood up. Sir Humphrey was at the door and opening it as Françoise and Leo came forward.

"Not you, Mr Stuart. Please wait in the conference room next door."

Sir Humphrey then led Françoise down a long corridor and ushered her into an elegant sitting room full of antique furniture. The walls were covered with royal portraits, mainly of women.

"Mrs. Stuart, ma'am," said Sir Humphrey, in his plummiest voice. Françoise instantly recognised the side view of the Queen, looking out of the window over a garden.

"Do you like camellias, Mrs. Stuart?" she asked, turning towards Françoise and giving her a tired smile. Françoise was pleased not to be hit with a fresh unhelpful revelation at the opening of the conversation with the Queen, but confused by its direction.

"Yes, I do very much but our *Manoir* in France sits on solid chalk so we can't really grow them very well."

"You need to put them in pots, Mrs. Stuart. I love camellias, such wonderful flowers, and they do so brighten up the end of winter," she said, turning towards her again and walking slowly over towards her. "Did you marry for love, Mrs. Stuart?"

"Yes, of course, I was very fortunate," stammered Françoise, remembering her first sight of Leo, on the tennis court in London and at last sensing something of a direction in the Queen's tack.

"So did I," confided the Queen, "fortunately, my husband wasn't forced into an arranged marriage. We've been very happy together. Do you know who these women are?" she asked, turning to two female portraits on the wall.

"No," replied Françoise, lost in the royal meanderings.

"It doesn't matter who they were really. They were both Queens, beneficiaries and victims of loveless arranged marriages," she said, turning back towards Françoise. "They were deeply unhappy women," she added, a little venom creeping into her voice.

"They don't look very happy, but why does that matter today?"

"Yes, Mrs. Stuart that does bring me to the point. Princess Victoria is deeply in love with your Robert Stuart."

"Have they been seeing each other?" asked Françoise in a tone of shocked disbelief. She felt herself flushing with acute embarrassment at the news.

"They met through the rugby and were seeing each other discreetly before the news of Robert's true identity broke. It hasn't been going on for very long. It was love at first sight, apparently. Isn't that romantic, Mrs. Stuart?

"I thought he already had a girlfriend. I don't know her but she's been mentioned in the papers."

"They're so much in love, Victoria and Robert. They would make a wonderful royal couple as Queen and King of Scotland, don't you think?" asked the Queen, ignoring Françoise's reply.

"So, you want an arranged marriage?" Françoise, felt faint as the implications sunk in. She was torn between branding Robert a traitor to the cause and screaming for joy at such a romantic outcome.

"An arranged love marriage; love is the key word Mrs. Stuart, as we've been saying, something that the ladies on the wall did not enjoy. It would be good for your side, too, Mrs. Stuart. It would end all the competition that's going on and settle everyone down again."

"I see exactly what you mean," replied Françoise, still struggling to cope with the enormity of the proposal.

"Think about it and talk to Robert, he'll have to agree, of course."

"Does your daughter want this?

"With all her heart. That's why we're here, Mrs. Stuart."

"It's not something that our side ever contemplated," replied Françoise, who could only imagine what Leo's response would be.

"Good, excellent progress, I look forward to your reply. Let's sit down now and I'll tell you how to pot a camellia, and we'll have a glass of something, shall we? It's thirsty work arranging marriages, is it not Mrs. Stuart? And I must ask if you play tennis?"

****

Leo sat fretting in the small conference room beside Sir Humphrey's office. It was worse than a dentist's waiting room or a surgeon's consulting room because of the complete uncertainty. What were they playing at, dividing him from his wife? As the time of his enforced wait lengthened to half an hour he could stand it no longer and went out into the corridor, just as Sir Humphrey reappeared with Françoise.

"I'm so sorry that you had to be separated like that. The Queen insisted that it was women's work. I trust we are all on the same side now?"

"Yes, but whose side?" answered Françoise, a little bitterly.

"Can you deliver?" asked Sir Humphrey, looking at her more impatiently.

"Deliver what?" asked Leo. His wife put her hand on Leo's arm to calm him.

"I'll do my best."

"Please feel free to use the conference room for a few minutes if you want to discuss it. I'll be next door if you have any questions."

"What's going on, Françoise? I've never felt so naked in my life."

"I was taken to see the Queen. According to her, Robert and Princess Victoria have been seeing each other secretly and are in

145

love."

"Robert in love with a Hanoverian Princess? I don't believe it."

"It's worse than that Leo, the Queen is proposing that they get married."

"Marry the enemy, that's ridiculous. I can't accept this."

Leo turned pale as an earthquake shook the carefully constructed anti-Hanoverian mountain, from the top of which he viewed the world. He was plunged into a depressive flurry, where the collective imagery of his list of grudges and hates wheeled behind his eyes, inducing a kind of stupor, like a thick alcoholic haze without the headache.

"Robert has some explaining to do. Let's get back to Edinburgh to confront him. I'll just have time tonight. And Leo, it might be easier all around if I see Robert alone about this. I don't think you would handle it very well." Leo did not reply.

****

Back in Edinburgh, Françoise arrived at Robert's in a taxi at 7:30 p.m. He had just come back from training and his hair was still wet. It had been something of an ordeal. All the publicity had made it difficult for him to behave as he used to. He was getting a lot of stares and occasional comments from people, mainly encouraging but occasionally negative. And then there were the photographers who became increasingly intrusive. Birnie had come into his own as his shield against this less pleasant aspect of his new found fame.

"Aunt Françoise, come in, what a wonderful surprise," he said, kissing her on both cheeks, genuinely pleased to see her, but at the same time, wondering why she was visiting him without warning. He sensed her slightly cool approach to him, as though she was prepared to scold a child.

"Robert, I'll come straight to the point. I've just come back from Buckingham Palace. You can imagine my surprise and embarrassment when the Queen told me about you and Princess Victoria. Can it be true?"

"Yes, I've been seeing Victoria. We met through rugby and she invited me to Holyrood Palace and then to country house weekends," he replied, guilt welling up in him and yet he was glad that it was out in the open.

"But, didn't you realise the danger to our cause or think of the impact on your family, especially your Uncle Leo? Can you imagine

146

what he's thinking?"

"That's the thing that troubles me most. I feel terribly guilty. Uncle Leo's simple world of good Stuarts and bad Hanoverians is being turned upside down and he'll see me as a traitor."

"That's exactly how he sees you."

"At first, I was fascinated by the idea of getting close to the enemy, getting into their heads, but it didn't stop there, it got out of control very quickly and we fell in love."

"Anyway, it appears that she's besotted with you. Not only that, the Queen's proposing that the two of you get married."

"Married! Did she propose that? I can hardly believe it. I never thought that would be possible. I thought that they would forbid it." Robert's heart sang at the prospect.

"The Hanoverians aren't stupid and they're pragmatic. Although the Queen sold the whole thing on a powerful love match, they can see that they're losing the battle for Scotland. You could see it as a cynical calculation. Having a Hanoverian Queen of Scotland is better than nothing and the love affair is the icing on the cake."

"Yes, I've been through the calculations myself and can see advantages to our side as well. But really Françoise, I'm very sorry that you had to hear about this from the Queen. I saw little point in telling you about the affair because I genuinely thought it would end when they found out who I was. I'm still waiting to hear from Victoria. The Queen hasn't given her an answer yet."

"So, how would you feel about marrying Victoria?"

"I love Victoria and do want to marry her. I can't see that it damages our cause; in fact there could be advantages for us as well. Hopefully, Uncle Leo will get over any sense of betrayal and fall in behind what's best in the new situation."

"While we're still on the subject of your love life…any more news about Tina, the girlfriend from the newspapers?"

"As I said at our meeting, the newspapers have exaggerated all that, I've only seen her a few times and anyway she seems to have disappeared. I tried to contact her again, but she's not at her flat and her mobile's dead. She's not turning up for work at the club either, so I don't know what's happened to her."

"It's very odd that she should go without contacting you. I hope nothing bad has happened to her. You do need to have Tina inside the fence, under control. We don't want any loose cannons firing kiss and tell stories, do we?"

"So, do I have your blessing at least, Aunt Françoise?"

"Robert, it's the most romantic thing I've ever heard of. Of course, you have my blessing, but I can't say the same for your Uncle Leo."

****

After Françoise left, Robert phoned Victoria to confirm the manoeuvrings of their elders and repeat his delight at the turn of events. They were desperate to see each other and Victoria agreed to come up to Edinburgh. She agreed to arrange a secret meeting for them in the apartments on the top floor of Holyrood Palace.

****

The next afternoon, Robert's team assembled in the oasis of Sir Duncan's New Town flat. There was a profound sense of occasion, a sense of creating history, depending on which way they jumped in the Hanoverian love affair.

Françoise began by describing in detail the events of the previous day at Buckingham Palace, although all those present had been made aware of the basic facts the night before. Sir Duncan then turned to Leo and invited him to start the discussion. Leo declined, stating that he wished to hear the others first, especially Sir Duncan.

"Part of me says "tell them to f.... off," but we need to be practical. I think it's good for us. It gives Robert more credibility and lifts him into a different bracket as a candidate for monarchy. Added to that, the public has an endless appetite for glitzy royal weddings; a wedding correctly timed would greatly boost our chances. I see this development as entirely positive for us. I support Robert in accepting the proposal," said Sir Duncan, nailing his colours to the mast.

"What do you think, Françoise?"

"For me it's very simple. If there are no negatives in the proposal then we should let it take its course. We're talking about two young people in love, who want to marry and I'm sure that Robert will do a far better job if he is married to the woman he loves."

All eyes then turned on Leo who had listened to the contributions with a gloomy expression that said it all.

"Calculated pragmatism and love; strange bedfellows, aren't they?" he began, with his arms splayed out on the table and his head low, looking down. "You all know where I stand. I'm not going to trade it for a mess of potage called a Hanoverian marriage, even if it did improve our chances. Were we not confident that Robert could succeed anyway on his own merits?" asked Leo, sitting up straight and looking round them, daring anyone to challenge his entrenched position.

"This is all very difficult for Leo," said Françoise, putting her hand on his arm.

"Well, can we all at least agree to let the PR people have a go at the issue? I know that you disapprove of our calculation Leo, but we have to operate in the real world," said Sir Duncan, playing for time.

"Who's real world? I've had enough of this, I'm going back to Paris," he announced, standing up and storming out of the room.

"There's only one person in the world that can pull Leo out of this," said Françoise quietly to Sir Duncan, as they were leaving.

Robert hung his head in shame at the realisation that he had driven away the man who had given so much of his life for him. However, a more pragmatic ruthless streak within him urged him to press on without the man who had for so long been indispensable, but was no longer.

Chapter 30

France, June 2038 - Paris

Leo crossed the Seine to have dinner with the Cardinal. It was almost twenty years since their first discussion of the Stuart Agenda in the left bank apartment. Leo was delighted to get the call. It pulled him out of the pit of despair that he had sunk into since walking out on the team in Edinburgh. He was unprepared for the impact of being separated from Françoise. He felt desperately lonely, a feeling made worse by the throngs of couples strolling around savouring the eternal sensuality of Paris. The Stuart Agenda had made enormous progress since his first meeting there with the Cardinal, but Robert's desire to marry the Hanoverian Princess had turned him inside out, an insult to the memory of his brother killed by the British.

The Cardinal was already in the tiny vaulted private dining room of the restaurant near the apartment. He was in mufti this time, showing a tell-tale strip of white neck normally encased in a clerical collar.

"You've made such wonderful progress since our last meeting on the left bank, Leo."

"Yes, but the very recent progress appears to have a very high price tag, at least for me."

"Françoise has told me. It seems you're at a difficult crossroads with Robert. I don't have any sons, Leo, but I feel that after everything that's happened, I have a tiny little share in Robert. Can you understand that Leo, and forgive me for poking my nose in?" said the Cardinal, as the waiter arrived with the menus.

"Of course, Cardinal, I appreciate your interest."

"You know, Leo, history is full of examples where yesterday's enemy is tomorrow's friend or even in-law, as in your case. New alliances are struck up that meet the needs of the day. It is a kind of pragmatism, but pragmatism isn't a sin. Call it enlightened self-interest, and it makes the world go round."

"Cardinal, this isn't the whole story. All these years ago when we last had dinner in the apartment, I kept a very important detail from you. I didn't tell you that the British Secret Service had killed my brother. David's murder has driven me ever since. I just can't let go," replied Leo, exposing his inner keep, his last place of refuge from which he would never be moved.

"Leo, I'm not sure that there's any truth in that. I don't think the Brits killed your brother. Who told you that anyway?" asked the Cardinal.

"It was Hervé Dubois, the French Minister of Justice," replied Leo, who felt his stomach tense at the sudden realisation that the Cardinal himself might not have been a neutral player.

"Have you ever considered the possibility that Hervé might have been setting you up, Leo, motivating you to take up the anti-Hanoverian cause seriously?"

"Set up, but why?" demanded Leo, as he faced the loneliness of separation from his faithful long term companion, the burning memory of his murdered brother. "Are you telling me that you were part of it?" he added.

"A very minor role. But if you remember, all I did was support what you clearly wanted to do anyway, although I'm ashamed of the subterfuge but delighted at the result," replied the Cardinal.

"So, can you tell me where the early funding actually came from? I had to meet a man called Albert Delavarenne in Brussels. It was made to look as though he was from an agency within the European Union but he looked more like a policeman than a bureaucrat to me. Who was he really working for?" pressed Leo, now that he had the Cardinal in confessional mode.

"I doubt if it was the European Union; I assumed it was Hervé Dubois but I was never told who was behind it. I didn't need to know but I believe that the hard cash came from England."

"England! Why England?"

"I don't know. Who had a motive? Who would have hated the Hanoverians enough? Perhaps we'll never know."

****

On the way home, Leo was relieved that the Cardinal had given him a credible way back to Robert's side in Edinburgh. However, he still struggled, as he had done many times before, with the puzzle of the magnanimous donor who had kick-started the funding of the Stuart Agenda. He vividly remembered his first meeting with the slightly sinister Albert Delavarenne in Brussels.

It was Armistice Day and he had travelled by train through

151

northern France, through the First World War battlefields where so many lions were slaughtered to satisfy the donkeys of Empire. Crossing the muddy Somme, he had the same eerie feeling that he experienced at Culloden. The sights of the First World War always depressed Leo and he was in sombre mood when he met Albert.

The Cardinal confirmed his suspicion that Albert couldn't have been representing the European Union and was pointing the finger at Hervé Dubois.

****

Next morning, Françoise arrived at the Sims' office at 9:00 a.m. feeling immensely relieved that Leo's wobble had been corrected and that he was on his way back from Paris. Everyone was now agreed that the marriage should go ahead. Amanda was already hard at work, but Françoise realised that she needed to be put in the picture about the Prince and Victoria immediately, because there was a vast PR problem looming. She quickly updated Amanda on the details of Robert's romance with Victoria and her meeting with the Queen.

"Crafty devils, they can't hang onto the crown, but a Hanoverian Queen is next best thing," was Amanda's response.

"Yes, all the cynics are saying that, but from our side it's a done deal," said Françoise, with finality

"What happens now?"

"I'm about to phone Sir Humphrey Grey, the King's Private Secretary to confirm our commitment. Is there anything else I should be asking him for?"

"This will be a PR nightmare for us. We have a girlfriend switch and a possible engagement to a Princess from the enemy camp. We'll need one of their PR people in this office, someone who can speak for them. On the other hand they may want to do it all from London but that would be a disaster."

Françoise felt confident as she called London from the Sims' office.

"Good morning, Sir Humphrey, how are things in London?"

"Hanging on your reply, which I trust you are about to give me?

"I can deliver the deal as we discussed," she said coming directly to the point.

"Splendid, Mrs. Stuart, and how wonderful. I'm so glad, and I know that the Royal Family will be thrilled as well," he added rather formally, keeping a fig leaf of security on the telephone conversation.

"So, what happens now?"

"You'll get a letter tomorrow detailing all that," he replied appearing to enjoy the subterfuge.

The following day the letter arrived in the morning by special royal courier, a service that Françoise did not know existed. Its contents were simple. Robert and the rest of the Stuart family were invited to Balmoral the following weekend, accompanied by any appropriate staff. By royal command, strict confidentiality was to be maintained, and the party was to be flown in by helicopter to help keep the visit private. Françoise was ecstatic, Leo grudging, about visiting the "lions in their holiday den," as he put it.

Chapter 31

Scotland, June 2038 - The Trossachs

The Independence Party Special Policy Conference was held in a large hotel in the Trossachs, an area of outstanding natural beauty to which most of the delegates were entirely oblivious. The first debate concerned the no confidence motion against Peter. A Robertson mouthpiece led the case against Peter for bringing the Party into disrepute over the funding scandal. Peter defended himself from the podium. He declared himself to be innocent in the deception; he had been instrumental in rebuilding the Party and anyway, the monarchy issue was turning out to be a pure vote winner, perhaps the key to power.

Peter knew that the leadership had badly miscalculated in trying to sack him. They lacked the long term perspective and objectivity to understand Peter's vital role in the Party. He knew that he was regarded as the father of the Party by the generation of young politicians that he had mentored, and by all as the fairy godfather of the Party for the largesse that he bestowed. He survived the vote easily.

Repelling the attack on Peter made the radicals led by Angela stronger, and the leadership weaker and vulnerable to counterattack. The victory set Peter up to undertake his most important task at the conference. This was now to rid the party of Robertson, paving the way for the accession of Angela, his most prized *protégée* and all that flowed from her restless political brain.

The following sessions were all concerned with policy, the eternal struggle between left and right. Angela and her supporters went through their list of new policies to contrast with the same old stuff sponsored by the leadership. In the voting, many of Angela's radical policies were formally accepted by the conference delegates, but the leadership, which had voted against them, would still have to approve them before they became Party policy.

Peter lobbied hard in the bars and even in private rooms to get the number of signatures needed to back a motion of no confidence in the Leader. It was all or nothing, and he ended up making some promises to individuals that he prayed the next Leader would honour. The requisite number of signatures gathered, Peter approached the chairman of the Agenda Forming Committee, demanding an emergency debate on a motion of no confidence in the Leader. Robertson was furious and tried to refuse on a procedural technicality. Peter then met Terry Wilkinson, Robertson's principal aide, privately.

"Terry, you need to know that if the motion of no confidence in Robertson isn't put to the conference, the radicals intend to leave to form a new party."

"I've already got wind of that from Angela."

"Robertson trusts your judgement, Terry. Can't you persuade him that the game's up? He needs to face reality."

"All political careers end in failure. Robertson knows that and he senses power slipping away from him. He's had visits from a few men in suits. Perhaps you could sweeten the pill. What could you offer him?"

"What does he want? We don't have much patronage up our sleeves yet, but the sky's the limit once we're in power."

"He knows that and he's prepared to be patient. He'll resign at the end of the conference, without a motion, if you promise him a Scottish peerage and a well-paid job running a Quango."

"I'm sure that we can do a deal on that," replied Peter, delighted.

Rumours began to circulate immediately and from that point in the conference, the policy debates were effectively controlled by Angela who got the overwhelming support of the delegates.

The final motion at the conference concerned the monarchy issue. One of Angela's colleagues in the Lomond Group argued that the proposal to place the Stuart Monarchy on the throne after independence should be written into the manifesto for the next election. It appeared to be an election winner from the polling data. There was a strong objection from the small republican extremist group whose mantra was, "a plague on all royal houses." Peter spoke at the end of the debate. He reminded them that an effective monarchy had to be above politics, and separate from the Party. He also reminded them that at his press conference the previous week Robert had stated clearly that he wanted the direct personal endorsement of the Scottish people. Peter's intervention swung most of the conference behind a compromise motion to give the Scottish people a choice about which constitutional option they favoured.

The final speech of the conference was made by Angela. It was not very long, but passionate about the need to reposition the Party and its policies and give the Scottish people the choice of constitution they wanted, a late change in her final draft. It was a leadership bid speech and nobody was in any doubt about that. The vote after her speech was on the proposal to change the Party name to New Independents. The motion was overwhelmingly carried. The Leader was dead, long live the Leader.

At the end of the proceedings, Peter, in his role as Party Chairman, announced that the leadership election would take place in two weeks' time, a shorter time than normal because of the proximity to the next general election. Huddles of delegates quickly began to form lists and quote odds; Angela was *odds on*.

That night, Peter held a small party for her in his suite. He was wound up reliving the highlights with his supporters. Amid the euphoria Angela was strangely quiet, suffering the anti-climax that bedevils many high performers after a major achievement. In that condition, more melancholic thoughts gripped her. She was supremely confident about winning the leadership, but was already fearful of the loneliness of high command. As she looked at Peter, he came over and pulled her out of the chair by the hands.

"Come on, Angela, this is your night," he said. At that moment, she silently thanked the French *vigneron* who had provided the key to unlocking Peter for her.

Angela declared her candidacy the following day, with the manifesto which had won the heart of the Party conference. The left wing of the Party also put up a leadership candidate. He was a younger protégé of Robertson, although not as young as Angela. The loony Republicans also put up a candidate as a gesture to keep their obsession in view. Angela won easily in the first round, gaining a sufficient majority to avoid a re-run against the second candidate. She was now Party Leader. Peter was over the moon. His personnel strategy had at last borne fruit after years of work and investment.

Chapter 32

Scotland, June 2038 - Balmoral Castle

On Sunday, the whole Stuart family gathered at Edinburgh heliport beside the main airport. Amanda Kennedy and Sir Duncan were already there. There were two helicopters waiting, and the party divided between them. The journey was noisy and uncomfortable but very scenic, crossing the Firth of Forth with its magnificent bridges and the Firth of Tay before heading into the Highlands across to Braemar. Robert made sure that he was the last to get out of his helicopter, and had a private word with the pilot.

The welcome at Balmoral was genuine if a little restrained. The programme involved lunch, after which there would be an opportunity for Robert to see the King privately. An afternoon walk in the grounds would take them up to departure time at 3:30 p.m.

The Windsor party was minimalist; just the King and Queen, Victoria and Sir Humphrey. Prince Henry, the heir to the throne, was conspicuously absent. This was not yet a family celebration. That would come later if all went well. The Queen and Françoise led the conversation over lunch in the gloomy, antler-heavy room with a magnificent view of the mountains. Victoria was placed well apart from Robert and had not even the opportunity to touch him since his arrival. Leo and the King did manage to talk quite a lot about France, especially the Cote d'Azur, which the King knew well. Amanda sat and studied every nuance of interpersonal dynamics around the table, storing it all up for possible lucrative memoirs far into the future. Sir Humphrey and Sir Duncan talked about the Middle East. Leo and Françoise's daughter, Nicole, had flown over from America especially for the occasion. She gave her end of the table a private lecture on the workings of the human brain, her research area at Harvard.

****

After lunch Robert got a nod from Sir Humphrey and followed the King to his study. Sir Humphrey closed the door behind them and stood guard outside, a faithful sentinel. The King poured two whiskies without consulting Robert and they sat down opposite each other in faded armchairs.

"This isn't easy for me, Robert, giving up part of the Crown but there's little that we can do about the politics. I must say it isn't as great a job as it looks. I'm pretty tired of shaking hands and smiling. I often wish I had a proper job," said the King, with a sigh.

"I hope that I'll be able to carve out a clear role for myself, sir."

"That's what I said, too. Anyway, I will miss Victoria, my only daughter. I suppose she's my favourite when I think about it, but the time comes," he added, looking expectantly at Robert, who took the cue and stood up.

"I would like to ask you formally, sir, for Victoria's hand in marriage," he said rather stiffly.

"I suppose your prospects are reasonable, especially now that the Independence Party has ditched the Republicans. There aren't so many vacancies for Kings these days," he said, indicating that Robert should sit down but without giving him a direct answer to his proposal.

"The Queen tells me that you're both very much in love. That's very important, it's a tough job and you have to stick together as a team."

"I agree, sir," said Robert who was hoping for a more direct answer.

"What kind of monarch are you going to be?"

"Of course, we still have several hurdles to cross yet, but I want to be a people's monarch, so I've insisted on a plebiscite. I need to be sure that I have the full support of the people of Scotland."

"Ah, just like the Danish Prince who was invited to be the first King of Norway when they separated from Sweden."

"Yes, I have read about him."

"What about religion?" asked the King.

"That's tricky, there's no escaping the fact that I'm a Catholic but the world's more secular now. I'm going to make the plea that religion should be a private matter, even for the sovereign."

"I think you might still have a problem. Don't forget that bigots aren't very religious people," said the King with a laugh.

"What if we announce that our children will be brought up as Protestants?"

"I'm sure that would make a difference. What a clever way out. Your religion would only be a temporary problem," replied the King, with obvious enthusiasm.

"I'm glad you agree, sir, but I haven't discussed it with Victoria yet."

"I like the sound of what you'll be trying to do, but do be wary of officials. They'll have their own ideas of what a monarch should be."

"Sir Humphrey seems very efficient."

"Watch out for Sir Humphrey. He'll try to control things from London. He's standing outside the door now, annoyed that he is not in here listening and interfering," replied the King, with frankness that astonished Robert.

"Thanks for the advice, sir."

"Anyway, you have my blessing, Robert," said the King. They both stood up and the King shook Robert's hand warmly. "Look after her well. I suppose that's what all fathers say."

"I'll do my best, sir."

"I suppose you'll stay in Holyrood Palace. Move into one of the upstairs apartments right away, Sir Humphrey can clear that. Then you'll have to get rid of the Palace keeper, he still has an apartment there. I'll leave you to find out about him for yourself. Go and see Victoria now and we can put Sir Humphrey out of his misery."

"Thanks for that, sir."

"One more thing before you go. I see you're still playing rugby. Don't you think you should announce your retirement from the game? You can't really continue, can you?"

"I suppose not, sir. I've been putting off making a decision. I'll announce my retirement after the official engagement," said Robert, trying to disguise the regret in his voice. He did not look forward to cutting himself off from his beloved game.

"Good man, why don't you take up golf?" said the King, steering Robert towards the door.

Sir Humphrey was still guarding the door when Robert left the King's study, intent on finding Victoria. Sir Humphrey looked perplexed as though the meeting had taken far longer than he considered necessary.

Victoria was lurking at the end of the corridor waiting for Robert to emerge. He smiled and nodded to indicate success and took her in his arms and kissed her. Sir Humphrey passed by, but diplomatically ignored them. Robert thought that was odd. Why did the Mandarin not want to be first to congratulate them? Robert then took Victoria by the hand and ran down the stairs with her and out of the front door. He then guided her over the lawn to the field where the helicopters were parked. The pilot of Robert's helicopter started the engine when he saw them leave the house.

"What are we doing, Robert?"

"I'm following your father's advice. Get in," he said, pushing her neat bottom up the few steps into the helicopter. Robert then closed the door and gesticulated to the pilot to take off. The chopper rose and swung round to fly northwest.

"Where are we going?"

"It's a surprise."

They put on the thick hooded anoraks and boots that Robert had left in the helicopter. The Cairngorm mountains looked even more magnificent from the air and the pilot pointed out large herds of red deer in some of the glens. As the land began to slope down, they could see water in the distance. The helicopter descended onto a moor with a biggish town in the middle distance. With the helicopter still technically airborne, Robert jumped down and lifted Victoria down after him.

"Ten minutes!" shouted the pilot, before he took off again. Robert looked around and led Victoria towards a flagpole about a hundred yards away. It was a cold but clear day and he could see the Black Isle very clearly, unlike on his last visit. It was still very early in the tourist season and there were not many people around.

"Do you know where you are?" he asked her, when they had reached their objective.

"Is it Culloden?"

"It was on this spot that I dedicated myself to recovering the crown of Scotland for the Stuarts. I thought it would be nice to propose to you here as well. Will you marry me, Victoria?" His heart pounded as he struggled to prevent the emotion of his previous visit from intruding.

"Robert, I accept with all my heart," she said, throwing herself at him ecstatically.

He took a ring box from his pocket and opened it to reveal a simple gold antique ring set with rubies. He put it on her finger.

"It looks old. Did this belong to who I think it belonged to?"

"Yes, it belonged to Mary Queen of Scots. It's a secret ring, for you to wear when you come up the hidden staircase to see me. We can choose the diamond version back in Edinburgh."

Robert then turned to look at the battlefield and the section of moor running towards the Hanoverian lines. He fell silent and distant from her, wondering how his proposal had been received by the shades of the highlanders buried nearby.

"Robert, it's over, forget about Bonnie Prince Charlie and the Jacobites. That's what this means," she said, lifting her ring finger. "Let's go back," she added, hugging him as they heard the helicopter approaching in the distance.

As he turned to go a strong shaft of sunlight burst through the light clouds, illuminating the Black Isle in the distance across the firth. He took it as a sign of a new beginning. He pledged himself to return again and again to repay the unsettled debt due to the Highlanders who had been so brutally treated in his family's name.

****

Back at Balmoral, the disappearance of the young couple had caused consternation and eventually elicited a polite invitation to the Stuarts to extend their stay for an impromptu afternoon tea with shortbread and cream cakes. The couple arrived back just as tea was finishing, still wearing their anoraks.

When she saw them, Amanda had a brainwave. They needed to leak pictures of the couple together to prepare the public for an eventual formal announcement. As they began to take their anoraks off, Amanda intervened and ushered them outside.

"You don't want photographs of us looking like this do you?" protested Victoria.

"Oh, yes, I do," Amanda insisted, as she got some pictures of them strolling through unidentifiable trees.

"Can I have a kiss now, please?" she called, not sure if she would need the picture, although, it would be the ultimate tabloid scoop.

****

Back in Edinburgh the following morning the Sims' office was a hive of activity. Justin Black, the refugee from Sir Humphrey's press office in London, was having coffee. He had taken the very early plane from London. Amanda and Françoise were still on a high after their helicopter ride and visit to Balmoral. Amanda immediately printed the photos taken at Balmoral the previous day.

"What do you think of the pictures, Justin? You've had more

experience of this sort of thing than we have."

"Good material for a tabloid leak. The pictures may be too good, though. They need to look like long lens paparazzi. The photo boys can work on that to get the right effect."

"How do we manage the leak?" asked Françoise, new to this aspect of media manipulation.

"I have a friendly journalist here in Edinburgh. I owe him one for asking a planted question at Robert's press conference," suggested Amanda.

"Do we need a source from within the couple's circle?" asked Françoise, "You know, to make the rumour more credible."

"Funny, I was just thinking the same and I have a name. Emily Douglas," said Justin.

"Who's Emily Douglas?" asked Françoise.

"A good friend of the Princess, minor aristocrat, nice country house and estate."

"Would the couple have met there secretly?" asked Françoise.

"I believe they did and the estate has already been besieged by the press," he replied.

"Fine, let's use your Emily to corroborate the story," said Amanda.

"And we could let it be assumed that the pictures were taken on her estate," chipped in Françoise.

"The storyline?" said Amanda, hands poised above the keys of her laptop.

"The couple have known each other for several years through the rugby connection. He played for Scotland and she was team patron. The romance with Victoria blossomed after Robert became Team Captain," proposed Justin.

"Yes, that spins well."

****

Later that day, Sir Duncan phoned Peter to update him on the Balmoral meeting and the timing of the leak about the couple. Peter then called Angela to warn her of the announcement and also called Dan Miller to prime him to undertake some more refined polling work, once the rumours of Robert's romance with a Hanoverian started circulating. The press leak was planned for the Wednesday of the following week.

Chapter 33

England, June 2038 - London, Cabinet Office

In London, Sir Humphrey was not looking forward to his next meeting with Underwood. He did not like violent changes in policy which made him look stupid, a plaything of events, even momentous ones. However, the new situation had the merit that they didn't have to do anything. The pressure to undermine the Stuart campaign was off.

"One of the things diplomats are paid to do is stand on their heads, Underwood."

"It's more difficult for us mere mortals, sir."

"Anyway, our enemy is now our friend, thanks to Cupid so to speak. I'm sure you've had to cope with this sort of thing before."

"Cupid my arse, it's expediency, the least bad outcome. Is it a done deal?"

"Completely, their engagement will be announced soon."

"Well, if you can't beat them, shag them," said Underwood.

"I'd rather call it a dynastic marriage, and apparently they are in love. It's really rather neat, don't you think? I certainly couldn't have engineered a solution as clever as that," said Sir Humphrey, warming more to the idea every time he repeated the details.

"It's certainly very convenient."

"From now on, you must think of Robert Stuart as one of us. You must protect him accordingly. Can you see any threats to him? Who would want to harm him as he looks like becoming King of Scotland? Is there a lunatic republican element that would go that far?" asked Sir Humphrey.

"We've not looked at that for some time," said Underwood, resuming his more normal pained serious expression. "The Scots have never been militantly republican, thank God, when you think of all the trained Scots killers in the Paras and the SAS. We'll have a look at it. It'll give the MacSpooks at Tartan Park something to do."

"Really, Underwood, you must try to think of our regional offices in a more positive light," chided Sir Humphrey.

"I'll try, sir," promised Underwood without any enthusiasm. "Are you still interested in the authenticity of Bonnie Prince Charlie's marriage contract?" said Underwood, reaching for a report on his desk.

"Oh, I'd rather forgotten about all that."

"The Prof eventually did get his hands on it inside the Vatican museum. He was wearing special gloves that absorb tiny flakes from the surface layer, enough for detailed analysis. The document looked authentic, correct for the period. The materials also conformed to what was expected. However, he found traces of a modern solvent in the ink. Probably more than could be accounted for by contamination, so there's a doubt. It might be a very good modern forgery using original materials."

"Is there any precedent for that?"

"Yes, according to the Prof, we're only finding the fakes now with powerful new analytical tools. What do you want me to do?"

"Well, it isn't conclusive enough to rock the boat. We're getting pretty committed. Sit on it for now."

"What would you do if I did prove that the Stuarts weren't who they say they are? What if he's just any old Tom, Dick or Harry Stuart?

"That's a hypothetical question, Underwood."

"I'm setting something in motion to get absolute proof. Bonnie Prince Charlie's tomb is actually inside St Peter's in Rome. We need to get it opened and remove one of the Bonnie Prince's teeth. We'll get enough DNA from that to nail Robert Stuart one way or the other."

"But they would never allow that."

"Their Cardinal McKerran looks squeaky clean, but there's an important English Archbishop who's been lifting shirts. It never goes away."

"But that's blackmail, Underwood."

"Fair trade I would say, an Archbishop's reputation for Bonnie Prince Charlie's tooth."

****

When Sir Humphrey left, Underwood phoned Jamie in Glasgow and asked him to update the threat analysis from extreme republicans who may have been stirred to action by the recent developments.

Chapter 34

Spain, July 2038 - Marbella

The week after the Balmoral meeting on Deeside, Françoise got a call from Robert's mother, Simone. It was not a social call.

"Françoise, it's Simone."

"What's happened, Simone? You sound worried."

"It's my ex-mother in law, Monique. She phoned me this morning from Marbella. She sounded drunk and confused. It was terrible, she was shouting."

"What did she say, Simone?"

"I think she must have seen something about Robert in the papers. She was going on about this being no way for the grandmother of a king to live."

"Did she want anything?"

"Nothing specific, she just said that she was going to tell everyone her secret, but she wouldn't tell me what it was. Oh, Françoise, I'm worried. Is there a secret?"

"Simone, we know all about Monique's so called secret. She's attention seeking. She's fantasising that Alexander, Robert's father, was sired by a lover and not by her husband, David. It's not true, of course. We've got the DNA results to prove it. All the same, it would be a disaster if something like that appeared in the newspapers."

"Oh, I'm so sorry Françoise. What should we do?"

"Someone will have to go and see her. She's Robert's grandmother after all. I'll get back to you." replied Françoise.

Françoise felt a little sorry for Simone who despite being Robert's mother was not in Robert's inner team. Simone lived a normal domestic life looking after the rest of her family in Paris. She had not been party to the details of the Hanoverian DNA challenge to Robert's authenticity as a Stuart. Françoise deeply resented the distraction being caused by Monique whom she detested. She considered it a miracle that the majestic Robert had somehow resulted from that corner of family chaos.

Françoise immediately phoned Robert, who was meeting with Sir Duncan, to report the alarming development. Robert volunteered to go to Marbella. As well as sorting out Grandma, he had several other reasons for making a visit. One was in the line of Stuart business but the other promised pure pleasure. He knew from Victoria that The Royal Family had access to a small very private palace on the outskirts of Marbella, owned by a member of the Saudi Royal family. He was sure that Victoria would be able to get access and join him there for at least some of the weekend. He satisfied Sir Duncan's concerns about security by promising to take Birnie with him.

In Marbella, Robert arrived at Monique's villa door at 11:00 a.m. on Friday, accompanied by Birnie. The property was nicely situated in a slightly elevated position with a distant view of the sea. In response to his knock, the dilapidated looking front door eventually opened an inch or two, limited by a security chain and Robert was aware of a pair of slanting sad old bloodshot eyes looking at him through the crack. An unpleasant foetid smell exploited the opening, wafting towards them.

"It's Robert, Grandma," he said loudly, imagining that she might be hard of hearing.

"Who?" she answered, in a sad weak voice.

"It's your grandson, Robert. I've come from Edinburgh to see you."

Robert suddenly wondered if the woman behind the door was indeed his grandmother. He had no clear picture of what she looked like in old age.

"Robert, what a nice surprise, I recognise you from the newspapers, but I was expecting Simone," said Monique, half opening the door to get a good look then closing it again against them. Robert put his hand out to stall Birnie's move to get his foot in the door to prevent her shutting it. As the two men looked at each other, they were aware of a loud clinking of bottles and shuffling about, coming from the inside.

"I think she's tidying the place for you, sir. I recognise that noise," said Birnie.

After a few minutes, the door opened fully this time and she welcomed them in. His grandmother's appearance pushed all the other sensory offences aside, claiming his full attention. She was dressed virtually in rags, dirty rags at that and her skin was wrinkled and pasty, but the saddest thing of all was her once beautiful face.

She had tried to apply some face powder after she closed the door. It was badly done. Patches of powder emphasised the red blotches around her mouth and chin and the yellow pallor of her forehead. The bright red lipstick was smeared, giving her the overall appearance of a lopsided clown with a serious skin disease.

Seeing past the human sadness of the old woman, Robert was aware of the chaos of the room. Clothes and magazines were strewn across the floor and many of the surfaces covered with dirty plates, containing half-eaten food and dirty glasses, which were all empty. Several ashtrays overflowed onto the tiled floor and the ill-concealed necks of empty booze bottles pointed accusingly from several hiding places, silent witnesses to his grandmother's problem. But perhaps the worst thing was the smell, much stronger than they got at the front door, an offensive mixture of dirt, fags and booze rounded off with the unmistakable ammoniac pungency of urine.

Robert was appalled. No doubt it was her own fault he reasoned, but nevertheless he was overwhelmed by guilt that his grandmother, who should have been a revered member of the clan, could be living in a pigsty in such misery. How could the family have allowed this to happen?

"It does need a tidy up," she said meekly, as Robert surveyed the chaos.

"We'll help you with that," replied Robert, as Birnie, without instruction, began the clean-up, leaving Robert alone with his grandmother.

"I've just been reading about you in the English newspapers. King of Scotland! We used to talk about that when we were young. My husband, David, might have made a good king," she said, and started laughing in a manic unfunny way. "If only he had fathered Alexander," she announced slyly. Robert caught her look, trying to gauge the effect of her revelation on him.

"Grandma, we know that's not true. David was Alexander's father and my true grandfather and we have the DNA evidence to prove it. It all happened a long time ago. You're just getting a little confused."

Her blotched face clouded, as science that she did not understand was used to refute her claim to the ultimate infidelity.

"I was there Robert, I know what happened. Well, if you won't listen..." she replied, not articulating the threat. "I do want you to become King of Scotland," she added, as a lone tear descended, snaking across a patch of makeup, leaving a snail-like trail.

"I'm glad that you're with us, Grandma, but we can't leave you like this. We need to get someone here to look after you. Sit out on the terrace in the sunshine. We'll do some more work on the house and arrange some help for you."

Robert ushered her towards the French doors that led to the rear of the house. As he stepped outside, the sense of disorder followed; the terrace had been decorated with a large display of potted plants. All were now dead and reduced to brown skeletons, victims of Monique's neglect. Watering had long since disappeared from her list of priorities.

"Can you find me a cigarette?" she asked, as Robert lowered her into a chair, the cover of which was badly affected by mildew. Beyond and below the terrace the small swimming pool was almost empty and on closer inspection he saw that the murky foot of water remaining in the bottom was colonised by frogs and smaller aquatic fauna. The mosaic-tiled sides were covered with flaking dried out slime. He pulled the roller cover over it.

Back in the lounge, Robert called Françoise in Edinburgh to explain the situation. He had somehow expected that the Stuart women would sort it out but he met with stiff resistance to his tentative suggestion that either herself or Simone should granny-sit for a period. He then called Sir Duncan and shared the problem with him. Sir Duncan did not have an immediate answer but wondered whether their new found friends in MI5 might be able to help. Jamie had established contact with him and appeared keen to prove his loyalty and devotion to the coming regime.

"I've gathered over a hundred bottles, sir," said Birnie, coming back into the lounge.

"I'm not surprised, have you found any cigarettes?"

"Just a couple, they're on the sideboard there."

"Give them to her. Then, could you go shopping? We need food and cigarettes for her and lots of plastic bags and stuff for cleaning."

"And booze, sir? There's none left. She'll start to shake soon."

"OK, get her a bottle of whisky, but we'll ration it carefully."

With Birnie out shopping and Monique planted on the dry terrace in a haze of smoke, Robert began a thorough search of the villa. He was searching for David's papers, anything that would cast light on why he might have been killed. He was looking for something that would finally slay Leo's demon, a new fact that would dissolve his fervent belief that David had been killed by the British. Robert sensed that the demon was still there, lurking beneath the fig leaf that Leo had patched over it. It was something that Robert wanted clearly resolved. He wanted his uncle at peace.

Inside the house, he looked in every drawer and cupboard without success. In the garage he found a very old tea chest in a corner, buried under a jumble of empty suitcases, discarded garden furniture and household effects. He cleared the corner and prised the tea chest lid off with the prongs of a garden shears to reveal a picture of regimented order, quite at odds with the surrounding chaos. The chest was full of files, stacked neatly in four vertical bundles, each tied with a different coloured ribbon. He started on the older faded brown files. The contents were handwritten on lined paper that was yellowing at the edges and clearly predated David. The subject matter was mundane, like an unbound diary and the writing style Victorian. It was tedious family history at best, although Robert did get a buzz from the thought that the writing might have been his great grandfather's.

Another file did contain some material on Edwardian Hanoverians but it was more of a scrapbook, the sort of thing that would be compiled by an admirer. Robert then turned to the newer typed files, glossing swiftly over those that had been prepared on ancient typewriters. At the bottom of the third pile lay a thin tartan folder tied together with red ribbon. The title, neatly handwritten on a white address label was *The Republican Brotherhood*. The hairs on the back of Robert's neck rose as he lifted the file out and undid the red ribbon bow. He was disappointed that it was a small file with just a few pages, not a complete work. The content, however, was explosive. It described a plot to retake Scotland with a subversive campaign along the lines of the IRA campaigns of earlier times. The *Brotherhood* was a clandestine army that would organise civil disobedience, blow up strategic targets and assassinate opponents. Robert was confused. Was it the outline of a real plan or the synopsis of a rip roaring yarn, the book that David was supposed to be writing? If it was a plan, its calculated viciousness would have started a civil war and certainly attracted the attention of the British Secret Service.

Robert was elated at the discovery but disturbed at the way the ante had been upped without giving him a clear answer. He couldn't possibly share his find with Leo. He was in no position to make an objective assessment of its possibilities.

As he was putting the files back in the chest he noticed a small brown paper envelope taped to the underside of the lid. Inside the envelope he found a key. It wasn't an ancient rusty iron lock turner. It was a shiny brass coloured modern number that looked much more serious than the average front door key. He slipped it into his pocket and re-nailed the tea chest lid in place. Just then, Birnie returned with mountains of shopping, including a very large pot of emulsion paint.

"Well done, Birnie, I can see what you're going to be doing this weekend," said Robert, nodding at the paint as Birnie handed him a sandwich for lunch.

"You'll dine better than this tonight, sir, at the Sheikh's palace."

"It might be sheep's eyes or something like that," replied Robert, screwing up his nose.

"They're not so bad, sir, with plenty of couscous."

"Have you ever seen a key like this?" asked Robert, delving into his pocket.

"I've stood beside enough men in vaults to recognise a safe deposit box key when I see one," said Birnie, taking it and examining it closely.

Robert was now clear in his own mind that he wanted the contents of the safe deposit box to be innocent. He wanted a good peace with his future in-laws, where he could safely look under the carpet. At the same time, his rapidly growing Machiavellian instinct told him that for the long term future of the Stuarts it would be useful to have a trump card in the bank, capable of squeezing Hanoverian testicles, if necessary. He was brought back to the present by his phone. It was Sir Duncan, confirming that Jamie was keen to cooperate and that someone would arrive on Saturday afternoon to take care of Grandma.

On the other side of Marbella, the Sheikh's palace was the most ostentatious building that Robert had ever seen. Victoria had no difficulty in getting them invited there for the weekend through the Sheikh's London office. The palace was not being used by any of the

Saudis. It seemed that the main design criterion had been expense, lots of it. For Robert, the acres of white marble and tons of gold leaf in the public rooms verged on vulgarity, yet there was an Arabian Night's fairy-tale feel to it. Not that Victoria and himself were allowed to stay in the actual living quarters of the absent Saudis. They were in a guest annex outside the main building, but crucially within the manned security perimeter. It was this feature that had enabled him to have a weekend apart from Birnie, releasing his minder for domestic duties and DIY at the villa.

Robert was eagerly awaiting the arrival of Victoria who had managed to get a lift in one of the many private jets that winged their way from London to Marbella at the weekend. Robert arrived at the palace around 7:00 p.m., to find a message that Victoria was running late, because of air traffic control problems around London. He spent about an hour on the phone to Françoise going over the build-up to the leaks and announcements. When Victoria arrived at 9:00 p.m., they went for a relaxing swim in the pool, a colonnaded replica, copied from a sumptuous Roman villa. The mosaic tiling featured classical Islamic patterns, in place of the original gods and demons.

They ate in the small dining room of their annex, where privacy and intimacy were guaranteed. After filling each other in on the details of their last few days, Robert could see that Victoria was playing with her main course of sea bass, clearly troubled by something. She went quiet on him and he had a sudden worry that his love was having second thoughts.

"It's my brother, Henry," she said finally. "He didn't seem too bad when he came out of the clinic but when he heard about us at the same time that the Army washed their hands of him, he had a relapse. He's saying some really silly things to me in particular, but everyone's noticing the change."

"What kind of things?"

"He called me a traitor. He said that I should be sent to the Tower."

"It's him who should be in the Tower."

"He keeps mentioning you. He refers to you as Pretender Prince Perfect. We all laughed the first time he said it, but it's wearing thin now. He's begun to call you PPP for short. He's getting more aggressive."

"I suppose I should be flattered."

"Mad King George is getting mentioned as well as other feeble minded Hanoverians and Windsors and Mummy and Daddy are getting really worried that he might never make any kind of a king."

"That's what I thought when I first came across him at Gordonstoun."

"He sees you as a competitor but, of course, there's no contest. He's not half the man you are and I think he knows that."

"He did save me at Balmoral. Simkins was going to kill me, so he can't feel that badly about me."

"That was before us. And Simkins is back on the scene whispering poison in his ear."

"I suppose I could try talking to him, let him make peace."

"Do try, it's destroying him."

"I'll do my best."

"I'm sure he'll come to the engagement party. Mummy's three line whip will get him there."

"Victoria, I've hesitated to mention this before but my cousin Nicole is doing research at Harvard. She's working on how to alter human behaviour by brain re-programming. The work's funded by the U.S. Military. They want to create super-soldiers, you can imagine."

"I've met Nicole at Balmoral, she's very pretty. But how does that work?"

"As I understand it, they copy the brain profiles of model individuals and transplant them into deficient hosts. They also implant nano-electrodes to reinforce the process and control the movement of data and emotions within the brain. Nicole gave us a half hour lecture on it."

"Do you think that could be applied to help Henry?"

"I would imagine that it could. They now know how the brain works. Surely they could copy his father's profile and insert that. The nano-electronics should be similar."

"I'll mention it to Mummy; could you find out more? How could we get him into the programme?"

Next morning, the couple rose late to breakfast served on the shaded terrace of their room, which had a distant view of the sea. They were then transported in a blacked out SUV the short distance to the marina at Puerto Banus, home to many of the most magnificent yachts in the Mediterranean and playground of the super-rich. From the car, they stepped directly onto the back of the Sheikh's small launch, which at fifteen metres in length was still impressive. The Sheikh's personal yacht was much longer and moored at the more opulent end of the marina where the berths were bigger. Free from the harbour, the launch reared up like a feisty horse and with a throaty roar headed straight out to sea as the couple changed for sunbathing and oiled themselves up. The day passed lazily and lunch of grilled John Dory was taken in a quiet cove at a table set up on deck under an awning. Back at sea, the afternoon traffic increased as the nocturnal beautiful stirred themselves to top up their suntans and helicopters buzzed around, delivering precious cargoes or taking rich punters on sightseeing trips along the coast. By mid-afternoon the wind had risen considerably and the experience was beginning to pale for Robert, who was not used to such forced if luxurious inactivity.

"I've had enough of this," he said to Victoria.

"Me too, I'm feeling a little seasick. You can have too much of a good thing," she added, as Robert asked the skipper to take them back.

Just after their return to the palace, Robert's phone rang. It was Sir Duncan.

"Robert, I've just had a call from the Sunday Net editor. He says that he's got pictures of you and Victoria together, taken at sea this morning off Marbella. He assured me that the pictures are clean, no toe sucking or bare breasts."

"Well, that's something at least."

"He's very surprised that the two of you should be together and because of the significance, he's checking the story."

"We were out on a boat this morning, so there's little point in denying it. I wasn't aware of any paparazzi coming near us, but there were lots of boats and helicopters going about."

"It'll be on the cybernet tomorrow, even if we deny it. I've talked to Sir Humphrey. We must get the two of you back in the UK before the story breaks. We can get a private plane to pick you up at Malaga Airport at 10:00 p.m. tonight," said Sir Duncan, without pausing for breath.

"I suppose this scuppers the carefully laid plans to leak the story out slowly, but I did wonder if our PR people were trying to be too clever. Does it really matter? We just need to get on with it."

"Yes, we'll have to bring forward the date of the engagement announcement. We're thinking of making it at the end of next week. How does that seem to you?"

"That's fine by me and I think Victoria will be happy with that as well."

"Good, the plane will pick you up at ten tonight, dropping Victoria off in London and bringing you up to Edinburgh, so it's not going to be a very comfortable night for you."

"Could you make that Paris Orly for me? I've got to see Leo urgently, and then I'll come straight up to Edinburgh."

Robert and Victoria then asked to be taken back to Monique's villa en route for the airport to pick up the rest of his luggage. When they arrived, they were amazed at Birnie's transformation of the villa, at least on the ground floor. The place was back to something like normality and the smell of fresh emulsion now dominated.

At 7:00 p.m. the doorbell rang. Robert was beginning to pack his bag for the return journey and Victoria was in the cleaned up lounge talking to Monique.

"I'll get it, sir, it'll be the granny sitter" called Birnie, heading into the hall. "You'd better come and have a look at this, sir," he called loudly, after opening the door.

"I didn't expect to find you here," gasped Tina, as she came in the door, past an unwelcoming Birnie to approach Robert.

"Tina, what are you doing here? What's going on?" he asked, momentarily confused at the reappearance of his erstwhile girlfriend.

"Watch out, sir, she must be a spook, she did a Mata Hari on you in Edinburgh. I wondered about her when she suddenly disappeared," said Birnie, who vigorously pushed Tina back against the wall and subjected her to a rough body search.

"Birnie, is that necessary?" asked Robert, who remembered thinking that Tina didn't quite fit for a fitness trainer. He also felt a flicker of anger at the way she had lured him.

"I'm just making sure she's not armed."

"We're all on the same side now, Robert," she pleaded, as Birnie finally let her go, her arms dropping to her sides. As she turned away from the wall, Robert could see paint imprints on her shoulder blades and buttocks from contact with the not quite dry wall.

"Well, I'm sure you two have things to talk about, but don't sit on the lounge furniture," said Birnie, smirking.

"Let's go onto the terrace, Tina, and perhaps the master painter could make us a cup of coffee," said Robert, who was feeling unnerved by the intervention, especially as Victoria was in the next room.

"I need to explain about Edinburgh, Robert. The electronic surveillance was giving us nothing so I felt that I had to get closer to you to find out if anything subversive was going on."

"Well, I was completely taken in. You must be very well trained. Have you a long list of field conquests?"

"Robert, please, this isn't easy for me. It may have started like that but I ended up in a different place. I was furious with Jamie for pulling me when your big hitters complained to the Home Secretary."

"Well, for the record, I enjoyed it, too, but things have moved on."

"I can't compete with her, can I? Did you miss me? Did you wonder what had happened to me?"

"Tina, I'm sure you have many interesting assignments in front of you, although perhaps not this one. Granny through there is threatening to spread harmful but untrue stories about my paternity, so we have to keep her quiet for a while."

Robert was anxious to turn the conversation away from them. He hadn't experienced any difficulty in drawing a line under Tina. At that moment, he turned to see Victoria looking out of the lounge window at them. He didn't know how long she had been there.

"Yes, Jamie's briefed me about it. He thinks I need a rest and this should be a nice easy assignment."

"Well, we need to pack. We're leaving in half an hour to get the plane back, so make yourself at home."

"I'm sorry you're going back tonight," said Tina, with a final tempting look.

"You might as well meet someone else when you're here," he said, thinking that Victoria would find it very strange if he did not introduce them. However, he didn't need to move, Victoria had taken the initiative, and timed her entrance well. Robert could see that she was quite calm but looking intently at Tina.

"Hi, I'm Victoria. Aren't you Tina, the disappearing girlfriend? I recognise you from the photo in the newspapers."

"Victoria, ma'am," she stammered, getting to her feet. "I didn't know you were here. When Robert said "we" I assumed he meant himself and his painter."

"Tina's come to look after Granny for a bit. It appears that she works for MI5, so her interest in me was strictly professional."

"Well, that's good news," said Victoria.

"Congratulations to both of you. It's an unbelievably good outcome all round, the stuff of novels really. Now I must go and find Granny."

Robert saw tears welling up in Tina's eyes as she swept past them into the house.

"You know she's in love with you," said Victoria, after Tina had gone.

Chapter 35

France, July 2038 - Fontainbleau

Robert was met at Orly airport at 2:00 a.m. by a tired and depressed Leo. Robert was unsure whether Leo's problem was lack of sleep or a continuing lack of enthusiasm for his marriage to Victoria. He had been told by Françoise that since the meeting with the Cardinal, Leo had experienced several mini-wobbles where he lapsed back to his anti-Hanoverian stance and turned negative about the wedding.

"Are you happy about the situation now, Uncle Leo?" enquired Robert, as they set out on the short drive south to the *Manoir* near Fontainbleau.

"I'm getting used to the idea. Did you find anything of interest at Monique's?"

"I searched the house thoroughly and found an old tea chest full of his papers. There was nothing of great import in the papers but this might interest you," replied Robert holding up the key. Robert had decided not to tell Leo about *The Republican Brotherhood* paper until he'd had more time to investigate it himself.

"A safe deposit key. Yes, he would surely have put anything of great value into the vault. He had a box in the same branch as me. It was the bank that father used."

On the drive to the bank next morning, Leo went silent, overwhelmed with images of his dead brother, especially of his body floating in the water after the explosion on the yacht, the defining image of Hanoverian treachery. At the station he hardly noticed Robert leaving them to catch the train to Paris. He declined Françoise's offer to accompany him into the bank and asked her to wait with the car. As he went through the bank door he had a surge of optimism that the box would deliver up the Hanoverian scandal that his brother had uncovered and died for. Leo had his own deposit box at the bank where he kept some of Françoise's valuable jewellery and Stuart memorabilia. He was able to get access to the vault in his own right and went straight to David's numbered box. He turned the key excitedly, savouring the prospect of damaging revelations and pulled open the drawer.

Inside was a modest brown envelope, which clearly did not contain a fat juicy manuscript or a large sum in cash. He lifted the envelope carefully by a corner and spilled its contents onto the bottom of the drawer. A youthful image of a naked woman with an equally young naked man stared up at him. He lifted out the batch of photographs and went over to the table in the middle of the floor. His hand shook as he laid the pictures out next to each other. He recognised the constant feature of the pictures as the magnificent body of the young Monique Stuart. She was receiving the enthusiastic attention of a young man, in a variety of positions, all of them wildly compromising.

None of the pictures gave a good close up of the face of Monique's lover and Leo began to forge an identikit image by combining elements from several of them. He then had to think back thirty years and more to revisit the gallery of faces from that time. Gradually an image took shape and the male head in the photograph finally turned towards him. The young features of Hervé Dubois, then a political assistant, coalesced before him, smiling smugly at his conquest. The smile was pure self-satisfaction, directed at the cuckolded David.

Leo had seen that smile once before, featuring Hervé's bizarre little teeth, standing in the shadow of Napoleon in the green room of the Ministry of Justice, telling him that his brother had been murdered by the British. The erstwhile mighty Minister of Justice and promoter of Leo's cause had been a close friend of David's, adding personal treachery to his lecherous sin, although as Leo knew, this was not an uncommon pattern in the tangled webs of French affairs.

Leo remained rooted in the vault. His next thought was sorrow for his brother. What pain and disgust must he have felt when confronted by such images of infidelity? How would he himself have felt about similar pictures of Françoise? And why had David kept the images, carefully storing the evidence of treachery? Not blackmail? Surely his beloved brother could not have been a blackmailer?

The photographs would have given David a hold over Hervé, certainly enough to persuade him to transfer his affections elsewhere, away from Monique. But then the body floating in the water intruded again, the body of his dead brother, his spilt blood dripping onto the photographs, mixing with the new facts, creating new possibilities.

That day long ago in the Ministry of Justice, Hervé had planted the killer bomb in Leo's imagination. A bomb covered with Hanoverian fingerprints, exploded to eliminate the alleged threat posed by his brother. The Cardinal had dismissed this version of events as Hervé's imaginary tale to motivate Leo to fight for Scotland.

Leo had not found any evidence of a Hanoverian plot, no smoking manuscript, not even working papers. So finally, he reasoned that the Cardinal must be right and edged yet further along the road to accepting that the Hanoverians were not responsible for his brother's death. He would finally have to confront and begin to root out the host of negative images that Robert's liaison with Victoria had built on top of his existing prejudice.

That thought left him feeling empty; he would miss the comforting familiarity of the stance which he had carefully nurtured and that had defined his being for so long.

Chapter 36

Scotland, August 2038 - Edinburgh

The reaction to the paparazzi pictures of Robert and Victoria in the newspapers was dramatic and quickly went worldwide. The timing undermined the carefully orchestrated leak strategy that was being followed in Edinburgh by Robert's PR team. The cautious statements put out by Sir Humphrey and Sir Duncan and their obvious choreography, led the world to assume that an engagement was imminent.

The printed output that was unleashed ranged from genuine historical features on the two families, particularly the Stuarts, at one extreme, to more prurient speculation that the Princess was pregnant. In the middle, thoughtful journalists analysed the likely impact of the rumoured union on the prospects for Robert becoming King. There was almost unanimous agreement that the credibility afforded him by the Hanoverian imprimatur greatly enhanced his already excellent chance of being accepted as King of Scotland.

After much infighting, especially between officials, the engagement was announced from both London and Holyrood, although the main focus was on Holyrood, where the Royal Family was gathered *en masse* along with the Stuarts.

Following the press release, they all posed for photographs and Robert and Victoria gave a short interview answering mainly safe questions agreed upon in advance. In response to a planted question, they announced almost casually that their children would be brought up as Protestants. The following coverage in the media was almost unprecedented from a huge international press corps; there had been nothing like it since the days of Diana. The marriage would take place in October. Much calculation, some of it cynical, had gone into the choice of date but because of the short notice, no detailed planning had yet been done.

Over pre-lunch drinks, an apparently innocent remark from the Queen sparked off a monumental argument. The Queen and Victoria were talking, not surprisingly, about wedding dresses.

"You would look lovely in that in the Abbey, darling," suggested the Queen to Victoria who was describing a top designer number.

"The Abbey, ma'am? Which Abbey are you talking about? Holyrood Abbey's a ruin," said Françoise, who was sitting beside the Queen.

"Why Westminster Abbey, of course, where the wedding will be. Won't it? It's the tradition after all," she said, looking around for support. All eyes turned to Robert who realised that this was his make or break conversation with the Hanoverian family. They had naturally assumed his compliance in continuing their traditions.

"We're starting afresh here with a new monarchy. It's going to be different. It'll be a monarchy for the people of Scotland. Our wedding is their wedding, so it must take place in Scotland and it must involve them. Once these criteria are satisfied I'll listen to detailed suggestions."

"Good man, breath of fresh air," said the King, tapping the table in front of him in agreement, cutting off the Queen, as she was about to protest at being denied her Westminster Abbeyfest.

"St. Giles is a very pretty church, ma'am, a very historic site," said Sir Humphrey, trying to float a helpful suggestion, as the Queen squirmed in her seat.

"Pretty grim I should say, with the statue of that ghastly man, John Knox, standing there."

"Who said anything about St. Giles? I'll let you know very soon where it's going to take place," said Robert with final authority. "And now, Madame, you haven't consulted me about the wedding dress, have you?" said Robert, with a broad smile, looking at the Queen. He had taken to calling her Madame, in the French way, in an ever so gently mocking tone, much to the amusement of the King.

"Oh, don't tell me we have to have a Scottish wedding dress. Couldn't she just wear tartan knickers underneath?" replied the Queen, who was famous for her waspish wit, thus far strictly under control in her dealings with the Stuarts. Everyone laughed at the royal lingerie joke, which was timely in defusing the escalating tension.

"I hope the weather will be kind to us on the day," said Victoria.

"Whatever the weather throws at us, I'm sure that Victoria will look wonderful in anything you choose Madame, as long as it is trimmed with Royal Stuart tartan." Robert was not yet exhausted on the sartorial front. The company laughed, less heartily this time, not quite sure whether Robert was following the Queen's humour or making a positive suggestion.

"I'll sew it on myself," replied the Queen, smiling.

"I'll be wearing Highland dress, just like today," said Robert seriously, clearing up any misunderstanding about the need for tartan trimming.

At the end of the interlude all eyes turned as Prince Henry, who was not present at the start of the reception, made a grand entrance. He was wearing Highland dress, not the elegant restrained ensemble of Robert, but a radically different version, that owed much to a Hollywood misconception of the real thing. The tartan was gaudy and improbable, but at least unique. Victoria had warned Robert that Henry was having his own personal tartan designed. The ruff at the neck splayed down across his chest in theatrical style, contrasting with Robert's neat bowtie. The lace cuffs of his shirt protruded too far from the sleeves of his jacket and took on a life of their own every time he moved his arms. Pinned to his chest was an insignia, which was so big that it could only have been awarded by a banana republic. Robert thought it was the garb of a man near the edge, who was clearly in his own warped way, trying to out Scottish Robert. Robert saw the looks on the faces of his family. Even legendary Royal self-control and discipline could not hide the distaste and sadness felt by those present.

Distracted by the garish spectacle of Henry's dress, Robert had not noticed that Henry was carrying something. He stiffened when Henry stopped in front of him and from behind his back swung a baseball bat into full view. Robert took a step back to give himself room if Henry took a swing at him. Victoria took a step towards Henry to forestall such a move.

"Don't worry, I just wanted to give PPP an engagement present," he said, holding out the bat horizontally in both hands for Robert to receive.

"Thank you, Henry, this is certainly the most original engagement present we've had. I'll treasure it," replied Robert diplomatically, shaking Henry's hand. Victoria led polite applause to mark the ceremony, which ended with bewildered looks on Royal faces.

"I didn't know that you played baseball, Robert," said the Queen.

"I did just the once, Madame," replied Robert, as they went in to lunch.

Chapter 37

Scotland, August 2038 - Glenfinnan

Robert had been cautious about engaging deeply with the old Scottish Jacobite landowners and aristocracy but finally succumbed to an invitation from Cameron of Lochiel to attend the Glenfinnan Highland gathering. It was the site of the raising of Bonnie Prince Charlie's standard on August 17th 1745 and so had a special significance for him. Lochiel himself was the direct descendent of "Lochiel the Gentle", the clan Chief who did most to support the Prince in his military campaign and ended up dying in exile in France after the tragedy of Culloden. His people fared worse; the bravest at Culloden were rewarded with the harshest treatment by the victors.

On the eve of the games, Lochiel held a small party for the organisers and helpers, mainly landed folk and their estate workers. Robert was the focus of most of the attention, although he felt that he was being paraded like a trophy. He was also inundated with invitations to go shooting, fishing and stalking. He remembered Sir Duncan's remarks about the fickleness of Scottish aristocrats. Their invitations were a good indication that he was going to win. Robert found himself relaxing in the warmth of the company and Lochiel's insistence that he learn to drink whisky, proper west coast whisky, where the malted barley is caressed with peat smoke before fermentation, blessing the final liquid with a heavenly aroma and a taste that the tongue will love forever. A group of imbibers gave a rendering of the song "Welcome Home" in Gaelic. Robert was touched.

Late in the proceedings Lochiel came over with yet another whisky for Robert to taste and sat down beside him.

"David Stuart was your uncle, wasn't he?"

"No, he was my grandfather. You met David, did you?" replied Robert, fighting through the whisky haze to concentrate on the unexpected turn of the conversation.

"Yes, he came to the estate a few times, rented the Shepherd's cottage."

"I didn't know that."

"He was very secretive about it; he didn't want anyone to know he was there. He said he was an author working on a book and he wanted to capture the atmosphere of the place."

"Did you know what he was writing about?"

"It was nonsense about a campaign to create a free republic of Scotland by force. He tried to talk to me about how it might work but I didn't want to get involved. He was a fantasist, but harmless really."

"Is it possible that he was planning something and that was his way of trying to get someone like yourself on board?"

"That's a bit farfetched but I did get a strange visit after his last stay. They looked like Special Branch types and wanted to know what I knew about him."

"Did you satisfy them?"

"Yes, they were happy with the idea that he was a writer on retreat."

Out of the corner of his eye Robert could see Birnie standing in front of the bar, whisky glass in hand. Raucous laughter was coming from the small group of estate workers gathered round him. Robert excused himself and ambled over to join them. The conversation stopped immediately as Robert introduced himself to the group and praised the qualities of the whisky he was tasting.

"I don't suppose you get many Frenchmen visiting here?" he asked, pointing his question at the oldest member of the group, a gnarled weather-beaten gamekeeper.

"Oh, we've had a few but not these last years. There was one who came a lot with a group of friends. Stuart he was called, just like yourself, sir."

"Did you take them stalking?"

"Aye, I did. They were nutters really, especially David himself. I'll never forget him with his Kalashnikov and his groupies. He was always going on about a Scottish Republic. They called him "The General" behind his back."

Robert was surprised to hear that his grandfather had republican rather than monarchist credentials. His knowledge of his grandfather had clearly been carefully sanitised by Leo.

"Did you take any photographs of them?" asked Birnie, who moved to fill the silence of Robert's distraction by the old keeper's story.

"Not me, but some were taken. You always take a photograph

when you shoot a twelve pointer. I'm sure Mr. Stuart got a few of them in his time. He was a nice gentleman, always gave me a good tip. Were you related to him, sir?"

"Distantly, but the family was saddened when he died," replied Robert.

"Yes we all were, that's true," said the old gamekeeper, shaking his head at some memory.

Robert then returned to Lochiel's table to take his leave. Lochiel was on his phone looking grave.

"There's been an explosion at Scone Palace. A car bomb at the front door. Nobody hurt," he said.

"What? Any idea who did it?"

"Something called *Scottish Republican Force*, is claiming responsibility."

"That's very bad news just days after we've gone public."

"And full of symbolism. That's the ancient coronation ground for the kings of Scotland. I'll ask for more police for tomorrow, just in case."

Robert felt sick at the significance of the target. This was a direct warning to him, opening up a new front of threats and uncertainty just as he felt that he had the Hanoverians on side.

Outside he complimented Birnie on his question about the photographs and kicked himself for not thinking to look for any at Monique's. He'd been too focussed on looking for documents. Despite the late hour he telephoned the villa in Marbella and asked Tina to conduct a search. An hour later a photo came through on his phone. It showed a group of hunters behind a dead stag, posed with its antlers vertical showing its twelve points.

Looking at the faces in detail he quickly confirmed the presence of David Stuart in the centre of the group but his stomach knotted when he saw the young face of his own father staring up at him from the paper. It was an image which must have been captured not long after he himself was born. Robert was well used to hearing Leo's conspiracy theories about his grandfather's death but was somehow troubled to see father and son in the same picture.

****

Games morning dawned to a cloudless sky and a bright sun, rising over the mountains behind the village, promising well for the day. The

185

sun and a good sea breeze kept the dreaded midges at bay. The games field was a hive of activity as the commercial side was put in place for the 11:00 a.m. start. The drones of practising pipers were momentarily drowned out by the comings and goings of helicopters. People began to arrive; the posh in tweeds, the weather-wary in anoraks and the inexperienced in T-shirts.

While Robert was a guest of the Chieftain, he was not prepared to confine himself to being a spectator. Robert was an athlete in his own right, although his strength and agility were untested in the Highland arena. He had always been fascinated by the heavy events and especially the tossing of the caber. He made his way down to the field where several heavy athletes were training for the rigours of the day. They were big men, carrying much more weight than Robert, but a friendly bunch. They responded well, if a little patronisingly, to Robert's request for assistance with the principles and practice of caber throwing. One of them helped Robert to raise the caber into the vertical position and lift it, with his hands cupped below the end and the length of the caber balanced on his shoulder before the short run and throw. After a few practice efforts he decided to register as a late entrant for the competition.

The opening ceremony was very impressive, beginning with a Gaelic prayer and a suitably sentimental Jacobite song. Cameron of Lochiel took the microphone to make the speech of welcome. It began with the usual eulogy to the bravery of the Prince and his followers, in taking on the Hanoverians without a French army, but then turned on Robert.

"Up to this point, everything that I have said has been said many times before, at this gathering and others like it in the Highlands. But today we have a new dawn. Standing at my shoulder is the descendent of the Prince who stood here nearly three hundred years ago next to my ancestor Locheil the Gentle. He's come back among us now to claim his throne, a claim kept warm in the hearts of Scots here and in exile down the centuries. And this time there will be no cannons roaring, no slaughter and banishment, no ethnic cleansing, only the wishes of the Scottish people will be heard. This young Prince has already achieved much in his own right as rugby Captain of his nation, and is now ready for that ultimate captaincy which is kingship and I commend him to the Scottish people. He has also found himself a wife, the Princess Victoria and we rejoice in that union which surely draws a final veil over our ancient conflict. Friends, go home and pass the message through the glens, down to the villages, towns and cities; the Stuart has returned. Long live the King."

Locheil's speech was greeted with loud cheering and quite a few tears from the faithful and new converts who were swept along on the emotional tide. Robert was very moved by Locheil's words which he felt seemed to strike the right balance between Stuart pride and reconciliation, perhaps going a little over the top at the very end. He moved forward to reply at Lochiel's prompting.

"Chieftain, brother Scots and friends; I've come here today to tap the spirit of the Prince himself and replant the Stuart roots that have succoured me in my long personal journey to stand before you here in the bright sunshine. I've come from France just like the Prince, without an army. My sword is my Stuart blood and my shield the strong desire of the Scottish people to manage their own affairs in the constitutional manner of their choice. If the people of Scotland ordain it, I will with great humility accept the call to become Sovereign, in their name. Scotland is a great country, we are a great people, let's seize the future together to make it even better."

As the rapturous applause died down, a piper appeared on the stage to carry on the age old tradition of celebrating events with a new tune, composed the day before at Lochiel's request. It was called "Bonnie Prince Robert". It started gloomily at the memory of sad times but quickly picked up tempo and spirit as the new dawn beckoned, finishing in a coronation crescendo. As the official party took their seats for the start of the proceedings, Robert made his way to the heavy field and with Birnie assisting, changed into some borrowed athlete's kit.

"Are you sure you want to do this, sir? These other fellows look a size. And the caber, it's a tree trunk," said Birnie.

"Don't worry, Birnie, it's mainly technique. I'm sure you could do it yourself."

"Not me, sir, I'd be scared of a hernia."

****

In the hotel bar after the games, Robert was again the centre of attention, receiving congratulations for his third place in the caber tossing competition. Out of the corner of his eye he noticed a woman hovering on the edge of the group. She seemed to be watching and listening, nervously waiting for an opportunity to intervene. Her dark hair was tied back with a wide band of fabric, the wavy tail spilling out down the back of a pretty flowery dress. She had a mature academic air about her, not at all threatening to Robert, who thought she looked attractive. Ever anxious to extend his public reach, he turned towards her.

"Were you at the games?" he asked.

"Yes, I enjoyed all your performances, especially the speech."

"So, what brought you to the games?"

"You did."

"That's very flattering. Are you a writer?"

"Not exactly, I'm Louise Stuart, your grandfather David's wife."

"My grandfather's wife? You can't be, he's dead," replied Robert confidently rejecting the woman's claim although inside, a chain reaction started.

"He needed everyone to think that but I assure you, he's very much alive. Look," she said taking a photograph from her handbag.

"I'm afraid I don't recognise him," said Robert, looking at the picture of Louise with a bearded older man and an adolescent boy.

"Here's a picture of him that I do recognise," said Robert, taking out his phone and showing the picture transmitted by Tina.

"Hey, I remember taking that picture with the stag. There's David and Alexander, your father. At the start I was his friend. After he was killed, David came back to Scotland. We got together despite the difference in our ages," she said rather shyly with a sweet little smile that accentuated her dimples.

Robert shuddered at the attack on the foundations of his carefully constructed position, all the more so because of the apparent innocence of the messenger. David's death had been kept alive and fresh by Leo over the years as his motivation for attacking the Hanoverians. They had killed his brother and he would get revenge by taking Scotland from them, using Robert as his champion Prince.

He was also unsettled by the hint of a relationship between his father and the woman in front of him. And the child; how old was he now? Was he a competitor for the title of Stuart Crown Prince? But worst of all was the realisation that David, if he was alive, would be the titular head of the Stuarts.

He suddenly felt angry, anger directed against Leo. How could Leo not have known that his beloved brother was still alive? Why had there been no contact? Was the filial affection one sided? He realised that he didn't know the exact circumstances of David's death. His yacht had blown up at sea, in the English Channel. His body was never recovered. Could he have faked his own death? Was his alleged murder by the Secret Service a story spun to ensnare Leo in a wider conspiracy?" His head reeled with the long list of questions posed by the woman in the floral dress.

"I need to meet him," said Robert.

"He'd like that."

Chapter 38

Scotland, August 2038 - Morar

The address given by Louise suited Robert and Birnie. Their immediate objective after the Games had been a walking challenge on the Isle of Skye, crossing over on the Mallaig Ferry. David's house lay on the way, five miles south of Mallaig at Morar. Robert had pondered hard on whether to tell Leo about the astonishing development and get him to rush over from Edinburgh to attend the bizarre reunion. However, he was concerned that the revelation would be too much for Leo on top of his fragility over the wedding to Victoria.

The lodge lay in extensive grounds up a steep track that afforded magnificent views of Loch Morar and the hills beyond. Robert felt nervous approaching the door; he was out on his own beyond the umbrella of his advisors and supporters.

David was sitting in the lounge on a large wooden chair with arms, a mini-throne. He was dressed rather formally in jacket and tie. The beard in the photograph had gone. It was David's face. The pieces of antique furniture looked too large for the room, misplaced baronial pretension thought Robert. The light was behind David, the sun in Robert's eyes, the choreography obvious. He was acting the part of King, making Robert feel like a supplicant. He didn't get up but did take Robert's offered hand in a weak limp shake, the clearest of opening remarks.

"I'm not going to explain to you why I'm here, only why you are here."

"But Grandfather, what's going on?" said Robert, confused by the aggressive stance.

"I'm not so sure I'm your grandfather."

"Of course you are; we've checked everyone's DNA. The Hanoverians challenged that at the beginning."

"Rubbish, anything can be faked but that's not the main point. I've watched your progress with interest and was prepared to back you until the Hanoverian Princess joined the cast."

"But David, we think that's an advantage, it helps our cause."

"Nonsense, it dilutes our cause and you're too fond of celebrity. It's turning into Hollywood not Holyrood. Next thing you'll be on chat shows," added David.

"Where is all this leading?" asked Robert, tension mounting as he feared that his future was about to unravel.

"We want you to stand down," said David.

"Are you putting yourself forward?" asked Robert, half prepared for the blow.

"Not me, my son, James," said David pointing at the young man who entered from the kitchen and stood beside David. Robert recognised the boy from Louise's photo. The young man was about his own age with similar looks and build. He could see that James looked uneasy and uncomfortable. Robert went over and politely shook hands with him getting a stammering blushing response.

"So, James, you must be my uncle. Do you think you can replace me?"

"It's not me, it's heredity."

"A blunt instrument when there's real work to be done," replied Robert, whose first impression of James was unfavourable. He lacked personality and seemed very shy.

"James is an officer in the Army, he plays football and he's not engaged to a Hanoverian Princess," announced David, as though those qualifications equalled or exceeded Robert's.

Robert continued to argue that he had a much better chance of winning the crown. David came over as deeply dug in and committed to his own son. For him, it didn't seem to be about winning. Robert wondered whether David wanted to preside over yet another Stuart defeat, wallowing in the continuing injustice and not having to face up to the realities and compromises of success. He had even called his son, James, the name of the last of the failed Stuart Kings. That would surely fit the psychological profile of a potential loser, a man who was able to disappear from the face of the earth for almost a generation.

Robert couldn't see past the roadblock that his grandfather represented. David was the Stuart Prince by birth and age and could pass the baton on to James; that was his call. Robert couldn't believe that such a trick of fate was denying him the inheritance that he and many others were now so committed to. The weakness of his position weighed on him as did David's cynicism in timing his move to coincide with the bookmakers' odds shortening dramatically on Robert. However, a new Stuart challenger out in the open would make the whole cause look ridiculous and both Stuarts would certainly fail. Was that his real objective? Was he a closet republican as his literature suggested, mounting a spoiling operation that he knew would probably destroy Robert's chances?

"What are we going to do, David?" asked Robert.

"We need to arrange a handover to James. He can take your place in everything except the Hanoverian marriage, of course." Robert was astonished that they expected him to step aside in his finest hour, giving way to someone who was likely to blow the opportunity created at such cost.

On the way out Robert excused himself and went to the bathroom, leaving Birnie outside alone admiring the view and swatting the midges beside the parked cars.

"I've just had a thought, Birnie. The bathroom in there was empty; not even a toothbrush. Could they be just camping there? Is it a set up?" asked Robert when he rejoined Birnie outside.

"Just what I'm thinking, sir. That boy has a Glasgow accent if ever I heard one. I've recorded it all," he said, holding up his phone.

"Well done, Birnie, and all that play acting bringing the boy in; someone wrote a script for that," said Robert, relieved to see immediate possibilities for striking back, given that he had initially been taken in by the charade.

"The other clue's the car. Who would have a BMW saloon to go up that unmade track? We need to park out of sight and watch."

They parked the car a hundred yards up a tree lined estate track and walked back to the main road. Ten minutes later the BMW made its way down from the lodge. Birnie confirmed through his binoculars that David was driving.

"We must follow him," said Robert.

"That's tempting, sir, but this is one for the professionals. My money's on them going to Glasgow. There's only the one road south, the new M82 from Fort William through Crianlarich and down Loch Lomond. Call our pal Jamie. I don't think Rangers are playing today."

Robert was tempted to return immediately to Edinburgh to consult his team, but decided on balance to stick to the plan. Jamie had eagerly agreed to take over the hunt for the new Stuart family and that would take some time to progress. Better to wait for feedback and a risk assessment before confusing things in Edinburgh. He also relished the thought of the hard physical exercise. It would help him to clear his head after the revelations.

Birnie drove them north, across to Skye on the Mallaig ferry. Robert had read about a gruelling walk done by the Prince, on the run after Culloden. The Prince and his companions covered the 30 miles from north of Portree to Elgol on the south coast, in 12 hours. In his darker hours searching for inspiration, Robert had imagined doing the whole walk, feeling the same pain and fatigue as he walked in the footsteps of his ancestor. In the new circumstances he was happy to limit the walk to the stretch over the Red Cuillin between Marsco and Ben Dearg, starting from the shore of Loch Ainot. As they checked the contents of their packs before leaving, Robert noted that Birnie had a serious looking handgun in his.

The two climbed steadily for about an hour up into the Cuillin, initially within range of the evocative aroma of peat smoke from a remote cottage. Robert went over the details of the morning confrontation again and again. He didn't want to discuss it with Birnie in case he ended up in a conversation about assassination, which would probably be Birnie's recommendation.

Their immediate objective was a high valley with a steep escarpment on one side and a gently sloping moor on the other. Herds of red dear pranced gracefully away as the pair intruded on their natural paradise. A golden eagle pirouetted on the up draught above them. Birnie raised his binoculars to see the bird more clearly.

"Christ, that's no eagle, it's a natural drone, it's watching us," shouted Birnie.

"Can it attack us?" asked Robert.

"No it's just a spotter, but it'll be directing an attack onto us. We better take cover just in case."

The pair then headed up the slope to the right towards a cave at the foot of the escarpment as a helicopter appeared over the brow about a mile away and dropped down into the valley, heading straight for them.

"You were right, Birnie," shouted Robert as they ran for their lives.

He had a good lead on Birnie as he entered the cave mouth to hear the loud hissing noise of a high powered laser gun striking behind him. Birnie hesitated and bravely turned, firing several shots at the helicopter from his pistol, before he stumbled and fell down. The helicopter overshot their position to turn giving them a brief respite. Robert rushed out to help the hobbling Birnie into the cave. The ex-SAS man pulled up his trouser leg to reveal the tangled mess of metal, plastic and wiring that was his lower left leg, melted by the laser.

"That was a present from my last tour in Afghanistan."

"Birnie, I had no idea."

"They're back, sir," said Birnie, as the insistent beat of the rotors penetrated the cave. The helicopter was descending outside, to line up with the entrance. "Let's get as far in as we can, they're going to put a missile in next."

"Look, I can see light at the back, there must be a passage up to the surface. Maybe we could squeeze through," shouted Robert, from the back of the cave.

"Go up and have a look, see if there's any cover," answered Birnie, as the rotor noise rose to a crescendo, indicating that the helicopter was now hovering at the cave mouth.

"They've been felling trees up here. Lots of trunks lying around."

"Tree trunks, sir?" said Birnie, as he clawed his way out of the hole. Robert suddenly twigged and quickly selected a trimmed slim trunk and dragged it nearer to the escarpment edge. Lifting the end in his cupped hands, he ran a few steps to build momentum then projected his missile up and out over the edge of the cliff with a throw that might have taken first prize at the Glenfinnan gathering. He watched the caber arc up and turn over hypnotically into the vertical position and begin its accelerating descent. He heard a rumble beneath his feet as the missile probed the depths of the now empty cave, sending a cloud of acrid smoke out of their escape hole into Birnie's face. Seconds later the air was rent by the gnashing of the disintegrating rotor, as it destroyed itself against the falling caber. A violent explosion followed, sending a searing flash of bright orange flame up beyond Robert, as the caber continued on its vengeful path towards the earth, bursting through the helicopter's fuel tank. Robert turned away, temporarily blinded by the flash, and staggered back towards Birnie.

"Well done, sir, what a throw," said Birnie, lying down against a tree trunk and exploring the damaged leg.

"Sure your leg's OK?"

"I think the flesh at the bottom's been warmed up a bit but it feels OK," he said removing the shattered prosthetic.

"We'll need to get help, you're not going to walk out of here are you?"

Robert called Jamie for the second time that day to report their situation and ask for help. Jamie reported that Birnie's guess was correct. The BMW had passed Crianlarich and was on its way down Loch Lomond.

As Robert was putting his phone away, Birnie roared "Down," as he drew his pistol and fired past Robert, who spun round to see a figure crumpling on top of a rifle at the edge of the cliff.

"The bastards," screamed Birnie, as Robert ran over to the face-down figure, whose singed smoking hair and melting neck and leather jacket fouled the clear mountain air with the stench of burning death. Robert turned over the squirming, moaning young man who had been hit squarely in the chest by Birnie's bullet. The face contorted with rage at the sight of Robert. With his last breath he tried to lunge up at Robert with his fist, as Robert had done to him with great effect at Gordonstoun. Simkins, more recently prosecutor at Robert's mock Balmoral Estate trial, expired before he could give voice to the evil words on his twisted lips.

"Thanks, Birnie, that was good shooting. You saved my life."

"Is he dead?"

"Yes, but he's still a problem. I recognise him. He's a friend of Prince Henry. I've had trouble with both of them."

"He's out to get you, sir, that Prince Henry, we'll need to deal with him."

"No, no, Birnie. Prince Henry isn't well. He's not in control, you must believe that," replied Robert.

Robert then went over to the cliff to inspect the remains of the helicopter which had burned out very quickly. He scrambled down the slope towards the blackened skeletal wreck which still had the charred remains of the deadly caber sticking up through it like hard worked battle colours. The carbonised shape of a man, without any discernable features, occupied the pilot's seat. His black bony fleshless fingers had contorted as he reached through the flames trying to release himself from his safety belt. The foul smell of burning flesh drove Robert back as he searched the empty blackness of the face.

Back on the cliff top he sat with the uncomplaining Birnie, letting the extreme tension subside. He had never felt anything like it, even in the roughest of rugby matches. The rush of adrenalin in response to the life threat had been overwhelming inducing a heady mixture of fear, aggression and elation. The memory of the morning's revelations soon dispersed the elation. He had nearly been killed for being something that he might no longer be, the Stuart heir. Elation turned to embarrassment at his complacency, his misplaced feeling that they were almost there; that one more heave would do, that they were onside with the Hanoverians, then the vicious sting in the tail and the big kick in the teeth from his own side.

Two hours later, Jamie arrived in a helicopter accompanied by a medic. A second helicopter arrived a few minutes later with a clean-up team.

"Thank God, you're not injured, sir," said Jamie, as he approached Robert, holding his stomach in relief at his arrival.

"Birnie's leg was hit by the laser gun. Thank God it was the plastic bit. He'll need to get his spare one," said Robert who then went over the details of the attack.

"It's a black operation against you, sir," said Jamie in response.

"Who exactly is Simkins?" asked Robert.

"As I understand it, he was trained in military intelligence, then left to be an equerry to Prince Henry."

"But who's running him? The drone, all this, he can't be acting alone? Could someone in the Service in London still be working against us?" asked Robert.

"It does look like it, sir."

"I realise this puts you in a difficult position Jamie. There's an obvious conflict of loyalty here for you."

"Loyalties change, sir. I'll try to find out who's behind this."

Just then Jamie's phone rang and he was soon nodding with satisfaction then shaking his head in frustration.

"Interesting, David dropped the woman and young man off at a flat in Glasgow but then he gave us the slip," reported Jamie.

"You'll be watching them I presume?"

"Like hawks, sir. We're already onto the woman; she's known locally as Mrs. Robertson. We've got the birth details for the boy. He's James Robertson, father not recorded."

"Jamie, with David on the loose we're very vulnerable; he's got to be found. Louise Robertson's bound to know where he is. Can we go to see her tomorrow after we get back, perhaps in the afternoon?"

"We're doing everything we can to find him but that might speed things up."

"Thanks, the first thing I have to do when I get back is tell Leo about his brother. That won't be easy for him."

"Rather you than me, sir. Anyway, I didn't know that you tossed the caber," said Jamie, as they climbed into the helicopter.

"I didn't until yesterday, and only today in anger," replied Robert, as the helicopter lifted them clumsily, like a pelican full of fish, above the burned out wreckage below. As he looked out at the majestic scenery of the Cuillin, he realised that he had not recorded the beauty that surrounded them. It had been washed from his eyes by the treachery of the sting in the Hanoverian dragon's tail and his own family's plan to change horses.

Chapter 39

Scotland, August 2038 - Edinburgh

Leo and Françoise were called to see Robert early on the Monday morning. Leo was looking forward to hearing all the details of Robert's weekend at the Games and on Skye. Instead he had to hear that his brother David was still alive; he hadn't been consumed by the English Channel all these years ago. He'd come back to haunt him.

Leo's first feeling was of betrayal that his hero could have voluntarily disappeared from his life without so much as a goodbye and then never getting in touch. And then there was a feeling of foolishness that he had built the whole Stuart Agenda on the premise that David had been murdered in the name of the Hanoverians. When the cold realisation dawned that David was still technically the heir to the Stuart pretence, anger boiled up within Leo. It was inconceivable that his brother should be mounting a hopeless spoiling challenge at the eleventh hour. They were now within sight of victory and the prospect of such a family-kicked own goal was too much to bear.

"I've got to see him. There must be some mistake," said Leo.

"He's disappeared again so that might be difficult."

"After the initial shock, I can't say I'm surprised. I often joked that David must be a spy. He didn't seem to have a proper job. He was a freelance journalist, away a lot of the time, but I never saw anything in print," said Françoise.

"What about the new wife, Louise? She said she took this picture," said Robert showing Françoise a print out of the photo that Tina had sent from Marbella as well as the pictures that Birnie had taken on his mobile phone.

"There's David and your father of course. I'm surprised he's there. I didn't know that he was part of the hunting set. I don't think I recognise anyone else. Wait a minute, who's that? Hold on, I need to get the weekend paper."

Françoise returned with the paper open at an article describing the formation of a new political party, Republican Alba. A picture of its first leader, Jim Robertson, accompanied the article. It described his motivation to keep a pure strain of republicanism alive now that the Independence Party that he had previously led was supporting a Stuart monarchy. Robert wondered what Angela would be thinking about that.

"Look, the guy in the photo standing to David's left. That could be Robertson," said Françoise.

"That would make sense; we've heard that David had republican sympathies."

"Louise is a Robertson. Maybe she's his sister. Did you ever meet her?"

"No, we were never part of that set in Scotland but I remember Monique telling me about a Scottish girl; she was crazy about Alexander. She used to come to Paris to meet him, even after he married Simone. The bitch found that amusing, can you imagine?"

"The gamekeeper we talked to hinted that there were a lot of women around David. Does that make sense?"

"Well, I would never speak ill of the dead but now that we know he's alive I'm prepared to tell you that he was just as bad as Monique; they were both serially unfaithful, although of course Leo won't like me saying it."

"Why not? I'm having to rethink everything."

"Françoise, could my father also be James's father?" asked Robert.

"That's what I'm thinking right now. That's possible; maybe she's not sure. Your DNA tests can sort that out. But even if he is your younger half-brother and not your uncle, David's still standing in your way, undermining your claim. He's got to be dealt with somehow."

Over in Glasgow at MI5 Scottish HQ Jamie was probing the records and had discovered that David Stuart was not unknown to the UK security services. He'd been deployed in Scotland infiltrating an extreme republican cell that was threatening violence. However that was after his faked death and re-emergence in Scotland with a new identity. Jamie didn't have access to the more detailed files covering the early period of David's service. He didn't trust his London contacts because of the phoney situation so he contacted the trustworthy John in Paris to try to find out what he could from that end.

John called back an hour later. The records were very incomplete and partly deleted. The only thing he could report with certainty was that Underwood had been deeply involved with David's work at the time of his disappearance. Jamie wrestled with the flimsy facts for an hour before smiling to himself. He called Underwood in London.

He relayed the story of the set up meeting in Morar with the new Stuart family. He then made up a report that Piers Ross was supposed to have received for publication, citing the new Stuart family's apparent superior claim to the Scottish throne. Jamie then added a final sentence.

"David Stuart claims that a British MI5 officer, Michael Underwood helped him to fake his death for reasons that he will explain in a book that he is preparing."

Underwood didn't answer. The phone went dead. Jamie felt the tug on his line.

Chapter 40

Scotland, August 2038 - Glasgow

Just after lunch time on Monday, Robert, Leo and Birnie met Jamie outside Louise Robertson's Glasgow apartment. It was in a fashionable refurbished tenement in a gentrified street. They confirmed with the surveillance team that Louise was at home. James had gone out earlier, ostensibly to college, and was being followed.

Robert had been thinking about what to do as they drove across from Edinburgh. He wanted Louise and James removed from the scene; removed from the possibility of making contacts that could propagate their claim and undermine him. Jamie's reaction was lukewarm; he wanted to keep them on familiar territory in Glasgow, bait for David and there for possible contact with the Scone Palace bombers. They both wanted to put pressure on Louise to find out where David was hiding.

Leaving Leo and Birnie outside, Robert and Jamie knocked on Louise's door. The look of surprise on Louise's face indicated that she had not expected their visit.

"I'm sorry to turn up like this, Louise, but we need your help."

"I don't know where David is. He didn't say where he was going," she replied defensively, before they asked the question in the untidy lounge which seemed to have books covering every free surface.

"We've got to find him, Louise. He's a loose cannon we have to control before he undermines me. Surely you can see that he has no chance of becoming king himself and we now know from the DNA database that James isn't David's son. He's a dynastic dead end."

"I'm not sure that David wants to be king. He's always been a republican, not a monarchist."

"Speaking of republicans, I don't suppose your hothead son had anything to do with the Scone Palace bombing?" asked Robert.

"James is just a student, he's not involved in anything like that."

"What was that about him being an Army Officer, then? That's what David said at Morar."

"That's David fantasising a bit. James is in the University Army Officer Training Corps, not quite the same thing."

201

"Weapons training all the same. We could fit him up for the Scone Palace bombing, couldn't we Jamie?" said Robert, hoping that Jamie would allow him some rope.

"One finger print would do it," added Jamie, much to Robert's relief.

"You bastards! David has a yacht at Inverkip on the Clyde. I think he'll be there," said Louise glaring at Jamie, visibly angry that her son had been threatened.

"Jamie, why don't you and Leo check out Inverkip? I'll stay here with Louise until I hear from you," said Robert, making it sound like a friendly gesture rather than a security essential to prevent her warning David. As Jamie left, Robert asked Louise to make a cup of tea to create a break with the aggression of the previous scene.

Louise visibly relaxed over the tea. Robert wanted to know how she met the Stuarts. She told him how she first met them at a republican summer school in Scotland with her older brother. Alexander was there with his father and they started a passionate love affair. The affair was sustained digitally and with occasional meetings until Alexander cooled and married Simone two years before David's reported death in a boating accident.

She was therefore astonished when three months later David appeared in Glasgow. He explained that his life was in danger, certain people were trying to kill him and that he'd been obliged to leave France quickly and secretly then change his identity. Sworn to secrecy, he had asked her to do him a great favour. He asked her to make a trip to Paris to collect something from his son, Alexander. The car crash happened when Alexander was driving her back to Charles De Gaulle Airport. The car veered suddenly, bounced off the central reservation barrier then rolled over. Her own injuries were slight but Alexander had suffered a fractured skull. The resulting internal bleeding caused his death. She had been distraught but David was a great comfort to her and naturally assumed parenthood of the boy, James. David, of course, blamed the French Secret Service for his son's death. It was a very high price to pay for collecting the first draft of David's novel, *The Republican Brotherhood.*

"But you did bring something else back, didn't you," said Robert.

"You're very perceptive. James was Alexander's parting gift."

"What was the book about?" asked Robert.

Louise explained that the work was a fantasy where David led a Scottish republican army to victory and set himself up as "Chieftain." He wouldn't entertain her suggestion that he should call himself king. Louise thought the whole plot very naïve in assuming that a terrorist rabble could actually take over the country. She was surprised that he never tried to get it published. It was as if he lost interest when life refused to fill out and occupy the clothes of the fiction.

"However, he started to write again recently when you came on the scene."

"Did he begin to write me into the story?"

"Oh yes, the charade at Morar was part of that. It was a test."

"Did I pass?"

"I'm sure you will. He thought that you'd come after him, perhaps not as quick as this. I think he'll enjoy this bit, fighting alone again."

"What did he think of me getting involved with the Hanoverians?"

"He didn't like that bit. He wasn't sure what to do about it."

"What's he doing now?" Wouldn't he like to come to the wedding and the Coronation. Why can't he join us? He's my grandfather."

"He's a Jekyll and Hyde about you. At a safe distance he's happy to take credit for you, but close up he retreats. Most of the time he says he's not your grandfather. I think you heard him say that at Morar, despite the results of the DNA tests."

Robert's phone went. Jamie was reporting that Leo had gone on board the yacht at Inverkip. Robert took his leave and rejoined Birnie, feeling profoundly sorry for Louise and ashamed of the treatment she had received from his Stuart relatives.

****

Leo was quiet on the short journey to the coast. He had so much to say to his brother, so many questions he wanted to ask. He didn't know where to begin. He was clear about one thing. He wanted to see David alone without the intimidating presence of someone from MI5.

The marina was vast, greatly expanded since the rise in temperature that was making the West coast of Scotland Europe's newest playground for the super-rich, in the vulgar big yachts that matched their egos. David's yacht was a serious sea going sailing boat, moored on a set of pontoons well away from the opulent end.

Leo was relieved when Jamie reluctantly agreed to let him approach the yacht alone. He was a little apprehensive walking out onto the pontoon to the chorus of pinging from the sheets on the masts and the flapping of the flags. It was a perfect accompaniment to the view across towards the hills above Dunoon on the other side of the firth.

Leo climbed aboard the yacht quietly and made for the door at the back of the cockpit. As he approached he heard raised voices. David was not alone. Leo put his ear to the door, resisting the temptation to barge in.

"You've got to be joking Underwood, we can't call this off now, especially if you're telling me that the family tree's been rumbled and you know that they're not pukka Royal Stuarts. Bonnie Prince Charlie's tooth my arse!" he heard his brother shout. Although the authenticity of the voice was strangely comforting he was deeply troubled by what he was hearing. He knew of Underwood and his fearsome reputation. What was he proposing to call off; but worse still, were they not Royal blood Stuarts?

"Look, David, I think getting rid of Robert isn't right now. Everyone's happy with the outcome. Let's face it, many kings in the past grabbed kingdoms without much regard for the niceties of birth-right. Your Robert has been a worthy latter day champion."

"You've gone wet, Underwood, seduced by the fairy-tale marriage. A story with a happy ending. Jesus, Underwood, give me a break, I don't like happy endings. I'm sticking to the plan."

"I hoped it wouldn't come to this," said Underwood in a threatening voice, from just inside the door.

"Put that thing away, Underwood," pleaded David as Leo launched himself at his side of the door with all his might, knocking the spook forward to the floor where his pistol shot ended up. David stepped in and struck the MI5 man viciously with a heavy frying pan, the only weapon to hand.

"David, stop," pleaded Leo standing in the doorway as David made to continue his assault.

"Christ, it's you, Leo. Thanks for that but what the hell are you doing here?"

"David, I couldn't believe it when Robert told me he'd met you. I just had to find you to be clear for myself," said Leo, who was appalled at his brother's appearance. The handsome face of his youth was now hollow and drawn like a torture victim. He also seemed shorter, shrunk by time and the ravages of his strange life, thought Leo.

"Your hero's a bit tarnished now, Leo. I wish you hadn't come."

"But why David? What drove you to leave us and your family?"

"Family! That nightmare bitch, Monique and her bastard son, Alexander. I had nothing to live for there. Anyway, my work was very dangerous. I had to make myself scarce or else. Know what I mean?" he said, passing his hand across his throat.

"But now? Isn't that all in the past?"

"You of all people should know that the future is the past, Leo."

"I couldn't help overhearing what you said about the Stuarts. We're not who we say we are?"

"Well, Underwood says that they got one of Bonnie Prince Charlie's teeth analysed and the DNA didn't match up with ours. The work I did on the family tree traced back very well so I'm not sure what to believe. Perhaps you could check with your Cardinal friend to see exactly what happened at the Vatican."

"David, you're making me very nervous, casting doubt on our lineage like this," said Leo as the main plank of his Stuart Agenda creaked below him, threatening to split and crash him to the ground. Would he soon be exposed as the biggest charlatan in history?

"Leo, I didn't know you were stalking the Scottish throne. It's the law of unintended consequences."

"How many people know about this?" asked Leo, thinking already of a damage limitation exercise.

"Don't worry, the only other people in the know are the King and Queen, who want it buried deep. But they're not stupid, Leo, it's a bargaining chip with the Stuarts, a hand on your balls, if ever they need one."

"What about Sir Humphrey?"

"Yes, I'm sure he knows. He was the link between Underwood and the King and Queen.

Leo immediately thought of Robert and what the impact of the new knowledge would be on him if he found out. As he wallowed in that uncertainty David pushed past him through the cabin door closing it sharply behind him. Leo heard the key turn in the lock followed immediately by the growl of the engine being started. Seconds later the boat was underway as Leo tugged furiously at the door to try to escape. He searched around for something to attack the door with but nothing in the cutlery drawer was heavy enough to prise it open. Finally, he managed to batter out one of the door panels using the same heavy frying pan that had stilled Underwood. As he put his head out a pistol touched his nose.

"Get back in. Check Underwood," said David.

"He's dead. The back of his head's pulped."

Inside the cabin, Leo racked his brains for a way out. He pulled out his phone and called Jamie.

"Throw that to me," said David from the gap in the door.

"Help," shouted Leo into the phone before complying.

"Sit down in that corner and don't move. I don't want to have to shoot my brother."

Leo crumpled into a heap on the bench, utterly distraught at the revelations and the evil intent of his brother, the full extent of which he didn't understand but feared. Minutes later he heard the roar of the outboard motor on the dingy. He gingerly stuck his head out of the door panel in time to see the craft with David on-board, heading at high speed towards the coast.

Leo managed to squeeze himself out through the gap in the door to find the boat sailing beautifully on automatic pilot heeled over in the brisk breeze. The heading was southwest down the Clyde estuary towards the Isle of Bute. Leo was wondering how to disengage the steering when he heard the throaty roar of a high speed launch coming at him through a great cloud of spray that bore Jamie's voice enhanced through a loud hailer.

"Put on a life jacket and jump in the water," was the shouted instruction. Leo complied immediately and nearly passed out from the shock of the cold water on top of all the other assaults he had suffered. Leo was truly relieved to see Jamie's smiling jowls looking down on him from the side of the launch as he grabbed the rope that would haul him to safety.

"Thanks, Jamie," gasped Leo as he rolled onto the deck. Behind him, the sky ahead of the launch lit up as the flash reflected from the low cloud and the blast rattled the windows of the launch. Leo struggled to his feet and looked at the burning remains of the boat, Underwood's grave and nearly his. The joy of his escape was nothing to the pain of the realisation that his brother had intended to kill him. What had turned him into such a monster?

After debriefing Leo, Jamie smiled to himself and mock punched the air. He'd succeeded in flushing out Underwood. It felt as good as Rangers beating Celtic 6-0. Surely justice had been done for him masterminding the attacks on Robert through the hapless Simkins on behalf of the compromised Prince Henry. On the negative side, David Stuart had escaped, disappearing into the sea again, leaving them uncertain about his motives and plans. From Leo's description, it sounded to Jamie as though they were looking for a dangerous psychopath, drunk on a perverted sense of history.

As the launch nosed into the Inverkip basin, Jamie's mind drifted onto the fish and chips that he had already planned he would pick up on the way home.

Chapter 41

Scotland, August 2038 - Clyde Coast

As David got into the dingy, leaving his yacht in the hands of the automatic pilot and Leo, he felt a pang of guilt. Not for Underwood or even Leo but for abandoning Louise again, as he had done so often in the past. At that moment, he had a strange feeling that he might never see her again. He certainly couldn't go near her flat or make direct contact. The only possession she had of his was the book manuscript that he had finished updating just before the visit to Morar. He didn't need it; he had an electronic copy posted remotely and anyway, the story was now final, there would be no more changes to the script.

He was also very annoyed with Underwood for turning up out of the blue. They were never supposed to meet without careful planning. He was heartily sick of Underwood patronisingly reminding him how he'd been saved from the wrath of the French and provided with a new identity and employment. With Underwood it had been a question of time. Back in the yacht he'd seen the mixture of distaste and finality on Underwood's face, looking every bit the executioner as he drew his pistol.

He'd always worried about Underwood trying to get rid of him because officially, he didn't exist, so wouldn't be missed. So it wasn't surprising that their long term arrangement had hit the buffers of age and changing times. Just Underwood's bad luck that Leo turned up to spoil the party.

With Underwood out of the way, at least he now had a pension in the secret funds squirreled away to fund his operations, although he wasn't a poor man, having creamed a lot out of the projects that Underwood cleared him to undertake, especially the simulated drug runs that were used to flush out crooked officials and illicit supply chains.

Then there was Leo, who had stumbled into his argument with Underwood and witnessed his murder in cold blood. He had always found his little brother a bit pathetic and needy, following him around, hanging on his coat tails. Once in Scotland, Leo had hidden in the bushes, watching him screw Monique. The sibling relationship at best meant nothing, at worst it was an annoying negative. However, he was impressed at the way Leo had led his project and got Robert into place without spilling a drop of blood. If his own project had come to fruition, a lot of blood would have been spilled. He thought that spilled blood was a very effective seal for a victory.

Just off the town of Largs, he turned for the shore towards a brightly lit hotel complex. Splashing up the beach, he headed around the back to the staff car park where the oldest and easiest to steal cars could be found and disappeared into the night on the back roads of Ayrshire.

Chapter 42

Scotland, August 2038 - Douglas Estate

Robert and Victoria had hardly seen one another since the announcement of the engagement and the rather tense meeting between the families. They wanted a quiet weekend together to take stock. The Douglas Estate held such memories for them that they decided to exploit the Douglas's hospitality one more time at least. They were torn between the peace and simplicity of the country cottage and the formality of the big house. Robert insisted on the privacy of the cottage as they had so much to discuss. The compromise was a boring dinner with the now sycophantic Douglas pair who revelled in their role as early secret hosts for the emerging couple.

Back at the cottage, Victoria had good news for Robert's ears only. Henry's bizarre performance at the Holyrood engagement celebration was the last straw for the family. It was finally clear to them that in his current condition, Henry would be unable to perform his duties as future King. The medical view was that conditions like his would get worse with age, so something had to be done. The family had followed up on the work being done in America on the control of personality by Robert's cousin Nicole and her colleagues, and were prepared to take the risk that a reprogramming using his father's personality profile and reinforcing nano-implants would improve his condition. The operation was to be done in great secrecy the following weekend in a private clinic in Switzerland. Assuming the operation was successful, Henry would resume the military career that had effectively been abandoned except for a few fig leaves that allowed him to appear in uniform from time to time.

"I'm really glad about that. I was attacked by Simkins at the weekend and just made it," said Robert, who then gave Victoria a potted version of the Skye attack.

"Well, I'm glad that Simkins is out of the way, that'll help Henry, I'm sure."

"Henry's the least of our troubles now. We've stirred up a hornet's nest with the engagement. We now have a terrorist group called the Scottish Republican Force who claimed responsibility for the Scone Palace bomb. The new political party Republic Alba is its mouthpiece. Jim Robertson's leading that. He's got pretty extreme republican form going way back, with my grandfather, David, involved. That brings me to the best story of the weekend."

Robert then reported on the meeting with Louise and the visit to Morar and the aftermath in Glasgow and at Inverkip, involving David.

"But surely the police and the Secret Service can sort them out?"

"Yes, but my reincarnated grandfather is the first Stuart in line. He might be trying to undermine me. If all that becomes public I'm finished."

"Don't worry, Daddy's already said that if the Scottish Crown thing goes belly up, he'll make you a Duke. You can sort out English sport and help Henry, and make babies with me. That last bit's mine."

"I like the last bit. I'm not sure about the rest."

"Can't David Stuart be dealt with?"

"You women, that's what my Aunt Françoise said."

"Speaking of women, you were very tough with Mummy about the wedding location," she said.

"Madame forgets who you are marrying, and the national significance of that. We can't be married in England. Surely you understand that?"

"Yes, I can see the argument but Mummy really had her heart set on Westminster Abbey. Robert, we've never spoken much about religion. I know we've announced that our children will be brought up as Protestants but what are we going to do about the wedding ceremony?"

"I'm seeing the Cardinal in a few days' time. He's pretty broad minded, I'm sure he'll have some good advice. Have you spoken to the Archbishop?"

"Not yet, should I talk to him?"

"Let's wait to see what the Cardinal says."

Chapter 43

Spain, August 2038 - Marbella

In Marbella, Tina was shattered to hear about the engagement of Robert and Victoria. With little to do, she dwelt obsessively on the injustice of her position in the oppressive sweltering heat of the Spanish summer. Robert, the object of her scrutiny had become the object of her affection and more. It had already happened before during her assignment in Ireland where she had fallen in love with the CIRA man who she had under surveillance. She seemed to be fatally attracted to dangerous or unobtainable men. And yet, in the case of Robert Stuart, in that instant when she was confronted with him again as she came into the villa in Marbella, her heart had soared. She thought that he was there for her, ready to resume their relationship, ready to return her love, only for her hopes to be cruelly dashed when Victoria appeared and took control. How could she compete with the likes of Victoria?

Should she have got herself pregnant by Robert? She imagined herself carrying his heir, and then presenting him with a sweet smelling baby son. Her unsatisfied hormone streams flowed without check, and jealousy nudged towards hate.

At first, Tina spent a lot of time re-teaching Monique how to do her hair, apply makeup and generally recover her femininity. At the same time, Tina scrupulously rationed out the booze for both of them, but as time went on and she delved deeper into the injustice of her position, her ration increased. Monique began swimming again in the cleaned up swimming pool and regained something of a shape. As Monique recovered her confidence and normal looks, she began to see some of her old friends again and her old flirtatiousness returned. It came to a head one evening when Monique drank almost a whole bottle of wine at dinner.

"Tina, do you know that Felix has asked me to marry him?" she slurred. Felix was an old flame attracted by Monique's improved condition.

"That's interesting, what are you planning to do?" said Tina who did not inform Monique that such an act would be bigamous. She had not told her about the reappearance of David and didn't intend to.

"How can I do anything with you watching me all the time?"

"Oh, Monique, how can you say that? I'm here to help you. You know how things were before I came to stay."

"No, you have to leave. I can manage perfectly well on my own, and Felix will be here to help me."

"Let's talk about it in the morning when you're feeling better," said Tina, who knew that Felix was every bit as bad as Monique.

"No, I want it settled now, or my secret will be out," said Monique, raising her voice. It was the first time that Tina had heard the threat from Monique.

"Ah your secret lover, the father of Alexander, the skeleton in your Stuart cupboard. But, Monique, it's not true. Leo has proof that David was indeed Alexander's father."

"We'll see who's believed when I go to the newspapers."

"How did you come to meet David anyway?"

"He was a beautiful big Frenchman. The family used to come for the summer fishing on my father's estate in Scotland. He was desperate for me, in bed, in the barn, even in the bushes, although we were caught one day by creepy gooseberry little brother Leo, who was jealous of me doing things with his hero."

"So what was it like when you arrived in France?" asked Tina.

"It was hideous from the start. They were all against me and eventually David cooled so I had to look elsewhere for love. You don't need to look far in France, they were queuing up, especially David's so-called friends."

"Oh never mind, that's all in the past. Let's have a nice brandy to finish, shall we? Then I'm going to have a little swim."

"That's more like it. Perhaps you should stay after all," replied Monique, taking a swig from the very large brandy that Tina poured. Tina, already in a bikini, pulled off her evening wrap and took the few steps into the swimming pool. She found the water temperature refreshing, if a little cool, and swam around weightless, making soothing noises until Monique had finished the brandy.

"Come and join me, Monique. I'll give you a massage in the water."

The thought of one of Tina's massages and her severely impaired judgement got Monique into the water, without too much coaxing.

"OK, now lie floating on your back."

Tina couldn't get to sleep after the action in the pool. She was looking forward to going back to Britain but couldn't see herself remaining in MI5 for very long. She had come to the reluctant conclusion that she just wasn't the right type. She wondered whether her Patrick in Ireland would be an escape route. She knew that she was the love of his life, and while she had loved him in Ireland, every time she conjured up his face now, she was looking over Robert Stuart's shoulder.

She remembered the highs and lows of working undercover there in one of the periodic flare-ups caused by the latest Irish Republican splinter group. She had watched Patrick for months and then met him innocently one night in a pub off duty. Sleeping with the enemy was thrilling at first but got more dangerous as the risk of her cover being blown increased. It came to a head one night when she had to jump from Patrick's bed and leap out of the bathroom window scantily clad, as the police were knocking down the front door. Her reports back to base glossed over all that and fortunately the group that he was a member of was persuaded to stand down by the mainstream Republican leadership. She knew that he had now reverted to being a legitimate business man and wondered whether he had found anyone else. She made a vow to contact him when she got back from Spain.

****

The following morning, Tina called the police, to report finding Monique dead in the swimming pool. It looked like an accidental drowning, following very high ingestion of alcohol. It was not the first such case in Marbella.

Chapter 44

France, September 2038 - Fontainbleau

News of Monique's death, however unlamented, still cast a pale shadow over a corner of the Stuart family's euphoria at their dramatic change in fortune. Despite the obvious temptation to do otherwise, the family had decided to bury Monique beneath the headstone that had been erected in memory of her apparently dead husband, David Stuart, after he disappeared.

The funeral was a surreal affair. Leo's local priest had been persuaded to hold the brief service in the chapel beside the *Manoir*, before burial in the family plot behind. A veneer of Catholicism had been added by importing some wooden crosses and religious wall coverings. The funeral had not been advertised and was a family affair, extending to a few close friends.

The coffin was bizarrely balanced on the flat part of the olive tree designed for goddess's buttocks. Additional supports at either end ensured that the departed remained on an even keel. With the coffin shrouded in a faded tricolour, Leo could not entirely blot out images of Bernard performing the fertility rite at the same spot. He was sure that Monique would have appreciated the sexual irony of the situation. Wasn't there a certain symmetry in performing a death ritual at the same spot?

Leo glanced towards Bernard who was staring directly ahead, toughing it out if he felt any embarrassment at the echoes from the walls of the chapel. Standing beside his wife, Angelique, his face was an innocent picture of denial. Seeing Bernard in such a pose, Leo did a quick mental calculation to work out whether Bernard was old enough to have been one of Monique's lovers.

Glancing in the other direction Leo felt a surge of anger at the sight of Hervé Dubois, although it was hardly the same young buck as he had seen in the photographs from the bank vault. He was stooped with age, his face a picture of sadness, marking him as the only person in the chapel who appeared to be grieving the departed. His once vertical stand of black hair was white and thin, collapsed on top of his head, making him seem smaller than ever.

After the short graveside service and lowering of the coffin, Leo was surprised when Hervé stepped forward to throw a handful of soil into the grave, an apparent final gesture of affection for the woman who was universally detested by her family.

Back at the *Manoir* after the interment, the atmosphere lightened considerably as the family members followed the time-honoured habit of not mentioning the deceased over drinks and canapés. Leo was undecided about how to deal with Hervé but matters were taken out of his hands.

"She was the love of my life," said the old man tearfully to Leo, who did not associate the pornographic realism of the photographs from the vault, with such a romantic sentiment. To Leo the photographs had a vile sadistic quality, but above all they expressed Hervé's treachery towards his once beloved brother.

"Was it worth it, destroying their marriage?" asked Leo.

"I know how it must look, Leo, but she was impossible to resist. She wore me down until I gave in and betrayed my best friend. I still feel so guilty about that."

"I've seen the photographs," said Leo, who found himself feeling a little sympathetic, having seen the effect that Monique's pursuit had on the young David.

"She insisted on having them taken, without showing my face, of course. She wanted to taunt David, she could be very cruel."

"So how did it end? Did David blackmail you with the photographs?"

"No, he didn't need to. She was a sexual butterfly. She got tired of me and moved on to her next conquest. There was something of the devil in her. She loved the challenge of seducing faithful men. I was very hurt at the time. I was obsessed with her and wanted to marry her but she just laughed in my face."

"David's still alive you know. We found him in Scotland. Actually he found us," said Leo. He wasn't sure why he said it. It just came out. The old man looked at Leo, his eyes narrowing almost to closure, obviously struggling with the response he wanted to make to Leo's revelation.

"We caught David spying for the British, military and nuclear stuff. I tipped him off and got him to his boat at Honfleur."

"Then the boat was found drifting in the Channel, halfway across," said Leo.

"The British really didn't want him back. That's what it looked like to me," said Hervé as Robert approached them, visibly perking up the old man.

"Robert, I'd like you to meet Hervé Dubois," said Leo more than a little irritated that such a productive line of conversation had to be closed off.

"Monsieur Dubois, it's a pleasure to meet you. I've heard a lot about your role at the start of our project. A personal thanks for that," said Robert shaking Hervé's now feeble hand.

"I've so longed to meet you," said Hervé, looking up at the much taller Robert and taking hold of his forearms as if to embrace him. Leo saw Robert stiffen at this unexpected show of affection, causing Hervé to back off as Françoise who had been standing nearby, appeared in their midst.

"You must be hungry, boys. Hervé, come and get something to eat," she said, guiding the old man away towards a seat at the end of the table with Leo in impatient pursuit. He was desperate to continue the conversation about David.

Chapter 45

Scotland, September 2038 - Edinburgh

Angela was exhausted after the election but victory meant that there was no respite; she had to work harder than ever on the myriad of detail that confronted her. Even she was impressed by the scale of her victory. Her party had won 85 seats in the 129 seat assembly, giving her the mandate she needed to implement her programme. She was especially pleased that she had not made any commitment to a referendum on independence. It had been the main manifesto pledge and the Bill to implement it was her first priority for the new Parliament.

She wanted to move quickly to exploit the vacuum before it was filled by a host of voices and competing claims. To move fast she had to get a quickie divorce from England and fate had delivered her the partner who needed one as much as she did, but for different reasons. The Tories had scraped a tiny majority as she had anticipated in her clandestine meeting with their leader several months before. Accompanied by Peter, she met Newbold at a Country Hotel near Carlisle to cement a deal.

"Congratulations on a wonderful victory," said Newbold, kissing her on the cheek.

"So, Morris, your result is good in principle but in reality it's a poisoned chalice, isn't it?"

"Yes, the majority isn't enough. I don't have much chance of getting my programme through."

"Governments in that situation tire very quickly and often fall apart in recrimination," added Peter, unhelpfully.

"Angela, I know this is difficult and we're in unexplored constitutional territory, but what are your plans?"

"We have a choice; it's a bit like the old song; there is a high road and a low road to Scotland. The separation process between Scotland and England could be spun out with a referendum, constitutional commissions, and lots of votes in both Parliaments and the House of Lords. It could go on for years, certainly for the lifetime of a Westminster Parliament."

"That's not the answer I want to hear. Tell me about the other road, Angela."

"I didn't commit us to a referendum on independence. That was the centrepiece of our manifesto. We've got a convincing majority. A simple vote in Edinburgh could be justified. The nobles who were bribed to dissolve the Scottish Parliament in 1707 didn't consult the people, did they?" she replied.

"That's more like it, Angela, so could you declare independence within a month?"

"Yes, I have the Bill drafted already." She looked at Newbold with a disguised smile of triumph on her lips. She did not tug sharply on the line. She knew that large fish, if played gently often come to the bank without much of a struggle.

"Then I could certainly be rid of all the Westminster Scottish MPs within say six months," he replied, sitting back in his seat to savour the prospect.

"Getting rid of the Scottish Labour MPs will give you a very respectable working majority. That must be worth a lot Morris."

"I'm waiting to hear the price," he replied, as she reached into her brief case and drew out a document, a copy of which she handed to him. It was entitled *Accelerated Separation Agreement with England*, and detailed her demands.

"Take a few minutes to read it while we make a cup of tea." She then headed for the kitchen with Peter. She was very pleased with the document that she had just handed over. She realised that with a compliant partner in power in Westminster and no second chamber in Scotland, she was in a constitutional vacuum, where nobody could stop her.

"I thought that quickie divorces were supposed to be cheap," said Newbold, when they returned with the tea.

"But Morris, for you this isn't a divorce; think of it as an opportunity to get rid of an inconvenient relative who stands between you and a legacy that history wants to bestow on you, the right to be the natural party of government in England. Isn't that priceless?"

"You're right there, Angela, but we still have to be able to afford to live in England," he countered, setting the document down.

"How long do you think it would take two teams of civil servants and lawyers to negotiate their way through all the issues in there?" she asked, waving her copy at him.

"Too long, far too long. Where do I sign?"

****

The first session of the new Parliament was opened by the Presiding Officer and not by the British Sovereign. There had been an unholy row about Angela's refusal to respect the prevailing constitutional niceties. She did, however, look forward to Scotland's own King performing the ceremony, although not dressed for Hollywood.

The Bill declaring Scottish Independence was tabled and after the formal committee hearings it was duly passed. The Bill contained the constitutional details covering the position of the new Scottish Monarchy that had been worked out between her staff and Sir Duncan. Angela had dismissed Robert's demand for a plebiscite. She didn't want the King to believe that he had been in any way elected, that he had a personal mandate that might clash with hers. Angela was pleased that many Tories and Liberal Democrats voted for the move. A new paradigm had been established. There was now broad political agreement that Scotland should be an independent country and with that issue out of the way, she could focus on the country's long neglected problems.

Robert had watched the election results come in at a party held in Sir Duncan's New Town apartment. He had cheered with Françoise and Sir Duncan as they thrust their fists in the air each time a good result came in, but didn't join in booing the opposition successes. Leo had fallen asleep as the results began to come in. When victory was finally declared, Robert thought of telephoning Angela but pulled back and asked Sir Duncan to relay his congratulations.

Victoria called from London to congratulate him. She was also ecstatic about the results of the operation in Switzerland. Robert was moved when Henry came on the phone to add his congratulations and apologise for all the bad things that had been done in his name. He also expressed his eternal gratitude to the Stuart family for providing the key to his deliverance from the torment of his medical condition. He'd made such progress that he was about to restart his Army training as a helicopter pilot. While that remark stirred up unpleasant memories for Robert, he was delighted to hear the transformation and looked forward to normal relations with his future brother-in-law.

Victoria and Robert then talked more about the final elements of the wedding and Coronation plans. He had insisted on keeping tight control over the details for both ceremonies. That had meant stepping on Hanoverian toes by refusing the help of the English Lord Chamberlain who would have been there to implement the Queen's wishes. He had, however, given way on one thing. There would be a public religious wedding service. Not the Westminster Abbeyfest that the Queen wanted, but a St. Giles Cathedral equivalent. He also had a secret plan that he needed to discuss urgently with the Cardinal.

Chapter 46

Scotland, October 2038 - Edinburgh

On the wedding morning, before the Palace was awake a car driven by Birnie left Holyrood and made its way south, crossing the bypass and arriving at the still sleeping village of Roslin twenty minutes later. Robert squeezed his beautiful fiancée's hand as she looked up adoringly at him getting out of the car.

"This is it then," he said, taking her hand as she got out of the car. "When we walk out of here we'll be man and wife for the first time today. You'll be Mrs. Stuart; nervous?"

"Absolutely not, this is the happiest day of my life," she said, her face shrouded in the long dark-blue hooded robe, identical to the one he was wearing.

"Come on," he said, as he led her in the darkness up the path to the door of Rosslyn Chapel.

The scene, which awaited them inside was breath-taking. The chapel was candle-lit. The flickering lights cast shadows on the spectacular carved arches and columns of the building adding to the surreal atmosphere. Robert paused and pointed out the face of his distant ancestor Robert the Bruce, a death mask that smiled on them as they passed below.

With their hoods still up, the couple walked slowly up the centre aisle and came to a halt beside the Apprentice Pillar. They were greeted by two magnificently robed clerics, their elaborate vestments slightly incongruous, demanding the stage set of a grand cathedral, not the intimacy of the confined space before the Rosslyn Chapel altar. Robert had never actually seen Cardinal McKerran in all his regalia, and was surprised at how tall he looked. He gave him a warm smile. The Cardinal beamed back. His mitred companion stepped forward, wearing a cloak of gold and silver, used by a previous Archbishop for the marriage of Victoria's parents.

"How good to see you both again," said the Archbishop of Canterbury in hallowed, hushed tones. "Now, if you are both ready, we'll begin." As they nodded their assent, Cardinal McKerran gently turned down their hoods.

In accordance with the couple's wishes, the ceremony was simple, and short, and weaved together key elements of the marriage service from both their traditions. The Archbishop and Cardinal McKerran stood shoulder to shoulder as they each performed their respective roles in the ceremonial vow taking, with the Archbishop leading Victoria's vows while the Cardinal guided Robert's. Birnie stepped forward from a discreet distance with the rings. After the couple had made their vows, the clerics wound a sacred cloth around their clasped hands.

"Those whom God has joined together, let no man pull asunder," they proclaimed in unison, with their own hands clasped together on top of the couple's. As Robert kissed his bride, a surge of emotion overwhelmed him. It was beyond the passion of Culloden or the glory of the famous try at Murrayfield; it was the raw power of their shared love pushing out the tangle of grudges and historical injustices that had driven him for so long. She had freed him from all that.

Walking back down the aisle with his bride, Robert felt elated under the gaze of the apprentice himself and Sir William Sinclair, builder of the Chapel to all religions.

The Sinclair stars all shone for them and every green man glowed with pride at witnessing such a historic union. Robert absorbed the mystical brew of earth, fire, water and latter day gods and felt at one with the world, inspired by the pantheon and prepared now to share the rest of the day with the multitudes who would claim a part of him. He looked across at his radiant bride, his earth goddess who would complete the cycle with him.

Outside the Church, the grey dawn was already probing the buttresses of the ancient building. At the Church door, Robert regretted not having the stirring call of the pipes to announce the end of the true marriage ceremony, to the shades within the Chapel. He knew that the coming day would be exuberant Hollywood, a Royal wedding fest designed to be consumed by the planet, putting his little nation at the centre of the world for at least a day, but promising more, a nation stirring from a long slumber.

"Congratulations, sir, on this fine morning," said Birnie, opening the car door for them.

"Thanks, Birnie, we need to get back before we're missed."

"And I'm hungry," announced Victoria.

****

223

At 11:00 a.m. the couple left Holyrood Palace in a procession of cars, which made its way up the Royal Mile to St Giles Cathedral. The streets were crowded with excited spectators; many were expatriate Scots drawn back by the call of history being made in their native land. The Prince was wearing Highland dress and the Princess a dreamy white silk creation, trimmed with Royal Stuart tartan, allegedly sewn on by the Queen herself. Layers of monarchs, presidents, politicians and dignitaries filled the old Kirk, arranged according to the arcane protocols of such events. The ceremony was all pomp and ecumenical fudge, led by the Church of Scotland, making heavy weather of the exchange of vows and rings, which prolonged the proceedings but made good television for the worldwide audience.

Despite his antipathy to the pomp, Robert did succumb to the majesty and symbolism of the occasion and exchanged vows again with complete sincerity, although he felt more like an actor playing a part in an extravagant production. He could not recreate the intimate emotion of Rosslyn Chapel.

For the next part of the proceedings, Robert had transformed the natural bowl of the West Princes Street Gardens area to form a ten thousand seat temporary amphitheatre equipped with big screens on which the crowd had followed the wedding ceremony. It had involved much stripping out of trees and the existing open air theatre. He planned this as a convenient starting point for a completely new King Robert Stuart Garden, which would be created after the wedding. It would be his first civic project.

The smell of venison being roasted on open wood fires already permeated the area, anticipating the wedding feast and mixing with the pipe music playing gently in the background. The centrepiece was the ceremonial dais. Warm-up acts included medieval jugglers, folk groups and choirs culminating in the light haunting melody of a Gaelic choir, which set the serious tone for the brief presentation ceremony when the Crown Prince presented his wife to the people.

"On behalf of my wife and...," said Robert, making the traditional start to a bridegroom's speech. His following words were drowned by the traditional applause that normally greets these words and the faces of the crowd were hidden behind a forest of Scottish flags, waved with enthusiasm and anticipation.

A Gaelic bard then appeared on stage with them and recited a poem specially composed for the occasion. Robert was moved by the lyrical simplicity of the words recited in the ancient tongue of his forefathers. The rhythms spoke of history, destiny and rebirth and looked forward to a bright and fertile future for the happy couple.

After the presentation ceremony everyone climbed out of the bowl up onto Princes Street itself, which had been transformed to feed the two times five thousand. Robert had insisted that every community in the land be represented at his Scottish medieval banquet. Ten thousand Scots and other guests were there, gathered in geographical groups of two hundred, starting with the Shetlanders and Orcadians at the west end of the street and ending with the Borderers at the end of North Bridge; almost a mile of Scots.

The whole street was protected from the potentially troublesome elements by a vast awning. Herds of red deer had been slaughtered to provide the meat. The salmon was from Scottish farms and whisky, the water of life, was in plentiful supply. Medieval dress was worn by most, and the ceremonial costumes of the great and good did not look out of place. Music from the different regions struck up, the fiddle merging into pipes and then the accordion. The main dignitaries were in a special pavilion with enhanced security, but by 3:00 p.m. at least half of them had left to join the fun outside, including the Royal couple who were making their way along the groups, stopping to speak to carefully selected guests, protected by an anxious Birnie and his security team.

Victoria had dispensed with her veil and uncoupled the train on her dress. At the Grampian tent the selected guest was Mrs. Margaret Mackenzie, the head gamekeeper's wife who had helped Robert escape from the Balmoral Estate. She was wearing the traditional dress of an eighteenth century highland woman.

"It's good to see you again, Margaret. I hope I don't look as knocked about as I did the first time you saw me."

"I'm so glad that I recognised you that day, sir."

"Thanks again for your help."

"What a story, it's so romantic. You look so beautiful," said Margaret to Victoria.

"We'll see you on the estate soon, I'm sure," said Robert.

****

At about the same time, an elegant looking Frenchman in his

forties presented himself at the entrance to the enclosure and asked if he could be introduced to Leo Stuart. The security steward looked at his list and came over to the Stuart family table.

"Who is he?" asked Leo, who had not heard the name very clearly when the steward first announced it.

"He sounds French, sir." said the steward.

"OK, bring him in and we'll see what he wants," said Leo, getting up.

"I am Philippe Delavarenne," said the Frenchman, extending his hand to Leo with a slight bow of his head, "I'm so pleased to meet you, Monsieur Stuart. I'm delighted to be present on this wonderful occasion. Perhaps you will recognise this?" he said, showing Leo a photograph.

"I do know him. It's Albert Delavarenne, of course, I recognise your name. How is he?" asked Leo, remembering the nervous days when he first visited Albert in Brussels at Hervé Dubois's suggestion.

"I'm afraid he died last year. He was my father."

"Oh, I am sorry to hear that, what a great pity. He did so much to get us started. We couldn't have done it without his help."

"I'm with the delegation from the European Union."

"Yes, I gather you're going to be very busy in Scotland."

"And you must be Madame Stuart," said Philippe, turning to Françoise. "I remember my father talking about you after he met you. He said that you were the most beautiful woman he had ever seen. He liked beautiful women."

Leo saw Françoise looking at him, first with a quizzical expression as he tried to remember when he had introduced Françoise to Albert. He quickly realised that he had never introduced the pair, nor would he ever have wanted to involve his wife in that clandestine side of the project. He looked at Françoise again, his turmoil showing as he desperately searched for the key to his wife's knowledge: how had she met Albert? It was like getting a speeding ticket through the post without owning a car, but much worse. Leo could see Françoise's anger, as she glowered at the unfortunate Phillipe, whose face was a picture of uncomprehending innocence.

"But Françoise, what does this mean?" asked Leo, ignoring Phillipe and looking at her as if he had just discovered her with a lover. At that moment, the Cardinal, who was sitting next to Françoise and had been keenly observing the proceedings, stood up and faced Phillipe, moving towards him and forcing him to back off, out of the immediate orbit of Leo and Françoise.

"Phillipe, thanks very much for coming over to see us. As Leo said, we're very grateful for the contribution your father made and I'm also very sorry to hear of his passing. Where did your father live?" asked the Cardinal, as he steered the Frenchman towards the other end of the table and introduced him to André and Simone, Robert's parents, and Bernard Frank.

Leo took his eye off the silent Françoise, who hadn't answered his question. He looked around the rest of the family party, searching for signs of complicity in their body language. He saw nothing in their faces; no knowing looks or nods and winks that spread the stain beyond Françoise.

"Leo, I've been wondering for years, who the mastermind of this operation was," whispered the Cardinal to Leo, as he returned. "We've all done our bit, but one piece of the jigsaw has always been missing, the big central piece. Suddenly, it's all clear. I think you have a very clever wife."

"Françoise?"

"Why don't the two of you get some air? It's getting very stuffy inside this tent."

"Yes, why don't we?" said Leo, who took little reassurance from the Cardinal's analysis. He stood up, waiting for Françoise to do the same, waiting for her to join him and tell him that it was all a misunderstanding and that she had never met Albert Delavarenne. He was in agony, feeling much more naked than he did waiting for Françoise when she saw the Queen. This time it wasn't a question of Robert's future, it was much closer to home. His wife, if the Cardinal was correct, had a secret life of some sort. He'd been completely unaware of a dark corner behind that beautiful façade, a disarming beauty that denied association with lies, deceit or intrigue. She rose heavily to join him and they left the tent, looking left and right for a quiet corner.

"When I wobbled over Robert's marriage to Victoria, I went to see the Cardinal in Paris. He suggested that I'd been set up by Hervé Dubois to start the Stuart project and the British hadn't murdered David. It got me off the anti-Hanoverian hook enough to be able to accept the marriage. I'd always assumed that Hervé was pushing the obvious politics. Europhiles trying to cut down Euro-sceptic Britain by carving bits off. Then just recently, I found compromising photographs of Monique and Hervé Dubois in a safe deposit box in Paris," said Leo.

"I did it for you, Leo," shouted Françoise, cutting him off.

"For me? You did what for me?"

"Leo, I was terrified of your depression, your Stuart melancholy was getting worse. I was afraid that it was taking you over, rotting your will, condemning you to join them as yet another one of history's failures. I didn't want that to happen. I wanted you alive, strong and fighting the demon. Like you, I could see Scottish Independence coming and that Robert was a remarkable child, capable of becoming a king. I thought so as I first held him in my arms in the hospital a few minutes after he was born, it was as powerful as that. So Leo, I had to make you do it."

"But Hervé, why Hervé?" asked Leo.

"He was a critical figure because he could give the political motivation credibility and it worked."

"Yes, but why was Hervé prepared to get involved personally?" asked Leo, looking very carefully at Françoise, fearing what she might have traded for his complicity.

"The clue's in the photographs. Obviously he was Monique's lover for a while. The important thing is that he believes he fathered Alexander," replied Françoise.

"So he thought that he was Robert's grandfather."

"And more important, he wanted his grandson to be a king."

"What a vanity," said Leo, who visibly relaxed when the spectre of infidelity turned away from his wife.

"Yes, it's a vanity of a kind I suppose, but one that we can well understand in our family. Monique had told me about Hervé in one of her less discreet moments. About his certainty that he was Alexander's father but she assured me that he wasn't, that as she put it at the time, *I have no intention of ever sullying the Stuart bloodline.*"

"Well, the DNA tests back that up, anyway," said Leo.

"And Leo, please don't be angry with the Cardinal. He wanted the same things as us and to help you at a personal level. He simply agreed to help me to nudge things along, to give you support for the project at the beginning."

"But what about the money? Where did that come from?"

"I laughed when I heard the Margaret Baird story that Bernard concocted for Peter Christie. It was a bit like that; I got an unexpected inheritance from Uncle Harry, who'd just died in America. It was sorted out through my solicitor in London. Uncle Harry triggered the whole thing; I couldn't have done it without Harry's money."

"I liked your Uncle Harry. It's a pity we rather lost touch when he went to America after our wedding."

"I still wrote to him every Christmas."

"Anyway, thank you, Uncle Harry," said Leo, looking up.

"With the money in place, Hervé produced Albert, who handled the transfer to the Swiss bank and fronted the operation for Bernard, posing as a discreet European Union official. The money couldn't be seen to be coming from either of us. You know it all now Leo, did I really do wrong?"

"Wrong, how could it be wrong, just look at the result, clever wife. It's just such a pity about David," he said, taking Françoise in his arms.

"Don't pity him, Leo. Don't forget he tried to kill you and we're not finished with him yet."

When they returned to the Stuart family area, Leo sought out the Cardinal who was still engaged in conversation with Phillipe Delavarenne.

"Thanks for tidying that up but there's something else. The Hanoverians are claiming that they've analysed one of Bonnie Prince Charlie's teeth and the DNA doesn't match ours."

"That can't be the case. The request to open the tomb was turned down flat. That would be the answer even for you."

"But why did they ever think you would do it?"

"They had something against one of our people. It was blackmail but we had a hold on them so the threat was neutralised."

"So whose tooth was analysed?"

"I don't know. Probably someone in their secret service made it up."

At the other end of the enclosure, Angela and Peter were the stars on the Edinburgh dignitaries' table, hosted by the Lord Provost. The couple basked in the normal mixture of approval and jealousy that attended success such as theirs. Angela was feeling self-satisfied, if not smug. She was still in the honeymoon period as Prime Minister and her methodical approach, allied to the deals that she had got from England and Norway, had given her programme a quick start. She was also delighted that her former leader and enemy, Jim Robertson, had been arrested for complicity in the Scone Palace bombing. However, she was even more pleased with her personal circumstances and was waiting for the right moment to make an important announcement.

"This must be a very proud day for you as kingmaker, Peter," said the Lord Provost.

"I still can't quite believe that it's happened."

"It must have been one of the greatest planned strategic operations in history."

"Well, there was some planning done, but Robert was a very worthy candidate, and then of course, it couldn't have happened without Angela's political vision," said Peter, giving her an admiring glance.

"Anyway, there should be a great honour coming your way. What about Lord Lomond? That sounds good, doesn't it?"

"That would be nice. I couldn't think of a better title for myself. But Angela hasn't told me yet if Scotland's going to have life peers."

"Well, there is *a man's a man for a' that* twist to the Scottish psyche that might be against peerages. On the other hand, we do have an existing Scottish aristocracy and they surely need to be diluted with deserving arrivistes. I'm sure that point will win the argument," said the Lord Provost.

"Yes, I would love you to be Lord Lomond, Peter darling. I would like our baby to be the son of a Lord," said Angela, using the public occasion to announce her pregnancy, obliging Peter to react positively to the explosive news.

"Angela, a baby? What?"

"Congratulations to you both," said the Lord Provost.

"I'm so pleased, Angela, really," said Peter, as the Lord Provost directed the conversation elsewhere. "It's just that I hadn't even thought of it. When?" he asked.

"I've just passed the critical three months. Don't worry, much older men than you have fathered children. Let's just live for the moment. Remember, a week is a long time in politics."

Chapter 47

Scotland, November 2038 - Edinburgh

Robert woke on Coronation morning well before dawn, leaving his beautiful sleeping wife. He wanted to free his spirit before the day began. He needed to go to a lonely place to prepare himself, like a high priest, for the sacred obligation that he would swear to uphold later in the day. The faithful Birnie drove him out of Holyrood through the ranks of crowd control barriers being assembled, past knots of the faithful who wanted the best vantage points and had stayed up all night to bag them.

They passed the Parliament which he would open each year, each time with hope of better things to come for his citizens. Birnie turned into the park beyond, towards the heights of Arthur's Seat, still lost in the darkness. The wind at the top of Arthur's seat tore at him, reminding him of his mortality and the short time he had to help wash the grime of centuries from the reborn nation.

From the top he looked east across the Firth of Forth as the sun warmed the horizon in a reassuring pink glow then burst out of the sea, a new dawn full of promise. As the first rays picked out the spires and chimneys of the Old Town he traced the route that would take him to his destiny. It was nearly three hundred years since his ancestor and inspiration, Bonnie Prince Charlie, had last visited Edinburgh. Robert wondered what his tragic hero would be thinking if he was looking down. Surely he would feel proud that the crown of Scotland had been recovered in the name of his family without the bloodshed and catastrophic aftermath of his own attempt.

****

Robert and Victoria were driven to Murrayfield for the Coronation. Dignitaries were present but had taken their seats quietly like everyone else. The ground was covered with a vast awning, coloured to represent a gigantic Scottish flag, the St. Andrew's cross dividing the ground into four quadrants. Scots representing every town, village and hamlet in the land occupied almost every seat. The crowning ceremony took place on a raised dais on a rotating stage in the middle of the field.

Seating filled the space between the stage and the terraces. A lone piper led the Coronation party up onto the stage to a tumultuous welcome from the crowd. The only furniture on the dais was the Stone of Destiny raised up on a carved wooden framework, and an oak table bearing the Scottish Honours: crown, sword and sceptre first used together for the Coronation of Mary Queen of Scots in 1543.

Robert sat down on the stone and Victoria stood at his side. A diminutive figure clad in orange robes stepped forward. It was the Dalai Lama, whom Robert had chosen as a mystical figure to sanctify the spiritual bridge between the King and his people. The orange clad monk placed the crown slowly on Robert's head, then the sword and sceptre in his hands.

"In the name of the Scottish people, I crown you King of Scotland," said the monk, in his thin high voice, which echoed out across the gardens.

The King then stood up, as his Queen knelt, and the monk placed a simple gold coronet on her head. The Royal couple were then led round the edge of the dais.

"Long live the King," called the monk to the crowd, throwing up his hands, signalling for them to take up the cry. The monk's words were taken up by the crowd and repeated until the beginnings of a song could be heard, the volume rising quickly as the words rippled round the stadium. Flower of Scotland had never been sung with such passion.

The singing took Robert back to the end of the field where he scored his famous first try against the Auld Enemy. The grass rolled over the crowd on the field as he relived that moment, charging invincibly through the Hanoverian ranks towards the Hanoverian banners, to score a sacred try and seal a famous victory. That day he had won his first battle in a long war. Today the war was over and the final blessed victory was his.

As the crown slipped onto Robert's head, Leo felt a weight lift from him, a yoke that he had been carrying since his fateful meeting with the Cardinal when he committed himself to the cause under the silent scrutiny of a gallery of Archbishops. The release from the yoke was doubly welcome since he still harboured doubts about the compromise with the Hanoverians and felt that even at the last moment they might be undermined by the falsehood of their genetics. He was feeling the burden of his secret and yearned now for the peace of retirement in France, leading a quiet rural life, according to the rhythms and mysteries of the land he loved. However, that was an unlikely prospect, given his wife's commitment to the cause.

He looked at Françoise sitting beside him, the true mastermind, her inscrutable beauty blinding all to the genius that she poured on him and Robert. He knew that Françoise was in her own mind the King's mother; had she not held him as a child minutes after he was born and listened to his first cry, hearing his destiny in it? And was she not now his trusted indispensable advisor, preparing herself to serve in whatever Robert invented to take the place of a court? Leo knew that she would not desert Robert in his hour of victory, now that he had power, something that she could have a tiny share in. She needed to feed her growing addiction.

The Royal motorcade left the stadium for the Castle where a VIP reception was planned in the hammer beamed Great Hall to allow the dignitaries to meet the new Royal Couple. Robert and Victoria were at one end of the hall receiving the congratulations of a chosen list of mainly foreign diplomats and representatives who would not be present at the formal dinner to be held later in Holyrood Palace.

Out on the floor, Françoise was talking to Sir Humphrey when his phone rang. She watched as his normally deadpan expression turned to horror at the news he was receiving. With an uncharacteristic snarl at Françoise he rushed out of the reception room without reference to his masters, pushing past Jamie who was keeping an eye on everyone from near the door. Jamie did not abandon his post but watched the camera feed on his phone as Sir Humphrey fled the Castle and went down the esplanade past the waiting horse drawn coaches and cavalry. As he disappeared into the crowd waiting at the esplanade exit, Jamie called the local security centre in the basement of the Pentland Hotel near the junction of the Bridges and The Royal Mile. He asked them to keep a lookout for Sir Humphrey on the battery of security cameras that had been deployed.

Tina, on duty in the centre, picked up the message and quickly spotted Sir Humphrey making his way down towards them. Zooming in on him, she could see that he was already out of breath at the brisk pace he was keeping up. He was also screaming into his phone, hardly normal Sir H. behaviour. When he passed the hotel and entered an apartment block, Tina leaped into action to follow him.

She raced up the stairs, checking the pair of doors on each landing. She reached the top fourth floor where the door of the flat looking over the street was slightly ajar. She drew her pistol and kicked the door open. Sir Humphrey was in the lobby corridor coming at her, apparently on his way out. He was carrying an old revolver which he raised towards her. She fired without hesitation, sending him flying back into the lounge. She had gone for a shoulder shot to disable his pistol arm; she didn't want to kill him.

Inside the lounge a figure dressed in a business suit was slumped at the windowsill, blood oozing from a hole in his head. Beside him lay a rifle with a telescopic sight. Tina bundled the groaning Sir Humphrey into a corner of the room covering him with her pistol.

"What happened here, then?" she asked

"I shot him, I've saved the King," said Sir Humphrey.

"Well done, Sir Humphrey, it looks as though you did manage to kill him. He won't be able to tell us anything now. Mind telling me how you knew he was here and why you didn't tell us? Shooting assassins is our job."

"I didn't think there would be time," he replied lamely.

"Not good enough, Humph, you're up to your neck in something," she replied, walking over to him with her pistol levelled. She saw the fear in his eyes and kicked him on the wounded shoulder, sending him writhing on the floor. As she was about to deliver another blow, she stopped. A crazy thought had entered her head. Was the setup she had stumbled on not a fateful opportunity for her? How often had she dreamed of ridding herself of the sorceress Princess who had stolen her Robert? Now that he was King, he'd surely be delighted to get out of the marriage arranged by the Hanoverians to save their skins in Scotland. She could repossess him and start again; she didn't want to be Queen, she just wanted Robert. She had already lost a great love in Ireland because of her loyalty to the Service; this was her last chance delivered by fate. She must take it.

She picked up the rifle and cradled it in her arms like a baby, caressing it, sensing its possibilities. Pointing it at Sir Humphrey she looked through the telescopic lens at the blurred follicles on his forehead, making him issue a pleading squeal and raise his hands to protect himself. The surging cocktail of adrenalin and other hormones drowned out the loud alarm bells triggered by all her training and hitherto ferocious loyalty.

"I'm not going to shoot you, Humph," she said pulling the assassin's body away and kneeling down in the window, taking up a firing position. "I'm going for the bitch. She's due to pass below us in a minute."

"Oh no," wailed the stricken Mandarin as the sound of the cavalry horses on the cobbles up the street penetrated the window that Tina had cracked open just enough to get the rifle point out.

"Here they come," announced Tina, rising slightly as she took aim, refusing to be distracted by a new noise entering the room.

"Drop it, Tina," said Jamie gasping from the exertion of running up the three flights of stairs two at a time. With his pistol trained on her head, Jamie saw her hesitate and lower the point of the rifle as the leathery smell of the cavalry horses added to the noise of their hooves.

"What the fuck are you doing, Tina?" he roared.

"I was just getting a better view through the telescopic sight."

"It was nearly your last," said Jamie overcome by a mixture of adrenalin and rage. He was angry at almost having to fire his first shot in anger, something he never imagined he would have to do. Worse still the target was a woman, a woman he actually liked. He was a dinosaur on that front, believing that women should be cherished, preferably at home and never put in harm's way. He was very relieved to see her submit but suffered a moment of self-doubt. Would he have pulled the trigger?

"What a fucking mess; what's he doing here?" asked Jamie, nodding in Sir Humphrey's direction, reasserting his professional authority.

"I met him coming out. I assume he shot the assassin."

"And who's the dead salesman?" he asked, kicking the lifeless leg of the business suited assassin. Jamie was appalled that such an attack on the Royal Couple had been planned and almost executed under his nose. Sir Humphrey hung his head, groaning as Jamie examined his wound.

"You're bleeding a lot but you'll probably live. Now talk. Who set this up?" he roared into the Mandarin's face, firing a small gob of spit into Sir Humphrey's hair.

"Who?" he repeated, shaking him by the jacket collars and bouncing his head off the wall, when the Mandarin did not reply immediately.

"Underwood," replied Sir Humphrey weakly.

"Underwood! Very convenient, he's dead; we fished him out of the Clyde."

"I swear it was him. He told me about the plan just before he was killed."

"But why did you go along with it? Why didn't you warn us?" shouted Jamie in frustration.

"These Stuarts; it's a charade. They're not who they claim to be. Underwood got the proof. They're not descendants of Bonnie Prince Charlie."

"Do you think we can trust Underwood's interpretation of history? He's been conspiring against the Stuarts all along."

Jamie let go and stood up, his anger dimmed by the cold counterblast of Sir Humphrey's claim. The revelation had tapped a buried gnawing uncertainty of his own.

"So what did your Royal masters have to say about that?"

"The Queen wouldn't accept it. We'd found out far too late and by then they were totally committed, it just couldn't be unpicked. In the end, the genetics didn't matter to her, she had her fairy-tale and they still had Scotland through Victoria."

"So why this? Why an assassination attempt?"

"I went along with Underwood from a higher sense of duty, beyond the current incumbents, protecting the integrity of the institution really. We can't have any Tom, Dick or Harry becoming King."

"But if I'm working things out correctly, you stopped it. You got a phone call at the reception and charged over here like a man possessed and took him out," said Jamie, pointing at the assassin's body.

"I got a frantic call from the surgeon who did Prince Henry's operation in Switzerland. I didn't understand the technical details but he said that if anything bad happened to Robert, the Stuarts had the means to destroy Henry's brain. That's credible, the whole thing was set up by Robert's cousin in America. I had to try and stop it."

"Well, I suppose I should be glad you got here in time," said Jamie, touched by a small flicker of sympathy for the Mandarin who had been obliged to act so quickly and violently on incomplete information.

"It's a pity you can't ask him what he thinks," said Sir Humphrey nodding at the assassin.

Jamie went over and rolled the suit onto his back. At close quarters, Jamie could see that he was wearing a very naturalistic thin rubber facemask to disguise his identity. Even after the horrors of the previous ten minutes, nothing could have prepared Jamie for the sight of David Stuart's pallid dead face. The death mask was chilling; a curled vengeful lip threatened him, promising unfinished business. It explained why face recognition software hadn't picked David out on any of the thousands of cameras in Scotland. Jamie wondered what family curse must inhabit the Stuarts to make a grandfather willing to shoot his grandson on the day of his Coronation.

"Last time I saw him he was heading out into the Clyde. I hoped he would disappear again for good. We've found out all about his republican past. Ironic really, but why would he go this far?"

"I don't know. Underwood set it up. He's apparently been running David Stuart off the books for years."

"We know that David didn't support the Hanoverian marriage. Could Victoria have been the target? Was he planning to shoot her, stringing all of you along?"

"That's possible. It would have pleased Tina if he'd taken out Victoria. I presume she's one of yours."

Jamie stood up and leaned against the wall putting the big picture together. The Queen was right. Whatever the veracity of the Stuart claim, the die of history was cast and had to be built on, there was no turning back. He had to end the conspiracy and just as important sweep its contagion away before it infected the body that they were all supposed to be protecting. Sir Humphrey was up to his neck in it; the other two key conspirators were out of the way.

Jamie walked over and pulled Sir Humphrey up by the hands. Sir Humphrey looked up at him with an air of mild surprise, as though he was being offered a cup of tea before groaning loudly from the pain in his shoulder. Jamie turned him and led him roughly out of the door of the flat on to the stair-head, turning him again so that his back faced the stairwell. He then pushed Sir Humphrey sharply and reached down, grabbing his legs to turn him over the top bannister. Sir Humphrey grabbed Jamie by the lapels, hanging onto his life. Tina intervened, removing Sir Humphreys hands from Jamie and pushing him back over the edge. They watched as the Mandarin rattled all the way down the stairwell to the ground floor, ending up draped at a spinally impossible angle over the bottom of the banister.

There was no repeat of the revulsion that swept over him when he faced pulling the trigger on Tina. He imagined it was something like the feeling of an agent of the Inquisition doing God's work. He had always known that a line was there but had never imagined he would cross it into the extra-judicial minefield.

****

That evening Robert and Victoria made a grand entrance into the Ballroom of Holyrood Palace to rapturous applause from the assembled company. Robert's smile hid his turmoil at the briefing they had just received from his Chief of Staff, Sir Duncan Flockhart. He couldn't believe that two people closely linked to him were now dead in almost inexplicable circumstances. His Grandfather's duplicity shamed him but he still couldn't believe that his own kin would carry out such an act against him. Sir Humphrey's role was beyond belief, even though the King had warned him about meddling Mandarins with their own agendas; this was going a bit far.

The corruption of power gripped him by the throat as he struggled to speak to the first of the guests in the long snaking line waiting to be greeted by the lined up Royal party. He wondered whether Victoria's father was right. Perhaps he should have got himself a proper job. Perhaps he hadn't been careful enough about what he'd wished for.

Across the hall out of the line, Robert could see Françoise and his cousin Nicole in animated conversation beneath the portrait of Mary Queen of Scots. Robert was sure that Françoise was revelling in what she had wished for.

****

"Tell me again how this thing works, Nicole."

"It's simple, Mother. Just think of this as a mobile phone. If you dial the number written on the back it sends a signal to the electrodes in Henry's head and scrambles his brains. He'll either be dead or a vegetable, certainly not a King. So you've got them by the balls, but obviously they have to know that. I'll leave you to tell them."

"Who on earth thought of that?"

"The U.S. Military funded the technology. They didn't just want to control behaviour. They wanted a way out in case of capture. Anything to avoid these embarrassing takes of U.S. troops on TV making confessions. So we added the "Death Programme" for them. I left it on Henry's suite of programmes, just in case."

"You are a clever girl, Nicole."

"This has to be kept very secret, Mother."

"Yes, just ourselves and your father; I don't want Robert to know about it."

"I think that's right, it would complicate his relationship with his in-laws."

"That's settled then, I know how this thing works; I'll have a chat with the Queen later tonight. We shouldn't have any more trouble with the Hanoverians. I'm sure she wouldn't like any harm to come to her newly restored son."

"I'd like to be a fly on the wall for that."

"Oh, and by the way, Victoria's pregnant, isn't that wonderful?"

"Did you have that in the script, too?"

"I must introduce you properly to Prince Henry. He's quite a charmer since his brain transplant."

"Mother! Don't even think about it."

Chapter 48

Scotland, November 2038 - Edinburgh

The Queen was deeply saddened by Sir Humphrey's death and the grim way that he met his end. She appreciated his diplomatic skills more than her husband and greatly admired the way he had handled the Stuarts. The worrying thing was his obvious knowledge of the assassination plot. It was difficult to conceive of an innocent explanation for his presence at the scene, although since he had apparently taken out the assassin, he could be presented as a hero. So far the Secret Service had established that a phone call from Henry's surgeon in Switzerland seemed to have catalysed Sir Humphrey's actions. That lead had taken a very worrying and sinister turn with the news that her son's head contained a programme that could scramble his brains, destroying him. The surgeon suspected that the Stuarts had the trigger to make it happen if they chose to. Fortunately, the Hanoverian powder magazine was not empty.

Her main consolation was the news of Victoria's pregnancy. It was perhaps several months too soon for old-fashioned decency but very welcome nevertheless. She was looking forward to a chat with Mrs. Stuart to indulge in a little anticipatory "granny talk", although she had to constantly remind herself that Françoise was not Robert's mother.

"We don't meet often enough like this, Mrs. Stuart."

"Yes, last time we talked about camellias before we arranged the wedding."

"That seems such a long time ago."

"I was very sorry to hear about Sir Humphrey."

"Yes, he was quite a hero, really, saving your Robert from his own grandfather's bullet."

"But who was grandfather working for? And how did Sir Humphrey know he was there? That's what's bothering me. It's all part of a pattern, isn't it? This is the third time that Robert's life has been threatened from your side and it's going to be the last."

"You look as though you're about to throw a killer punch, Mrs. Stuart. Don't tell me that you're inside Henry's head."

"We are. It happened by accident not design. They simply forgot to remove that part of the military programme they modified. I'm told that it would be very risky trying to remove it at this stage."

"So if anything bad happens to Robert, you pull the trigger, is that it?

"That's it."

"Do you know who you are, Mrs. Stuart?" asked the Queen, who had been expecting an approach of some sort from the Stuart side, but this was sooner than she had anticipated. She was glad however of the opportunity to clear the air.

"I'm Robert's great aunt, actually."

"Yes, Robert Stuart, scion of Bonnie Prince Charlie's direct line. It's rubbish, he's a fraud. He's no more descended from Bonnie Prince Charlie than you or I. The Vatican marriage contract is a goodish fake and the DNA doesn't fit. How would this look in the newspapers? He'd be written off as the greatest genealogical fraudster of all time. He'd have to abdicate, almost as bad as having your brains scrambled, except that you would be fully conscious of the humiliation."

"Steady on, ma'am. My information is that your dead agent, Underwood, who masterminded all the attacks on Robert dreamt up this as well. But it can't be true. We have an absolute assurance that the Prince's tomb in the Vatican hasn't been opened, so there is no DNA and there can be no such proof."

"Anyway, Mrs. Stuart, perhaps it's best we don't know. We were totally committed by the time we found out; and they are a wonderful couple, so much in love."

"So my little trigger is even more important than I thought."

"We've got the power to destroy each other, Mrs Stuart, shall we call it deuce?"

"OK, but it's probably more like fifteen all, with a long way to go."

"This has to be settled at the top. I'm going to get the King to talk to Robert. Now, what about this baby?"

Chapter 49

France, November 2038 - Fontainbleau

In the graveyard behind the chapel at the *Manoir* the low sunlight splayed past the stone crosses with an added sparkle from the coating of hoar frost. As David's coffin was lowered into the jaws of the grave, only recently closed over Monique, Louise Robertson saw the Stuart family members looking at her, trying to imagine the life she had with David. She tried to remember the sweet moments and push the negative thoughts to the back of her mind. The only good time was when James was small. She remembered David being very insistent on calling the boy James, a name that she considered old-fashioned at the time. David was often around and they had something that passed for a normal family life as he worked manically on his book, his republican masterpiece. The factual part came at the start and accurately recorded the republican summer school phase that she had so much enjoyed. The only inaccuracy from that period was David's assumption that he was James' father. That provoked a happy memory of Alexander, the love of her life, a love that had been concentrated into a short few weeks.

Back at the *Manoir* after the interment, Louise sought out Robert. She had a package for him.

"You need to read this, especially the last few pages. It's the final version of David's novel."

Robert excused himself with difficulty and withdrew to Leo's study with the book. The last few pages described the planned assassination in detail. He was astonished to read that David's target was neither himself nor Victoria but her brother, Henry, heir to the throne of England. So his grandfather was apparently on his side after all, aiming to get both crowns for the Stuarts, fully reversing history. But somehow, it didn't feel right. David had been prepared to kill his brother and had never made any gesture of support towards their cause.

A few minutes later, he came back to find Louise waiting where he had left her.

She looked apprehensive as if she was concerned that Robert might not believe what he had read.

"What do you think?" she asked.

"I think that you're a kind sweet woman. You rewrote the ending didn't you, to make us feel better?"

"Don't be so cynical."

"It's just inconsistent with everything else he did. He was even prepared to kill his brother."

"I know he admired the way that you got yourself into the role. You were able to seize the Scottish crown yourself with the help of your team. But he wanted the bigger prize for you, nothing less than both crowns so Prince Henry had to go. David was Underwood's hired assassin, you were Underwood's target but in the end who was in charge of the gun? So you can see why he couldn't come in from the cold. He had to finish the job alone. If he'd tried to explain himself he would have been stopped."

"I'm sorry Louise; I hadn't seen it that way. I'm glad it didn't happen, though. How would it have looked, my grandfather killing the Prince of Wales?"

"Perhaps you're right; it would have been very difficult for your wife and her relations."

"Might David have been kidding us with his republican stuff? When he conquered Scotland at the head of his freedom fighters. Don't you think he would have been tempted to declare himself King?"

"I once suggested that to him, it was a joke really on my part. He reacted furiously, overly so, I thought, so you may be right. We'll never know what went on in his head."

"Well, let's hope that things settle down now. I've had enough excitement already for one reign."

About the Author

Alan was born in Wick in the far North of Scotland and gained a Chemistry PhD at Aberdeen University before a career in Research and Development with ICI and Zeneca. Alan was appointed CBE in 1995 for services to the chemical industry.

He took up the pen in early retirement and enjoys writing contemporary thrillers with their roots in history, as well as poetry. He lives with his wife in Yorkshire, England near his grown up family. Summers are spent in Scotland, writing, fishing and doing heritage projects.